FOREIGN BODIES

BOOKS BY CYNTHIA OZICK

Nonfiction

QUARREL & QUANDARY

FAME & FOLLY

METAPHOR & MEMORY

ART & ARDOR

THE DIN IN THE HEAD

Fiction

FOREIGN BODIES

DICTATION

HEIR TO THE GLIMMERING WORLD

THE PUTTERMESSER PAPERS

THE SHAWL

THE MESSIAH OF STOCKHOLM

THE CANNIBAL GALAXY

LEVITATION: FIVE FICTIONS

BLOODSHED AND THREE NOVELLAS

THE PAGAN RABBI AND OTHER STORIES

TRUST

CYNTHIA OZICK

FOREIGN BODIES

Houghton Mifflin Harcourt

2010 BOSTON NEW YORK

For information about permission to reproduce
selections from this book, write to Permissions,
Houghton Mifflin Harcourt Publishing Company,
215 Park Avenue South, New York, New York 10003.

www.hmhbooks.com

Library of Congress Cataloging-in-Publication Data
Ozick, Cynthia.
Foreign bodies / Cynthia Ozick.
p. cm.
ISBN 978-0-547-43557-2
1. Americans — France — Fiction. 2. Paris
(France) — Fiction. I. Title.
PS3565.Z5F67 2010
813'.54 — dc22   2010005757

Book design by Melissa Lotfy

Printed in the United States of America

DOC 10 9 8 7 6 5 4 3 2

But there are two quite distinct things — given the wonderful place he's in — that may have happened to him. One is that he may have got brutalized. The other is that he may have got refined.

—HENRY JAMES, *The Ambassadors*

FOREIGN BODIES

I

Dear Marvin,

Well, I'm back. London was all right, Paris was terrible, and I never made it down to Rome. They say it's the hottest summer they've had since before the war. And except for the weather, I'm afraid there's not much else to report. The address you gave me—Julian left there about a week ago. It seems I just missed him by a few days. You wouldn't have approved, a rooming house in a rundown neighborhood way out toward the edge of the city. I did the best I could to track him down—tried all the places you said he might be working at. His landlady when I inquired turned out to be a pure blank. All she had to offer was an inkling of a girlfriend. He took everything with him, apparently not much.

I'm returning your check. From the looks of where your son was living, he could certainly have used the $500. Sorry I couldn't help more. I hope you and (especially) Margaret are well.

Yours,
Beatrice

2

IN THE EARLY FIFTIES of the last century, a ferocious heat wave assaulted Europe. It choked its way north from Sicily, where it scorched half the island to brownish rust, up toward Malmö at the lowest tip of Sweden; but it burned most savagely over the city of Paris. Hot steam hissed from the wet rings left by wine glasses on the steel tables of outdoor cafés. In the sky just overhead, a blast furnace exhaled searing gusts, or else a fiery geyser, loosed from the sun's core, hurled down boiling lava on roofs and pavements. People made this comparison and that — sometimes it was the furnace, sometimes the geyser, and now and then the terrible heat was said to be a general malignancy, a remnant of the recent war, as if the continent itself had been turned into a region of hell.

At that time there were foreigners all over Paris, suffering together with the native population, wiping the trickling sweat from their collarbones, complaining equally of feeling suffocated; but otherwise they had nothing in common with the Parisians or, for that matter, with one another. These strangers fell into two parties — one vigorous, ambitious, cheerful, and given to drink, the other pale, quarrelsome, forlorn: a squad of volatile maundering ghosts.

The first was looking to summon the past: it was a kind of self-intoxicated theater. They were mostly young Americans in their twenties and thirties who called themselves "expatriates," though they were little more than literary tourists on a long visit, besotted with legends of Hemingway and Gertrude Stein. They gathered in the cafés to gossip and slander and savor the old tales of the lost generation, and to scorn what they had left behind. They rotated lovers of either sex and played at existentialism and founded avant-garde journals in which they published one another and bragged of having sighted Sartre at the Deux Magots, and were proudly, relentlessly, unremittingly conscious of their youth. Unlike that earlier band of expatriates, who had grown up and gone home, these intended to stay young in Paris forever. They made up a little city of shining white foreheads; but their teeth were stained from too much whiskey and wine, and too many powerful French cigarettes. They spoke only American. Their French was bad.

The other foreign contingent — the ghosts — were polyglot. They chattered in dozens of languages. Out of their mouths spilled all the cadences of Europe. Unlike the Americans, they shunned the past, and were free of any taint of nostalgia or folklore or idyllic renewal. They were Europeans whom Europe had set upon; they wore Europe's tattoo. You could not say of them, as you surely would of the Americans, that they were a postwar wave. They were not postwar. Though they had washed up in Paris, the war was still in them. They were the displaced, the temporary and the temporizing. Paris was a way station; they were in Paris only to depart from Paris, as soon as they knew who would have them. Paris was a city to wait in. It was a city to get away from.

Beatrice Nightingale belonged to neither party. She had been "Miss Nightingale" — in public — for twenty-four years, even during her marriage and certainly after the divorce, and had sometimes begun to think of herself by that name, if only to avoid the accusatory inward buzz of Bea. To Bea or not to Bea: she was one of that ludicrously recognizable breed of middle-aged teachers who save up for a longed-for summer vacation in the more romantic capitals of Europe. That these capitals, after the war, were scarred and exhausted, drained of all their well-advertised enchantments, did not escape her. She was resilient, intelligent, not inexperienced (marriage itself had taught her a thing or two). She was, after all, forty-eight years old,

3

graying only a little, and tough with her students, high school boys sporting duck-tail haircuts who laughed at Wordsworth and ridiculed Keats: when they came to "Ode to a Nightingale" they went out of their way to hoot and leer—but she knew how to tame them. She was good at her job and not ashamed of it. And after two decades at it, she was not yet burned out.

She had signed up for London, Paris, and Rome, but gave up on Rome (even though it was included in the agent's package deal) when she read, in her noisy hot hotel room off Piccadilly, of the dangerous temperatures in the south. London had been nearly bearable, if you kept to the shade, but Paris was hideous, and Rome was bound to be an inferno. "That ludicrously recognizable breed"—these were her mocking words to herself (traveling alone, she had no one else to say them to), though likely parroted from some jaunty guidebook, the kind that makes light of its own constituents. A more conscientious guidebook, the one sequestered at the bottom of her capacious bag—passport, notepad, camera, tissues, aspirin, and so on—was not jaunty. It was punishingly painstaking, and if you were obedient to its almost sacerdotal cartography, you would come away exalted by pictures and sculptures and historic public squares redolent of ancient beheadings.

On this July day the page she was consulting in her guidebook was bare of Monets and Gauguins and day-trip chateaus. It was captioned "Neighborhood Cafés." All afternoon she had been walking from café to café, searching for her nephew. A filmy smear greased her vision—it was as if her corneas were melting—and her heartbeat either ran too fast or else meant to run out altogether, with small reminding jabs. The pavements, the walls of buildings, blew out torrid vibrations. Paris was sub-Saharan, she was being cooked in a great equatorial vat. She fell into a wicker chair at a burning round table and ordered cold juice, and sat panting, only half recovered, with her blurry eye on the *garçon* who brought it. Her nephew was a waiter in one of these sidewalk establishments, this much she knew. It was difficult to think of him as her nephew: he was her brother's son, he

4

was too remote, he was as uncertain for her as a rumor. Marvin had sent her a photograph: a boy in his twenties, straw hair, indeterminate expression. How to sort him out from the identical others, with their wine-spattered white aprons tied around their skinny waists? She supposed she could spot him once he opened his mouth and revealed himself as an American: she had only to say to any probable straw-haired boy, Excuse me, are you Julian?

—*Pardon?*

—I'm looking for Julian Nachtigall, from California. Do you know him, does he work here?

—*Pardon?*

— *Un Américain*. Julian. *Un garçon. Est-il ici?*

—*Non, madame.*

Doubtless there was a more efficient way of finding him. Marvin had written out, in those big imperious letters as loud as his big imperious voice, his son's precise address. Three times, so far, she had climbed the broken front steps of the squat brown house in the broken brown neighborhood her fastidious guidebook mentioned only to warn its readers away. A bony landlady erupted from a door at the top of the stoop; the boy, she said in a garble as broken as her teeth, lived overhead, one flight up, only no, he was not home, he was not home already four days. *Oui, certainement,* he worked in one of the cafés, what else was a boy like that good for? At least she got the rent out of him. *Dieu merci,* he has a rich father over there.

So! A wild goose chase, useless, pointless, it was eating into her vacation time, and all to please Marvin, to *serve* Marvin, who—after years of disapproval, of repudiation, of what felt almost like hatred —was all at once appealing to the claims of family. This fruitless search, and the murderous heat. Retrograde Europe, where you had to ask bluntly for a toilet whenever you wanted a ladies' room, and where it seemed that nothing, *nothing* was air-conditioned—at home in New York, everything was air-conditioned, it was the middle of the twentieth century, for God's sake! Her guidebook showed no concern for the tourist's bladder, and in its fervid preoccupation with the heirlooms of the ages never dreamed of cooling off. It recommended small quaint boutiques in fashionable neighborhoods — if you cared for something American-style, it chided, stay in America. But she had had enough of the small and the quaint and the unaffordably fashionable, and more than enough of that asinine wandering from café to café: what she needed was air-conditioning and a toilet, and urgently. She walked on through the roasting miasma of late afternoon, and when she saw before her a tall gray edifice with a frieze incised above its two stately doors, for a moment she supposed it was yet another historic site smacking of Richelieu. But there were letters in the stone: GRAND MAGASIN LUXOR. A department store! The cold air came rushing at her with its familiar saving breath. The ladies' room was very much like what she might have found in, say, Bloomingdale's, all mirrors and marble sinks. Call it American-style, condemn it for its barbarous mimicry, Louis XIII on the outside, New York on the inside — the place was life-giving.

The ladies' room led out through a corridor into something like a restaurant, though it resembled more a busy Broadway cafeteria, where shoppers sat surrounded by their newly purchased bags and boxes. The ceiling was misty with smoke; all these people were intent on their cigarettes. She looked around for a seat. Every table was taken. Then she noticed an empty spot strewn with ash-filled saucers, occupied by three noisy men and a woman.

She put her hand on the back of the vacant chair. "Will it be all right if I settle down here for a minute?"

The woman gave out a help-yourself-what-do-I-care shrug. It was impossible to know whether she understood English, or whether the gesture with the chair was enough. The men continued what seemed to be an argument. Here there was no heap of overflowing bags: presumably this intense little circle, like Bea herself, had no local purpose other than refuge from the griddle of the streets. Odors of eggs and coffee all around. Floating tongues of perfume: a mannequin sailing by, uncannily tall, feet uncannily long, a trail of silky garments over one long arm, breastless, eyes of glass, Matisse-red mouth, perfection of jaw and limbs and stiffened hair, the very model of a Parisian model, exuding streams of fragrance. The men stared, as if sighting a yellow tiger in a place that smelled of kitchen. *"Imbéciles,"* the woman muttered; these syllables, addressed to Bea, were roughened by an unidentifiable accent. The accent matched the woman's hard look: tight black curls sprouting from an angry head. The visionary living robot slid away, and the men resumed their quarrel—if it was a quarrel. Their talk was French and not-French, it had the sound of half a dozen languages all at once: Europe scrambled. A quarrel, a protest, a lament, a bark of resignation? Bea sank into the clear relief of sitting still and shedding warmth—she could almost fall asleep against these enigmatic contentious voices, wavering like underwater flora at the far rim of her fatigue. The deadly walk back to the hotel still ahead. These people, who were they, where did they come from? Too shabby, too provisional, to be ordinary citizens. They didn't belong, they were out of place and out of sorts. They hung their cigarettes from their lower lips only to let the time pass. The woman, with those impatient furious whorls springing up around a blotched face, stood up and was pulled down by one of the men. She stood up again, to go where? Where had they come from, where could they go?

Bea left them finally. She had seen their like strewn all over Paris.

She went one last time to find Marvin's son. The jagged-toothed landlady materialized as before, only now in cotton house slippers, with a wet mop in hand and a big rag wound round her waist. She was washing down the stairs. The boy was gone, since two days gone for good with his knapsack and a girl to help drag out the duffle bag. What did he have in there, iron bars? The room was his for one week more, it was a blessing anyhow that he owed nothing, that useless boy, because of the father in America. The girl? A quiet little dark thing, like an Arab or a gypsy.

—How should I know where he went? He didn't tell me, why should he?

—I need to talk to him, I'm his aunt.

— I'm sorry for you, a boy like that. My own two nephews, they have real jobs, not one day here, one day there, a different boss every time. Maybe he moved in with her, that one, not a kid like him, already a wrinkle between the eyes, that's what they do, after a while they move in with them. If you want to take a look upstairs, I don't object, only watch the steps, they're still wet. I looked in up there myself, to see about damage. A couple of nails in the wall, I don't mind, like if he hung a picture.

— Well, but did he leave anything behind?

— I found this up there, if you want it it's yours, it's no use to me.

The landlady held out a battered book.

In the taxi going back to her hotel, she examined it. Something like a dictionary, an indecipherable language across from a column of French, not a name inscribed, not a sign of anything. It was old; the pages were brittle and loose. Pointless to keep it, so when she paid the driver and got out, she abandoned it.

The next day she visited the Louvre, and for the rest of the week — as far as her money and the lethal weather allowed — she relied on her guidebook to lead her to storied scenes and ancient glories. Then she went home to her two-and-a-half-room apartment on West 89th Street, where the bulky shoulder of an air conditioner darkened a window and vibrated like a worn drum. And where to Bea or not to Bea was always the question.

3

Dear Bea,

You missed him? You were right there in Paris, you knew exactly where he was, you knew reasonably well where he might be employed, and I depended on you. And what do I get instead? A weather report! The business as you know has me pretty much tied up lately, I couldn't for love or money get out there myself, my sister takes a vacation and thinks of nothing but her own pleasure and leaves me in the dark. You simply didn't try hard enough. I realize you don't know Julian, but if you haven't got any family feeling, why not a little family responsibility?

You mention a girl. As if in passing. Julian is twenty-three years old. At this age to get himself mixed up with some girl over there is not what I have in mind for my son. You understand that Margaret would go if it was feasible, but as you are aware she is somewhat neurasthenic, and is plainly incapable of traveling alone. Of course we are both very distressed, Margaret even more than I. She finds it intolerable that we sometimes don't know Julian's whereabouts, he writes so infrequently. I recognize that he's at that experimental stage typical of his generation, they want to try out this and try out that, and if it's a little on the spiteful side, all the better, they go for it. The trouble with these kids is that they haven't had

9

the military to toughen them up, not that I'm not glad he's been spared what I saw in the Pacific. And considering that I got through it as an overaged LCDR it wasn't so easy for me either. A headstrong boy, I suppose we've indulged him. Or maybe not—there's nothing out of the ordinary with junior year abroad, they all do it nowadays. One year with the Paris meshugas, all right, but it's been three, and he shows no signs of returning to finish up. I can assure you that Margaret and I never anticipated a dropout! As an alumnus who's made substantial contributions to my alma mater, I'm embarrassed. There was no hint of his not finishing, even with all that crazy reading he was doing, Camus and whatnot, a waste of time for a science major. Or history of science, the soft stuff, he doesn't have a head for the real thing. Iris is the one, she takes after me, a commonsensical head on her shoulders, and a good head for chemistry too—halfway through a doctorate, in fact. I expect her to marry intelligently. You can never tell how genes ricochet, I sometimes think there's a bit of you in Julian, and God knows I can't have him ending up in a bad marriage, not to mention teaching louts on their way to the body shop.

As far as the 500 bucks are concerned, you imply this was to get him out of that slum into something better. Not so! I can imagine what sort of grimy getup he's been running around in, and I did speak of cleaning him up with something respectable, a shirt and an actual suit, etc., whatever the cost, but I told you explicitly, I want my son out of there altogether, out of Europe, out of the bloody dirt of that place, and back home in America where he belongs. He complains that his mother and I manipulate him—whatever he thinks that means—yet if anyone's doing the manipulating, it's Julian. I hear from him only when his pockets are past empty. Otherwise the few times he writes it's to Iris. They used to be close, those two, as thick as thieves, though with the three years between them and his head in the clouds they never had much in common that I could see.

But if anyone can dope out what he might be up to, it's his sister. Who knows what he tells her — she reads his letters and then they disappear. If you ask her she says he's fine, he's well, he's attending some sort of lecture thing, he's got some sort of job — it turns out he's wiping up tables.

Now here's my idea, and this time I hope you'll come through. As soon as we get wind of where he's at, I want you to take a week or so and go over there again and bring him back. I don't care how you do it. Do whatever you do when you get your body shop guys to swallow those nursery rhymes you keep shoving down their throats. You seem to think you're good at that. If you have to bribe him — I mean with $$$ — then bribe him. Just get him back to New York, for starters. He won't be willing to come out here to his own family, at least not right away. I suspect he'll be too hangdog. There's Iris who always has her little cat-that-ate-the-canary smile, and there's Julian, the sullen one, and what's he got to sulk about? He's always had his own way. When you get off the plane at Idlewild, I want you to take him home with you and keep him for a couple of days and calm him down. I don't say he won't be resentful, but if you can handle your regular louts, you can handle a boy like Julian. Talk books to him — he'll like that.

But that's only part of my idea. It's not that I think it'll be a cinch to pry him out of Paris. He's wormed his way into the life over there — Iris says he sometimes even writes to her partly in French. I'm not so stupid as to believe that a relative he's never met, who comes at him out of the blue, is going to be much of an influence, just like that. You have to <u>know</u> him, to figure him out, not that I've been able to. I can't reach him, that's the fact of it, and Margaret — Margaret's awfully tired. Some days she's just too tired to cope with the <u>thought</u> of Julian, how long he's been away.

So Iris is the one. I'm sending her east next week, to get you acquainted with Julian. A briefing, in navy lingo. I should have arranged something like this before you went off on that vacation — but then I found out about it too late to do anything except get the check to you. You ought to be in touch more. When I see how thick Iris is with Julian, I realize how derelict my own sister's been. Ever since mama and papa died, eighteen years since mama, ten since papa, what do I know of your life? That you had a bad patch with a fellow who played the oboe, or whatever it was? Iris's plane is due at LaGuardia Thursday afternoon at 4:10 P.M. She'll stay the weekend, and then it's back on Monday — she's got her 9 A.M. lab Tuesday morning.

As ever,
Marvin

July 31, 1952

Dear Marvin,

I am looking forward to meeting your daughter. Luckily I have no out-of-town plans as I sometimes do on weekends in the summer, and will be free to host her. I believe she was no more than two or so, the only time I ever saw her. It's very fine that Iris understands Julian so well — she would certainly make a better emissary than I, so why not? I'm afraid you are being a little high-handed when you suppose I can simply fly off again at a word from you. I do have a job, whether or not you esteem it.

Yrs,
Bea

August 3, 1952

Bea:

Don't tell me about your so-called job, they'll never miss you. You do what you do and you are what you are because you never had the drive to be anything else. Iris is on her way

12

to a Ph.D., I <u>told</u> you this, the hard stuff, the real thing—she's
an ambitious kid, she's on track, she sticks to what she starts.
It's you I want over there, I've explained why. You can make
the time—get yourself one of those substitutes from the
teachers' union or whatever. As I said, I'll let you know where
Julian's at as soon as we hear. Meanwhile Iris will fill you in.

Marvin

4

MARVIN'S RANT, Marvin's bluster, with all its contradictions and lame exposures. The brutishness of his language, even when he imagined himself at his fanciest. The old nasty condescension. An unwitting confession of desperation — his son was a hard case, that was the long and the short of it. And still he intended, with a wave of a seigneurial hand, to ship her out again.

Marvin aimed high. How happy he would have been, Bea told Mrs. Bienenfeld, who taught history (this was during lunch break, in the teachers' lounge), to have been sired by a Bourbon, or even a Borgia. A Lowell or an Eliot would have done nearly as well. Unfortunately, he was the grandson of Leib Nachtigall, an impoverished greenhorn from an impoverished village in Minsk Province, White Russia. Poor Marvin was unrelated to the Czar of All the Russias — unless he was willing to cite a certain negative connection: grandfather Leib had fled the Czar's conscription, arriving in steerage and landing in Castle Garden with nothing but a tattered leather bag to start life in the New World. Marvin, miraculous Marvin, was the miraculous work of miraculous America. By now he was a dedicated Californian. And the greatest wonder of all was that he was a Tory (a Republican, in fact), an American Bourbon, an American Borgia! Or, if you insisted on going lower in the scale, a Lowell or an Eliot. If you *did* insist on going lower — just a little — you would discover that he had married a Breckinridge, the sister of a Princeton classmate. Her blood was satisfyingly blue. She had relatives in the State Department.

New York rarely drew him—an infrequent business trip; the two funerals, nearly a decade apart, first for mother, then for father. Bea had never set eyes on Marvin's son. She had seen Iris, the older child, only once, on the sole occasion Marvin brought his wife and their little girl east, for a landmark class reunion. Iris and Julian: Bea could barely remember their names. When Julian was born she dispatched a present; it was politely acknowledged by Marvin's wife: "Many thanks for your good wishes, and surely little Julian will enjoy the delightful giraffe"—something of the sort, on thick perfumed letter paper with that preposterous crest at the upper left margin.

Yet Marvin kept the ancestral name, and Bea, in deference to her students, had not: what were those big rough boys, with their New York larynxes, to make of Nachtigall? What they made of it was a cawing, a gargling, a sneezing, until she surrendered—though Nightingale had its own farcical consequences. Miss Mary Canary. Miss Polly-Want-a-Cracker. Miss Old Crow. Miss Robin Redbreast —*that* one produced smirks and snorts and whistles, and a clandestine blackboard sketch of a fat bird wearing eyeglasses and flaunting a pair of ballooning protuberances. As a penalty she ordered the smirkers to memorize "To a Skylark," and tested them on their performance. Oh, what she had come to! Poetry as punishment. Wasn't the summer's trip to have been an antidote to all that, an earned indulgence?

"But can you imagine," she said to Mrs. Bienenfeld, "he's pushing me to go back, when I've just come home. He snaps his fingers and expects me to jump. As if I don't have a life—"

That letterhead! Out of raw California, an aggrandizing crest—a silver shield displaying a pair of crossed swords rising out of a green river. A tribute to Margaret's signal line: Marvin had found it in a book of Scottish heraldry.

5

THE AIR-CONDITIONING was on everywhere, rattling as always. It was eight o'clock. They had eaten supper on trays in the living room, where the machine ran cooler — poached eggs on toast. There was a pitcher of iced tea on a side table.

"Is it this hot in L.A.?" Bea asked.

"Mostly. Sometimes hotter. What was it like in Paris?"

"Worse. Horrible. Fainting-hot."

"Did you actually faint?"

"No, but I drank gallons. The hotel people said it was the worst summer they'd had in fifteen years. Are you worn out from the plane, or would you like to take a walk? There's still plenty of light. I can show you famous upper Broadway."

"I'd rather sit here with you," Iris said.

"We don't have to get down to business right away. There's tomorrow, and the two days after."

"Business? Oh . . . about Julian."

"What you've come for."

"What dad says I've come for." She stretched her neck to take in everything around her. "How long have you lived alone?"

Intrusive, impertinent!

Bea said, suppressing annoyance, "Nearly all my adult life."

"I guess I sort of knew that. I heard you were married once."

"Then your father's had me on his mind a lot more than I would have thought —"

"Dad mentioned it a long time ago. I remember it because he almost never talks about his family."

"Does your mother talk about hers?"

"Not really. But she can't help it, people talk to her about them. Especially about my uncle who died. You know he was in Congress, he was even thinking of running for president."

"So the papers said at the time."

"I never knew *him* either."

The girl had a way of flicking her hair out of her eyes with a shrug that was half twitch and half shudder. Yet there was nothing unsure in this. A sign of boldness rather: the shake of an impatient colt. Her hair was long, neither light nor dark—a kind of bronze. Metallic, and when she whipped it round it had, faintly, the sound of coins caught in a net. Her resemblance to her mother hinted at some indistinct old photograph, insofar as Bea could conjure up her faded impression of Margaret. Iris had the same opalescent skin—fragile white smoke, and the thin nose with its small ovoid nostrils, and the pale irises. Iris: had they named her for the human eye? Hers was more bland than vivid—a screen. She might look out at you, but you couldn't fathom what stirred behind it.

"I thought while you're here," Bea said, "you might enjoy seeing a play. I've got us some tickets—a little theater down in the Village. Would you like that?"

It was self-defense. What did Marvin expect when he thrust his daughter at her? A walk, a play, sightseeing, what was she to *do* with this self-possessed young woman? The Empire State Building, views of the city? How to fill the time, how long would it take to be made privy to Julian's habits, Julian's predicament . . . Julian's soul? And to what end?

"Those two days," Iris said. "Well, I don't have them anyhow."

"But I understood from your father . . . you won't be staying till Monday?"

"I'm leaving tomorrow. I'm sorry about the tickets, if they have to go to waste—"

17

Bea said, "Tomorrow?"

"Yes, and if you wouldn't mind phoning dad, I know you usually write, but he won't care if you call him long-distance collect. Especially if it's urgent. Just explain that you want to keep me the whole week, and by Friday I'll be back."

Bea took a bewildered breath. "Back from where?"

"From seeing Julian. It's all set, plane fare and everything, but only if you help. If dad found out he'd blow up."

"Your father told me you have to be back at school, that's one thing," Bea said. "And the other is you can't possibly go off to Paris all on your own—"

But it came to her that she had herself hinted exactly this to Marvin: Iris as envoy.

"I've got the fare and practically the whole rest of it left over. In traveler's checks. The money dad gave me to give you for the rescue operation, bring 'im back alive."

"You don't know where he is."

"Mom and dad don't know. There's been a letter, only not for them, for me. I sneaked it past them, I always do that, they never saw it. Part of it nobody can read anyhow, it isn't even French, it's in a weird sort of writing, one of Julian's jokes—he's a funny boy sometimes."

"I won't go along with this," Bea said. "I can't let you, your father sent you here, you can't just run off—"

"I'm not twelve years old, and *you* don't want to go. You told dad you have to teach, you can't leave."

"It wouldn't be so easy, not that I can see the point of it. Why won't Marvin send your brother some money if he needs it and let him be? Why all this ambassadorial traffic—"

"Dad won't let anyone be. Poor Julian—it's dad's scenario. I'm supposed to be the family Madame Curie, and Julian's . . . hopeless. He doesn't apply himself, he's a parasite, he hasn't got an ounce of practicality, he doesn't know what he wants, no focus, too emotional—all that."

Bea asked, "And *are* you Madame Curie?"

"I don't have dad's push, nobody does. He's got me going for the degree that's supposed to be Julian's, I'm the stand-in for the star. Only there isn't any star." The twitch-shrug of the head. "I mean I really *can* see it from dad's point of view. *Merlin*—that's a magazine they have in Paris? It's run by a bunch of Americans over there, and Julian actually had an article in it. About pigeons."

"Pigeons?"

"Well, I guess doves. 'Doves in the Marais,' he called it, people worthless as pigeons, nuisances pecking around in the streets, in everybody's way, nobody wants them. Then he had something else, sort of like poetry though not exactly, in a big thick thing called *Botteghe Oscure*. Some rich American woman started it, a princess actually, married to a real Italian prince. So he sent us these things, and dad got mad, and wrote him I don't know what. And after that he never let on what he was up to."

The girl was tumultuous—Bea saw that she had read her too quickly. What had seemed strong-willed was a leaf propelled by a storm. For the first time she noticed how the upper lip was tilted forward, like an eave, over the lower one; in profile it made a small round bulge. Marvin's mouth! The tie of blood, an astonishment after all.

"Iris"—she opened out her hand to ward off the recognition—"what if your brother's content as he is?"

"Dad's considered stopping the money. And for a while he tried it—only last month he tried it. But Julian's perfectly willing to live on the edge, hand to mouth, so that won't work."

"Then what makes you think he'll listen to you?"

"He won't, I know he won't. I just want to *see* him. And I want him to see me. I want to give him the money myself. Especially if it's the last he's ever likely to get. That's why it's better for me to go, Aunt Bea, better for me than for you—"

"You don't have to say Aunt." An unexpected jump of whatever lurked in the ribs.

"That's just what I mean. Why should Julian care? Julian and I practically never knew we *had* an aunt. Going over there doesn't make sense for you, whatever dad's convinced himself about it. He feels he's out of options, he says it's business that's keeping him, but it's not that. He understands . . . well, he understands he's lost all his power when it comes to Julian."

"And when it comes to Iris?"

"I'm no different from Julian. It's only that I let him believe I'm different. It's taken me longer."

"To do what?"

"To get away."

A stillness blundered between them. The girl stood up and began to roam here and there, from the bookshelves to the window — the late sun just starting to slant toward dusk — to the aging Käthe Kollwitz prints on the walls to the striped davenport with its worn brown cushions. And finally to the grotesquerie of the grand piano, too roaringly huge in this modest space: a stupendous lion in a cramped cage. Watching Marvin's daughter examining the entrails of her past (the museum-shop prints, the flaking paperbacks, the piano on its thick paws, Iris's finger striking a key), Bea took in with new knowledge how everything in this overly familiar room was foreign to the girl, and poor, surely, to this offspring of affluence. In Marvin's bragging snapshots the big house in California resembled a castle in the shape of a conquistador's hacienda. Marvin the conqueror! The girl wandered off into the bedroom and back again: how unblemished she was, how young, what a limitless tract of unsullied years stretched ahead, and what was all that, Bea scolded herself, if not commonplace middle-aged envy? Her entire body was no better than a latticed basket leaking stale lost longings. That damn piano! That damn Leo!

And now this trespasser who called her aunt. Aunt? Then like it or not, swallow the role and act the part.

"You must be tired," Bea said. "You can have the bedroom, and I'll take the davenport. It opens up quite nicely."

"I was really thinking a hotel—"

"You'll have enough of that in Paris."

"No, I'll be staying with Julian . . . Paris? Aunt Bea! Then you'll do it? You'll call dad?"

A conspiracy. Reckless. "All right," Bea said. She felt a kind of pleasure in disobeying—no, deceiving—Marvin.

6

THE GIRL LEFT the next morning. Bea walked out with her to Broadway, where even at that early hour — the buildings all around still gray with sleep — taxis were sure to be cruising. Iris had declined breakfast.

"I'll be fine, there's always something to eat in the terminal. Or else on the plane —"

"And meanwhile," Bea said, "your father will be eating me alive."

"I wonder how it started, you and dad, the way things are —"

Bea thought this worth no more than a grunt. "My brother doesn't like me, that's all."

"But why?"

"It's not so unusual. Cain and Abel, Jacob and Esau —"

But then a yellow light winked toward the curb, and Iris vanished. A phantom. A visitation. A brevity! And without an instant's intimacy. A young stranger who came and went. Or came, and touched a random key on the piano, and dissolved with its sound.

The call to Marvin turned out not to be a trial. Bea had expected bullying and booming, Marvin's blowhard tactic. But he was almost pacific, even ingratiating: not in the mood, it seemed, to eat her alive.

"Good," he said, "looks like the two of you are hitting it off. She tell you about those fool magazines the boy got involved with? Didn't pay a red cent. He won't grow up. His sister's worth two of him, you saw that. Sure, let her take a few more days, what's the harm? Pump the kid, she knows her brother inside out, so all right, as long as she can paint you his portrait, if you get my drift—"

Paint his portrait! This was Marvin struggling to put on the dog, *You understand that Margaret would go if it was feasible, but as you are aware she is somewhat neurasthenic,* or lurching into a foreign tongue, what he presumed to be Bea's language, the uppity language of Poesy: the featherheaded birds' choir. She could not accuse him of satire or even sarcasm. Forget white-shoe Princeton, Marvin at his most genuine had a voice out of the streets. There was a kind of innocence in it: he was earnest, he was oblivious, he was honestly trying to please her, he was working at being conciliatory. He was seeing her, for the moment, as useful.

"Even if Iris gets to miss her lab?" Bea said: edging toward peril. By this time, she calculated, the girl had already been three hours in the air.

"Leave it to my daughter, she'll make up for it, she'll manage. That kid can cope with anything—listen, if she didn't have this big exam coming up, some sort of big review, I'd have her make the trip herself, not that you didn't have the same idea. But couple more days with her aunt, I'm not worried, it's an investment. The more time with Iris, the more you'll get the picture, no big surprises when you see what you've got to tackle. So let her bring you up to speed, keep her at it, take her around if that helps, show her the city."

Poor Marvin: he was out of breath, making the best of it. Julian the hard, hard case.

"I've got us tickets to a play," Bea said. A truth that lied. To use up the extra ticket, she intended to invite Mrs. Bienenfeld. The play was *Othello*. Afterward, if Mrs. Bienenfeld agreed (she had a husband and a teenage son at home), they might stop for dessert in one of those barely lit Village places: candles in saucers.

"A play's fine," Marvin said. "If it was me, I'd pick one of those Broadway musicals, I hear *South Pacific*'s still on. So hey, did you fix it to get time off?"

"Not yet." The spore of betrayal.

"Well look, don't you wait till the last minute, I want you out there as soon as we know. Eventually he throws his mother a bone, he comes up with the new place he's at. Moves around a lot, that's how they do it. I mean the drifters. I want that boy back here!"

The booming was beginning.

"Regards to Margaret," Bea said, and hung up.

7

IN THE END — the end of what? ah, she knew, she knew — she did not invite Mrs. Bienenfeld to *Othello*. It was being put on in one of those avant-garde cellars in a part of the Village that was really still the Lower East Side. You went down a flight of cracked stone stairs stinking of urine, canine or human (evidences of both species, a dried-up turd pile, the lost heel of a shoe with the nails sticking up), and stepped into the dark, where rows of battered folding chairs faced a narrow raised platform. The costumes were makeshift and clumsy, and you could see into the wings where the actors were fiddling with wigs and swords, getting ready for the next scene. You could also glimpse a comical lineup of Heinz ketchup bottles, noble Shakespearean blood, on a wooden shelf. The idea of these places was to do the unexpected (the primal word was "transgressive"): the Moor played by a white woman in blackface and pantaloons, breasts suppressed by a wide silk band; Desdemona a lipsticked young Negro in a yellow peruke. Or else, to save on expenses, the whole thing would be set in Manhattan, with a backdrop of impressionistic skyscrapers and the actors in contemporary clothing.

So — in the end — she tore up the tickets. It was because of the piano: the connections might be invisible, but they were *there*, palpable and audible. Audible for sure! The piano was Leo's; years ago he had left it behind. Not permanently, he said, only for a few weeks — one day soon he'd send the truckers for it. Bea herself was a musical blank. A deaf chromosome, a missing vertebra. Leo knew this when they married: he valued it. Bea, thinking it over (she often drifted in that direction, even nowadays), believed it was this spinal absence, more pronounced than a mere lack of aptitude, that had pleased him from the start. It kept him immaculate: she could not contaminate him with half-knowledge or meaningless praise. The piano was his mind, his mind was the piano. She had never once touched it, except (obviously!) to dust the legs, the looming sheen of the frame. Her obedient cloth barely skimmed white teeth and thin black lozenges; she didn't dare set off the secret hammer within, shaped like a foot in a velvet sock, the crier of the cry. The piano was protected territory. She had no entrance there, partly out of ignorance, partly out of reverence. The piano was worshiped.

And out of the ether, uncalled for, invading, this calamitous foreign body, this unknown niece, this Iris, this scrutinizing violating blue eye, had fingered a key and brought out a sound. A single sound, lone, unattached, desolate. Even chaste. Whereas Leo had sent out thundering swarms, armies clashing, raging unkempt battalions, war whoops, warplanes arcing and plunging, great crushing tanks on giant crashing treads. The noises of ecstatic gods who could kill.

In those days Leo was a beautiful boy. There was no other way to say it. Handsome is outer and ephemeral. Leo's beauty was Platonic, embedded in a theory of the world and its implausible reality. His round eyes hinted at the cycle of eternal things, and an inch above them were the faint, just-beginning lines of an intelligent frown. He was not very tall, but this only drew more attention to his head. Leo's curly head seemed larger than it was because of the very black hair that pushed aggressively upward from his ears and forehead, with no admixture of commonplace dark brown or traces of the Jewish tendency toward the reddish. Out of the forest of wavy blackness, its puffs and folds and spirals glinting as sporadically as foliage in sunlight, two steel eyes took you in with an unrelenting judgment. The nose was severely ideal, like a schoolgirl's drawing; under it the mild grin. It was this unsettling contradiction—the kindly mouth and Leo's brazen, strict, assessing stare — that shocked Bea into what she scarcely wanted to admit: an instant wash of infatuation. He acknowledged that they were bound to meet. Destiny was opposed to their never meeting; if you tried to defy destiny, especially if you happened to live merely one city block away, you would implode. And again the careless grin.

Leo was Laura Coopersmith's cousin, and Laura was Bea's classmate at Hunter College: the two of them, in the new low-waisted frocks that showed their knees, sat together in history and English. Laura had contrived a pair of spit curls, each one a brown comma set in the center of a cheek. From her neck waggled a long loop of fake Woolworth's pearls: it was, she said, the "flapper look," copied from the pictures in society columns featuring debutantes and nightlife. But this was as far as she would go in boldness. She was serious about her future as a high school teacher and had chosen history as her subject because, she believed, it was factual and objective and couldn't be argued with. She admired Leo and disliked him: when he wasn't teasing her, he ignored her. He was an out-of-towner from Chicago, studying piano and composition at Juilliard. To satisfy his frugal parents he had agreed to board with his uncle's family in New York — Laura's father and Leo's father were brothers. Both were salesmen, Laura's father in paper goods and Leo's in textiles. The music, Laura explained, was from Leo's mother's side. She had hoped to become a professional singer, and once gave a concert of Schubert *Lieder* at the local Y in Des Plaines. Somewhere in Leo's gene pool there lurked a remote yet renowned cantor. Folklore had it that cantors, when they were not outright fools, had low intelligence. Such defamation could not apply to Leo. He was reading Nietzsche and Aldous Huxley.

Bea, in her private way, hid her infatuation from Laura, who would only have jeered at its pointlessness: *Leo isn't for the likes of you.* The likes of Bea! Laura's goals were meager. In her senior year she became engaged to Harold Bienenfeld. Her wedding dress had a six-foot lace train. At the close of the ceremony the ring boy, in charge also of the rented cage, released four practiced white doves. They circled over the startled guests and then flew docilely back into their cage. Its floor was thick with mottled droppings.

"I suppose you'll be the next one," Leo said.

"The next what?" Though of course she knew.

They were standing side by side near an ice sculpture — twin mermaids embracing — at the base of which lay wide oval platters of sliced melon, layer upon layer of pink, orange, green, studded with swollen strawberries still attached to their leafy stems. The strawberries resembled surgically removed organs freshly lifted from the gash in an anaesthetized belly.

"Bride, wife, mother, teacher."

"I'd rather be an Indian chief," Bea retorted.

"There can't be two chiefs in one tribe."

"Who's the other?"

"Your sibling, Prince Marvin. Only he's the other kind of Indian, a Princeton rajah. And you're the pauper who got sent to a public college, for free."

"Marvin's good at math. They gave him a scholarship."

"And what are you good at?" Leo asked. She was almost certain he wasn't needling her. He was looking for useful information. Or else — it was what she feared — whatever she might say would mean nothing to him, it was only prattle to pass the time.

At nineteen Bea was truthful. "I want to make my mark in the world," she told him. The instant it was out, she felt humiliated.

"An aspiration as admirable as its expression is trite," Leo said, and gave her an impatient little push. "Hey, come on, a waltz, even if they're lousy at it. Baboons on harmonicas, who cares?"

Trite: should she be hurt? Truthful was reckless. He judged her by his cousin Laura, by the intertwined frozen mermaids ("Sapphists," he muttered), and by the second-rate wedding band; he judged her by Harold Bienenfeld, who was going into his father's accounting business. If you mean to make your mark, how else can you put it? Better never to tell. If you told, it was only natural that you'd be ridiculed.

28

At the end of the dance, he let her drop backward in a dip, a ballroom maneuver she had seen only in the movies. The fast swooping motion, thrusting her nearly all the way down with her head close to the floor, and up again into the cavern of his long jacket sleeves breeding warmth, whirled her into a moment of vertigo. His face streaked in her vision.

"A mark? Any old mark?" — as if nothing had intervened. "Or is there something explicit you have in mind?" A stir of nausea. She slowed her breath, hoping to thwart an upward-creeping gas bubble. It broke silently in her throat. "Because," he said, "I'm all for the explicit. You've got to *know,* and you've got to know that you know. Beethoven of the twentieth century, for instance, that's me. Maybe Stravinsky. Hindemith maybe. Kiddo, just call me Doctor Faustus. Captain of my fate."

She saw that under the mockery — of her, of himself — he was as driven as Marvin, the Princeton rajah. But still he was only a poor Chicago boy stuck with his father's relations in a five-story Bronx walkup. Laura had told her that he slept on a foldaway couch in the dining room, where in the mornings he was in everyone's way.

"You're not a bad dancer," he admitted. "I've been with worse. But you're never going to make it with the Bolshoi, so how about it? What're you after?"

He was someone who could hold on to a thread. He let nothing dangle, he followed through. The heat in his voice — was it artificial, pumped up? Anyhow she let it draw her out. "You'll laugh," she said, "because I've had different ideas at different times, and they all add up to the same. Sometimes I think I could be a foreign correspondent, or even a sort of detective, going all over to figure things out. And sometimes I think about archaeology, digging up old secrets everyone's forgotten. But lately" — she was babbling, and did she dare? — "I've thought about making up a sort of dictionary."

"Miss Samuel Johnson, lexicographer. Pleased to meet you." A relief: he wasn't laughing. Instead he was examining her as if she was some unfamiliar insect or bird, or a kind of unknown root rumored

29

to be edible. "But Miss Johnson, ma'am, one can't help observing that none of these have any sensible connection—"

"Oh, but they're all just alike. They're things that start out hidden, and then you find them out. I mean it wouldn't be a dictionary of *words*, nothing like that. Nothing that's ever existed before."

"How about cloud shapes? Elephants, giraffes, shoes, chimneys with smoke coming out, pies, puddings, cheese. Balloons, obviously. Tuna fish in or out of the can, with little cloud-drawings all around. Or what about a dictionary of famous crooks, serial killers, say, in alphabetical order—"

"If you're going to do *that*," she said (a tug of confusion just behind her eyes), "I won't tell it." And immediately did: "A dictionary of feelings. Moods. Smells. Feelings that everyone's somehow felt, only there's no name for them. Look," she cried, "you *can't* make fun of everything there is!"

"I can of everything that isn't. It sounds to me," he said mildly, "that you're well on your way to being a run-of-the-mill high school teacher. English lit, possibly—all that sensibility."

"And you," she shot back, "are just a run-of-the-mill false prophet. And what's more, you're not on your way to it, you're already there."

She was shamed: why hadn't he heard what lay beating below that unlucky spew of wayward nonsense? It was inchoate; it was worse than clouds, it had no shape at all. *I want to make my mark:* this wasn't what she meant really, it was foolishness, it was trite (yes!), a fantasy, a kind of crippled poem; she was incriminated. The trouble with liking poetry (she did like it, she liked it immensely), exhaling the words almost aloud but mainly under your breath so that no one would hear you freakishly murmuring, was that it inflamed you, it made you want your life on this round earth to *count*, the way the poet and the poem counted. *Ah, love, let us be true to one another! for the world, which seems to lie before us like a land of dreams, so various, so beautiful, so new* . . . A mark, a mark, a dent in history, a leaving—even (even!) if not her own. She all at once seized on it; *this* was what she was after: to be attached in some intimate way to a marvel, a force, a prodigy, the other side of the moon, where ordinary mortals could never go. Or to plummet into the sun! The big dark room was over-heated: gilt cornices, mirrored walls, dim chandeliers sprouting fat electric candles, statuettes of gods on fluted pedestals. A male singer in an oiled pompadour was whining slowly into a microphone, elon-gating the vowels like stretched taffy. The band had lurched into a foxtrot; couples pressed shoulders and hips close, the men's bowties coming undone, the women's armpits seeping sweat. And now the wedding cake was wheeled in on a cart, like a belated and infirm guest gallantly overdressed in too many fringes and tassels. On its topmost ledge stood the stiff little sugar bride and groom with their tiny black staring licorice toy eyes. A child in a long pink gown and a garland in her hair ran up to it and picked out the eyes to suck, and then spat them out. The ice sculpture was melting quickly. Nobody minded; its glory was past, and Leo, loitering, held his palm under the cold drip-ping tail of a mermaid, catching the drops that fell with the regular-ity of a metronome. Bea felt him burning there; it was as if his hand had caught fire and he was cooling it in ice water. Looking all around, and finally down at her blue satin party shoes with their nasty narrow toes that hurt, she knew him to be made of sulfur—he was a match, he could strike flames!

The two of them despised Laura's wedding.

He began to take her to student concerts. Sometimes he played in them, but more often not. He complained that he was not doing well enough at the piano—the practice rooms at Juilliard were too much in demand, the waiting lists were too long, he didn't get suf-ficient time. There was a piano at his uncle's (Laura had been given lessons as a child), but it was a second-hand upright, wildly out of tune, and hardly adequate. He worked at it anyhow, wincing when a note turned up sour, until his aunt protested that she couldn't en-dure the racket one minute more, her ears were ringing, the neigh-bors were warning her that the noise was drowning out their favorite radio programs.

"Look at my dumb cousin," he told Bea. "She and that dimwit Mister Debit-and-Credit have three whole rooms to themselves, and what've I got?"

"Laura's bed," Bea said promptly. "At least you're off the couch now. Besides, they can afford it, Harold has his job and Laura's applying for her teaching certificate —"

"I need a place of my own. I need a decent instrument. A grand, and the space for it."

"You could change to something else, couldn't you? Something smaller, and . . . portable."

"Portable? Put it in a sack and drag it around. How about a kazoo? A kazoo would do me just fine, it could go right in my pocket. Maybe a whistle? Bach on a blade of grass, it wouldn't cost a cent. I could just sit with it in a closet and not bother anybody. Or an oboe, that's the rajah's idea, don't tell me it isn't —"

It was the oboe that stung — Marvin's private taunt, not that Marvin would know an oboe from an organ grinder with a monkey. The ludicrous word itself: *oboe, oboe,* a monkey bleat, a jungle sound. Marvin had long ago declared war on Leo. Leo, he said, was going nowhere, and what did you expect from an oboe, what could you get out of a type like that? Two years before, Marvin had been pledged by Kappa Beta Kappa; he was elated. They had never before taken in anyone on scholarship, and certainly never a Jew named Nachtigall. A Lehman, a Schiff possibly, those old Hebrew bluebloods. He didn't have the looks, he didn't have the money, he couldn't exactly figure why he had been chosen (they actually called him the Chosen One), and it was true that they made good use of him, though not always to the point of abuse — he helped with math and chemistry, and wrote their papers now and then, in that fake pretentious hifalutin prose he supposed their professors liked. He liked it himself, and tried it out in letters to Breckinridge's sister. He was a kind of convenience, an in-house tutor. He suspected that his wasn't the only frat to keep a Jew for this purpose, but he put the thought away: it was too cheap, a cheapness to be overcome. If helping out (he didn't think *serving*) was the price, it was worth it, an investment, it would pay off in the future. And he got a lot from *them:* he saw how they dressed, how they talked, their shoes, the crease in their trousers, their boredom between syllables. He was learning to drink as they did, cheerfully and boisterously. They were all good fellows. When they drank they ragged him: he was the Chosen One, he was Hardware Boy; sometimes—affectionately, frat-style—he was Jewboy. And sometimes not so affectionately: *Will it be bagels or knishes for breakfast this morning? Or the blood of a Christian child?* But they had taken him in! The grandson of an immigrant who sold pots and pans. "And you," he admonished Bea, "want to get stuck with an oboe." Kappa Beta Kappa—it stood for Courage, Boldness, Conquest—was honing his power to insult. From the very beginning Marvin hadn't comprehended Leo.

And Leo was quicksilver: Bea could not keep up with him. "Still," he threw out at her, "if I have to do it with a blade of grass," and veered into his sidewise grin. It was the kind of self-satisfaction she had come to recognize: he was single-minded, he had a strain of what now and then struck her as fanaticism. But Marvin too was a fanatic. He had set himself on a straight course upward. He was shrewd, he hustled, he had a campaign. He had his eye on Breckinridge's sister. There was money there, and an attractive diffidence, and a quiet, almost suppressed, way of watching him, or pretending not to. Marvin didn't covet the money—he intended to make his own—but it was the shyness and the quiet that lured him, Margaret in a white dress, her head down, glancing up at him with her nervous inquisitive anxious look. Her napkin tricornered on her lap. A tiny blossom, a mere three petals, stitched into her gloves.

Leo's course was strangely, almost mystically, inward—it wasn't a course at all, it was the opposite, it was indefinable, to know it was not to know it, it was the pulse of a river, it was a rod of light, he would go where it led, he was mercurial, he was protean, he wasn't for the explicit after all, he was illumined! He explained that the instrument itself didn't matter, that all the world's instruments were joined in an operatic clamor in his brain; whole orchestras. He wasn't born to regurgitate or copy — he wasn't destined to be a commonplace musician, however skilled (here he sniffed out a nostrilful of scorn) at "interpretation." Let those practitioners, those inspired mechanics, interpret as they pleased: he was the horn of plenty who fed their French horns, their clarinets, their tubas, their flutes and cellos and violins! He was the thunder-maker who commanded the bass, the drums, the cymbals! They were the fingers, the tongues, the lungs, the hands merely; the creatures of the notes, the score, the skin of the thing. He was a seer — their Wagner, their creator, their god. What he divined, they must obey. He was the thing itself — the vibration that steamed up from a cauldron stoked by demons, or out of a tornado stirred by a rush of an armada of divinities. He was going to compose symphonies, couldn't she grasp this?

Poor Bea protested that she took him at his word, but wasn't he contradicting himself, and if he didn't need a piano really, then why . . .

"Are we back to the kazoo in a sack? Your famous principle of portability? Listen, Beatrice," he scolded, "man doth not live by Tao alone. There's the reality principle too. I have to have a piano, a Baldwin if not a Steinway, I need a place of my own — how many times do I have to say it? Especially when you're in a position to help, and you do nothing."

Bea in a position to help?

"Your parents," he said.

"They're in the store all day."

"That hole in the wall. Your mother speaks of it as though she's in steel, she's running an empire."

"My aunts think she would if they let her."

"They" was Bea's father. Bea's mother had a head for business. She was ambitious; her husband was not. He was content with his modest legacy, the product of his father's ascent from customer peddler — door to door with three monstrous suitcases packed with knives, ladles, spatulas, can openers, sieves, frying pans, screwdrivers, pliers, even tea sets — to shopkeeper. Bea's mother had arranged

34

for a grand neon sign that swung crimsonly from a creaking metal arm: AMERICA'S HOUSEHOLD EMPORIUM. But it was still only Leib Nachtigall's small shadowy hardware store, despite the newly installed fluorescent lighting. Bea's parents knew every nail, every washer, every picture hook in the tiny drawers set in tall wooden cabinets ranged side by side along the dark walls. Her mother hoped to enlarge the business; she planned to buy the vacant store abutting theirs. But her father demurred: one shop was enough, he said. It was commonly understood (by Bea's three aunts, her mother's unmarried sisters) that Marvin had inherited his push from his thwarted mother, who subscribed to *The Cutlery Courier* and *Hammer & Saw Digest* and dreamed of founding a chain of hardware stores, while Bea's father, when there was a lull up front, rested in a private rear nook and read George Meredith and Henry James. The lulls were frequent.

Leo said, "It doesn't have to be anything like Laura's. The mob, that extravaganza of a dress, the silly cake, those damn birds, the ushers, the bridesmaids, my God, the *flower* girl, the bloody *ring* boy, the whole thing a pageant, a parade, a cavalcade, a saturnalia, a phantasmagoria—"

Leo's affectations. *Bloody?*

"Leo, what are you talking about?"

"Parsimony, my dear, bloody parsimony. We'll skip the wedding and keep the honeymoon."

So it was a marriage proposal. It was also a directive. Bea was to persuade her parents to forfeit the usual wedding palace and its paraphernalia (*phantasmagoria, saturnalia!*). The cost of all that stupidity would very nearly pay for a Steinway grand, even if it had to be a reconditioned one—but anyhow Leo had a connection at Juilliard who had a connection with someone at Steinway who might get them a good price on a new one. They would need only one room big enough to hold the piano, an icebox, and a hotplate, and that would suffice. As for the rent, Bea should do what Laura was doing, and teach. It was all sensible and practical; it was operating on the reality principle.

"Besides," Leo pointed out, "your college hasn't cost your family a nickel, so they owe you something, don't they?"

"Leo, I don't want to teach."

"What else could you do? Anyhow it would only be for a little while, until I get on my feet."

"Do composers ever get on their feet?" she wondered.

"This one will," he said; it was the certainty principle.

To their tiny new apartment (but Leo called it "my atelier") Bea's father brought boxes of useful things: an array of carving knives, half a dozen aluminum cooking pots in graduated sizes, a set of sil-ver-rimmed spice jars, an egg timer, a pepper grinder, a scissors, a cutting board, a tea kettle, a strainer, a steamer, a pitcher, and three tall bottles of furniture polish. He stared respectfully at the piano — it wasn't a Steinway after all, but it was certainly a grand, and costly enough. Wherever you tried to walk, it was always in the way. To get to the bed, you had to go around the piano. The bed itself was a pres-ent from the aunts, who were feeling cheated: it wasn't responsible, it wasn't respectable — to sneak off to City Hall, without so much as a ceremony, without family, without a normal *wedding!* The aunts be-lieved that just as Marvin took after his mother, it was Bea who took after her father: he actually thought of the piano as his daughter's dowry. It gave him a veiled chill, like something out of an old tale.

"Well, Beatrice," he said, "it looks like you've married a future concert artist, so don't forget to keep the wood oiled. You don't want to let such beautiful wood dry out."

Bea's mother blew out an exasperated breath. "Concert artist, they're nothing but a pair of senseless kids, they don't know what they're doing." And then, *sotto voce* (but Bea caught it), "Marvin will do better."

Her parents were quickly gone. They rarely left the store together; one or the other had to stay behind to tend to any stray customer in search of a wrench.

Leo threw himself on the bed and pulled Bea down with him. Her toes were inches from the piano's black flank. "Nasty old virginal voyeurs," he said.

"Who?" Nearly everything Leo uttered was new to her, and unexpected.

"Your mother's old-maid sisters. Why do you think they gave us a bed, of all things?"

"Generosity," Bea said bravely. "They haven't got a lot of money, but they heard we needed some furniture—"

"And why is it you're always bringing up money?"

Unfair: it was Leo who was fixed on money, or why else had he urged her to follow Laura into that terrible school? Those wild raucous young thugs who worked on greasy engines, why should they care about *Sir Gawain and the Green Knight,* and how could she possibly make them care? Laura's principal had been willing to hire Bea, even without experience; he had an urgent opening for an English teacher. And as Leo had promised, it was Bea's job that paid for their atelier.

"God only knows," he persisted, "what those old-lady sex maniacs imagine we'll be doing in their bed—"

Bea had never imagined what her aunts might imagine.

"Then I'll show you," Leo said.

The bed and the piano, the piano and the bed: it seemed to Bea that the piano, so hotly close to the bed, fevered it with unpredictable paroxysms. She could not tell when it would lunge; each time it was the same, and also different. The piano was a delirium, a maelstrom. It rocked her and tossed her; it swallowed her up and threw her out. It was insidious, it swam in her blood and then coughed her out as foreign matter. Leo, steadfast at the keys, was inventing those sounds: they were, he said, the crash of his footsteps through a wilderness, he was battling his way into a mighty thicket where no one before him had gone, he was creeping upward toward an undiscovered peak as arduous as Everest, or else he was on tiptoe, lullaby-soporific, or as explosive as twenty tons of TNT. He told Bea to listen for gunfire, and groaning war machines, and the treble howls of falling planes or women keening. He was at war with the piano; the piano was at war with itself. And then he would drop onto the bed, a spent runner returned from an alien kingdom bristling with cannon.

Bea went every morning to her classroom. It smelled of male sweat, of seats fumy with uneasy odors, of salami sandwiches, of sneakers rubbery and faintly urinous. It smelled of beer. The brutish muscles of young men bulged under their sleeveless shirts. Their dark voices made a blue-black din. They laughed at *Julius Caesar,* so she tried "The Midnight Ride of Paul Revere." They laughed at that too.

Leo was beginning to grumble about his days at Juilliard.

"But you told me the training's important, it keeps you channeled," Bea countered.

"It keeps me trammeled. I feel cramped, I'm stultified over there, I can't breathe. The place is a vault, it's airless, not that it's anyone's fault exactly, it's just that they don't know what to do with you if you're an original."

"Aren't there lots of composers who come out of music school?"

"Lots? *Lots?* For God's sake, Bea, the real thing doesn't crop up in clumps, they don't graduate them a dozen a year, it shows up maybe once in every five generations, why can't you understand this? And 'music school,' very nice, I like the way you put it. Music school, high school, allee samee, what's in my head all day is no different from what's in yours, is that what you're telling me—"

"Well," she said, "what do you want to do?"

"Do! That's just it, I want to do it, actually *do* it, not go on pretending to be just another up-and-coming composition drudge when I'm already there. I feel it, I know it, I know what's in me, I've got my ideas. Gershwin, Schönberg, Cage, don't think I'm not on to them, what they're up to, and you bet your life I intend to leave them all behind—"

Leo, burbling, gurgling, winding on and on, half satiric, self-seduced, concealing what he really meant by telling what he really meant: he meant to make his mark in the world, she saw this, she believed him, it was nothing like her own insubstantial fantasies, she had abandoned these, oh easily, easily, they had evaporated, leaving not a rack behind; her fantasies were no more than a dictionary of clouds. Leo's talk was artifice and rattle and shuttlecock; but (she knew this) it masked the detonations of his will. It was as zigzag and made-up as the crashing music in his mind.

Which was why, in the end, Bea tore up the tickets. The nerve of that girl, that so-called niece: a stranger, an intrusion, an invasion. A violation! Those secretive roving eyes, that casually encroaching finger daring to strike a note, any note, one key interchangeable with another, one poison as bitter as any other, a trespass, a violation! Laura might have been accommodating, she was always willing to do a favor, but what was *Othello* to her? Laura and Harold preferred the movies; they went often.

So did Bea, but alone, clandestinely: she had her reasons.

8

Dear Aunt Bea—you don't want me to call you that, but it's
hard to change. I've always thought of you as the Unknown
Aunt, and maybe you've thought of me as the Non-Existent
Niece. When I barged in on you in New York (that has to
be how it felt for you), we weren't really at home with each
other, were we? It was only one night, and even if it sounds
unreasonable and selfish, I did want you to know me a little, at
least enough to defend me. What must you have been thinking when I didn't turn up last Friday, as I'd promised? A whole
week's gone by, and I wonder whether you've heard from dad,
or is he still stuck with whatever it was you cooked up to tell
him, some nice soothing story about how you just had to have
more time to get the lowdown on Julian.

What I hope you'll help with now is another big fib to ward
off dad, though I can't think what it should be—I know he's
going to have himself a meltdown, and the truth is I can't face
it. So I'm leaving it to you to do it for me, maybe out of that
family feeling dad's suddenly discovered he wants from his
long-lost sister. You saw the postmark, you've already figured
out that I haven't left Paris. I'm not coming back, anyhow not
for a while, I never meant to, and you're right to condemn me
as the most horrible liar in the world, but I <u>had</u> to fix it somehow to get away without dad breathing down my neck every

40

minute. I'm here with Julian and Lili (Julian calls the two of us, Lili and me, the Botanicals), and I can't tell how long it'll be—there's a lot to take in. I can't explain it all in this letter, since I want finally to get it in the mail, and I know I should have written days ago. Please don't blame me too much, it's only that it's so complicated here, more than I ever guessed. Whatever you can do with dad, I'll thank you forever.

Iris

P.S. You might let him know that Julian's not living in any sort of rathole if that's what he's worried about. It's more like a palace. Also it's probably best not to mention Lili right now, don't you think?

The Botanicals! It was the first clue Bea had that Julian, sulky and stubborn, had a wisp of wit. The rest was wisp upon wisp: the girl-friend, hardly more solid than the rumor or dread she'd been before. And that infuriating *I'll thank you forever,* with its tone of entitle-ment, its expectation of being served; its command. Iris might wear Margaret's bland look, but oh! she was Marvin's daughter. And she was at it still, duplicity engendering duplicity: having inveigled Bea into outflanking Marvin, she was ordering a second maneuver. The first had been easy enough; he had swallowed it almost benignly, and wasn't there more than a touch of triumph in outwitting Marvin? But to do it yet again, another round of sleight of hand, when she had no interest in these young people's lives, their plots and intimacies, their alien bodies and whatever effluvium might pass for their souls. Iris and Julian, niece and nephew, flesh of her flesh, who had never cared to seek her out, or she them. They were mutually incurious and mu-tually superfluous. It was fear (Marvin's fear) that was tossing them all into a single dirty drawstring sack—Marvin, at home in Califor-nia, tightening the cord. He was afraid of Europe. He was afraid of Paris. Bea saw in him a kind of terrorized primitive—his Paris was no more than the platitudes of the postcards, Eiffel Tower, Arc de

Triomphe; and grimly below, diseased and bloody dungeons engulf-
ing his boy. Beneath those famed public monoliths were interiors a
visitor could never fathom; and in Marvin's naked grasp of it, his
son, no longer merely a visitor, had penetrated that unnatural dark.
Julian was a captive of Europe. He was gradually turning foreign.

His sister was abetting him. Worse, she was coercing Bea into a
further scheme she ultimately had no taste for — what was she to say
to Marvin? If Marvin was a lion to be bearded, then Iris ought to take
on the bearding herself. She had lied and run off — let her feel the
poundings of her father's roar. It was only just, it was what she deserved; Bea, for her part (but she had no part in any of it), intended to
remain an outsider to this California crisis — California, where the
capricious seductions of too warm air and too much sun melted away
familial ties, parents from children, husbands from wives; where, for
years and years now, Leo had, after all, become the captain of his
fate, and where, though they lived in their fancy houses with those
red-tiled Spanish roofs and hanging balconies, possibly less than a
mile apart, Leo and Marvin would never meet.

The girl's urgings: arrogant, dictatorial — but also a plea. A plea
for fraudulence and fabrication. It came to Bea that the two of them,
Iris and Marvin, had ceded to her the means to punish: the father for
his tyranny, the daughter for her evasions.

Then what was she to say to Marvin?

The cold and dangerous truth.

9

Dear Marvin,

It's a bit surprising that I haven't had so much as a word
from you about the many days' delay in Iris's return, though
by now you must be getting somewhat impatient. Even knowing that she's missed her lab work (I recognize how this must
upset you), you've given her, and me, a good deal of leeway.
In fact, I've been half expecting the telephone to ring itself
hoarse. I can only attribute your indulgence to your trust in
me, and to your belief in the worthiness of your plan. I write
now to tell you a hard thing, with this caveat. If when you
receive this you attempt to phone, I promise you I will absolutely not listen to a rant. If you begin one, I will instantly
cut you off. I do not agree to be yelled at, or accused, or
belittled. I have no responsibility for any of it. Here are the
facts. Your trust, and your plan, and my mistaken trust in
your daughter, have all failed. It seems that Iris never had
any intention of schooling me in her brother's character and
circumstances—as far as she's been able to surmise them
from a distance. She has now closed that distance. She is with
Julian in Paris. This was as much a bolt from the blue for me as
it will be for you. On the positive side, you will recall that you
yourself considered, if only fleetingly, the idea of sending Iris
alone. Apparently this was her thought as well. She feels for

43

her brother, and she, more than anyone, certainly more than I, will have the means to persuade him to come home. On the negative side, she gives no sign of her own return — make of this what you will.

As ever,
Beatrice

•

August 23, 1952

Bea:

All right, you've given me a shock. I suppose that was the idea. And no, I won't be phoning. At this point I simply don't care to hear your voice and whatever cock-and-bull story you'll come up with in that schoolmarmy sleaze of yours. It may shut up those slum kids you've decided to sacrifice your life to, but it won't get to me. And please don't tell me you had no inkling my daughter was heading for Paris! It won't hold water, I'm on to what you've been up to, I knew it the minute I got back and found this pile of shit you've sent me. Actually I've been in Mexico on a deal — we're selling them helicopters, not that some of those honchos down there can tell an engine from a horse's ass. The plain fact of it is I assumed Iris was back at school. She's got her own little place just off campus — she said she wanted her independence so I set her up out there at never mind the cost. I've always done what I could to please my children, and for what return! Anyhow it wasn't easy on Iris living here with Margaret the way she's been. Right now, for the last month or so, Margaret's being treated in a very good rest home, the Suite Eyre, here in Beverly Hills. I came back to an empty house, except for the housekeeper, and I won't deny that I deliberately keep this woman as blind as a bat — I don't need a servant to snoop into my family's comings and goings. I sacked the last one when she started asking why Margaret sleeps so much in the afternoons. Of course I can't let Margaret know about Iris, at least not right now,

I'm afraid she'd just slip over the edge. She's always had her
nerves, but what's made her sicker than usual is Julian's disappearance. That's how she says it, Julian's disappearance. As
if he's gone up in a puff of smoke, as if something horrible's
been done to him. And now Iris! So I ask you, why did you let
this happen? Why did you let my daughter do this? What's
this crazy business about her not coming back? Why in God's
name didn't you STOP her? You shit, you never stopped her!
My kids are running from me, and why? What have I done?
What haven't I done? Did I neglect them, did I hurt them?
Sometimes I feel it's a curse, but for what? I don't know, I
don't know. All I know is that I want my son to come home.
He doesn't belong there, it's the wrong place for him, they've
swallowed him up over there. You tell me Iris will get him
back. But what if whatever it is over there swallows her up the
same as Julian? I'm a dead man, I'm dead, for God's sake, Bea,
can't you understand what I'm going through?

                                                    Marvin

You shit. This pile of shit. Marvin back in street mode. Marvin
undone.

10

THE NEW HOTEL was surprisingly full for September, and though it was less expensive than the last one, it was also, for the money, surprisingly shabby. But on short notice she was lucky to find a room at all, and she could afford nothing better — what foolishness, a second trip two months after the first! Summer was officially over, the tourists were still swarming, and the better-off Parisians who habitually escape the city in August were trickling back. The taxi from the airport had dropped her in front of a narrow pair of steps at an ordinary wooden door, when she had expected a marquee and a man in uniform. She was obliged to prop the door open with one foot while struggling to swing her suitcase over the threshold and into the tiny lobby. The young clerk at the reception counter made no move to help.

The room turned out to be stifling. Its single window, partly blocked by a battered wardrobe, looked out on a dirty alley. A wide bed with a gully in the middle of its belly consumed nearly all the space there was, and a narrow pathway at its flank led to what had been advertised as "Spacious Private Bath with Shower." The toilet and the washbasin were jammed together catty-corner, almost obstructed by a huge tub in which a serpentine hose lay coiled.

But in the morning she found the lobby transformed by a circle of little breakfast tables lit by sharp slashes of sunlight and crowded with staccato British chirps and the low catarrh of German. She drank the very good coffee, nibbled at a bit of brie and a croissant, and set out.

She had left behind her guidebook — it was useless for her present confusions — but had extracted from its pocket a compact map of Paris. The map was a mystery anyhow — you could see the names of streets, and where they met or diverged, and, in spread-out red type, the Roman numerals that identified this or that arrondissement: all of it meaningless. In New York you readily knew the difference between the glittering Fifth Avenue of the museums and the impoverished Fifth Avenue of the tenements, though no street map could hint at what a mere two miles' distance might signify. Here in Paris, what was it to be mad about Proust (she had brought her yellowing copy of *Swann's Way* to read on the plane), or bookishly familiar with history and kings and revolutionaries and philosophers? It counted for nothing when you were puzzling over how to get from the IXth to the VIIth on an unexceptional Tuesday in the middle of your unexceptional life, and when you were feeling dismissed by the conscientious weekday faces streaming past, faces that had mundane tasks and were set on exactly what they were and how they were to be done. She could not understand this city, it was an enigma, or else it was Paris that comprehended whatever passed through its arteries, and it was she, the interloper, who was the enigma.

She was an enigma to herself. She had come away calmly enough, a curious calm, a sleepwalker's calm: the bus to the bank, the hypnotic mechanical packing, the interview with her rough-hewn principal.

— You ask this *now?* At the last minute, just at the start of the new term?

— Mrs. Bienenfeld says she'll cover for me, won't that take care of it?

— It's too much, she has her own classes. And she isn't credentialed to teach English, you can't mix puddings!

— She'll be fine. She's glad to do it, she's a friend.

— You mean she's your patsy. Well, if she's that willing, she can take two of yours, but for the other two it'll mean an extra teacher from outside and extra pay, and we've got guidelines and a budget. All right, you're worth something around here, you give us some class, so I'll go for it, but Mrs. Bienenfeld better keep your guys in line, you've been good about that. Hell, what's this really about, Bea, another run to Paree, you got a French kisser hidden away over there? Miss Nightingale, lady of the night, oo-lala!

And then Laura:

— Bea, I can't do your syllabus the way you have it, all this Whitman and Hawthorne and God help me, *A Tale of Two Cities*, they'll spit it out! Can't you change it to stuff I can handle?

— Wing it, Laura, wing it.

Her rough-hewn principal, rough-hewn Laura. Her own life ragged and low, scorned by Marvin, scorned by Leo — by Leo, who had put her there! Then why hadn't she climbed out of it?

On the rue Mouffetard (she saw this on the side of a building) she stopped and looked all around. She had been walking in the wrong direction — she was nowhere near the numbers on the back of Iris's envelope. The morning cool had begun to retreat. Despite the growing mob, a frenetic swirl of tourists with their cameras and bags, she was sickeningly alone. She had smuggled herself into this unnatural scene, displaced, desolate, and to what end? Marvin, hollow Marvin — she hadn't answered his letter, she had told him nothing. She was all contradiction — resentment and indifference — and then this . . . this harebrained plummeting into Paris. To do what? To rescue whom? Marvin from his torment, the brother who abused her? Bea from a low and ragged life? That note, that broken blow, as of glass splitting, a wallop to the brain — she had thought herself content, reconciled, resilient, orderly days, an orderly life: until Iris's finger hurled her into turmoil. The stab at that single uncanny key, a short-lived overturning looking-glass sound — it had a pitch, an accent, she could not recall whether bass or treble, boom or screech, a splinter of glass that wormed through her veins and flowed with the flow of her blood . . . Leo's untouchable instrument. The girl's touch, a golden girl, and what was Bea, if not aging, ragged, and low?

She turned down a street of cavelike stalls hung with souvenirs, key chains, rings, ashtrays, bracelets, each engraved with a minuscule

Eiffel Tower, painted ties and scarves and banners, row upon row of porcelain trivia. And squeezed among these importuning shops in this unidentifiable neighborhood, yet another outdoor café. She ordered scrambled eggs and cold juice, more out of politeness than hunger, and showed the elderly waiter her map, pointing to the street she wanted. Madame—laughter in an old creased Levantine face—it is far from where you are now, very far! Madame should not think of walking, under this hot sun she will drop in the road, the police will come and place her in hospital, hospital for foolish Americans who drop! Never mind, he was one who liked Americans very much, he especially liked American cinema, back there in America did she know *Weesperin Weens?* A very good film, the woman so beautiful, only in the American cinema do women have such red lips and whole teeth, in fact she is right now in a cinema just here, not ten meters away . . .

Yes, she said, *Whispering Winds*, I know it. And paid for her uneaten meal (but thirstily drained the juice) and stepped out toward where the waiter gestured, and there they were: the big crimson garish posters, the two familiar stars entwined in a kiss, the heroine's blouse unbuttoned just enough to display the upper cushions of her ample breasts, the man's arms bare and almost cartoonishly muscular. To her surprise the box office was open for business, though it was still early in the afternoon. In the startling sudden night of the auditorium, she felt a seedy stickiness: fresh gum underfoot, spills on the patched carpet. The movie was already under way; she shut her eyes. She had nearly every movement by heart, and much of the dialogue. She had no desire to look at the screen. At home, uptown and downtown, in the Village, in the Eighties, on Times Square, she had pursued this spoor from movie house to movie house, secretly, alone, listening to Leo's mind. Leo's mind! "I intend," he told her once, "to throw out the usual components of the conventional orchestra, you see what I mean?" She did not see. He knew she did not see, but it gratified him that she listened. In the evenings, after five or six hours with those deafening boys in that deafening classroom, she listened.

49

Leo in bed since morning, dreaming symphonies, dreaming operas. "What I'm just getting hold of is what nobody's ever done before, two electric pianos, two bass guitars, two alto saxophones, a percussion ensemble, a boy soprano, a female chorus . . ." And another time: "The idea is to have a choir of fifty, a mezzo-soprano for Anna Karenina, or I haven't decided, maybe it ought to be Bovary" — Leo exalted, carried away (and rested, Bea couldn't help thinking), pouncing on the keys to show her a string of noisy passages, but then it was enough, it was only to give her the gist of it, the dramatic theme, steering her by the nape, his blazing look, the blazing engine of what he liked to call their harmony and counterpoint . . . The lovers were embracing, the movie was over, the credits were rolling past, almost too quickly to be read, but her eyes were busy now, she was ready for the name, it slid by in a second, *Music composed by Leo Coopersmith,* and then the lights came on, and she took in the unswept dirt all around, and the four other moviegoers scattered in the seats, one of them a derelict stinking of something foul.

Leo's mind!

The street was as brilliant as before: it was a Parisian sun renowned for setting as late as ten o'clock. Finding Julian could wait another day. She scouted a taxi and went back to her hotel to sleep off the deadly exhaustion of a foreign time zone.

II

A PALACE, Iris had written. To Bea's American eyes that Sunday morning, it was venerably European—Romanesque windows, the lower ones swelled by rounded wrought-iron barriers, dark thick oblong stones rising like a vast wall, heavy wooden double doors carved into bunches of bursting grapes and a fat-stomached glowering Bacchus, all of it giving out some nearly olfactory opulence. Or else it was a latter-day mimicry, war-stained Paris refurbished, an architect's willful deception or obsequious homage, stale modern Europe pretending to be ancient Europe. One of the doors stood open: a lamplit dimness, a marble desk and a concierge behind it—so this ducal manse was, after all, only another middle-class apartment building, though not of a kind you would ever see in New York.

Julian lived here.

She said his name to the concierge, who, it turned out, spoke English with a cockney sound, and was eager to explain why: it was lonely to sit all day in the half-dark without a living soul to talk to, only the comings and goings of the people upstairs, and nothing in her ears but the lift's funny whistle. And of course she was English, anyone could hear it straightaway, she couldn't be mistaken for anything else, she had married her second husband, a Frenchman from La Rochelle on the coast, they had met when she crossed over to Normandy to visit her first husband's grave, a British soldier, you know, and here she was, stuck now in Paris, because her second husband was dead from the disease you can only whisper about . . . Please say again?

"Nachtigall," Bea said. "Julian Nachtigall."

"I've got nobody like that on my roster, and believe me" — she tapped her forehead — "I've got them all up here."

"A young man. In his twenties. An American."

"There's an American doctor on the top floor, he speaks French pretty well. But almost never here, you don't mean Dr. Montalbano?"

"No, no, Nachtigall."

"All these foreign names, you'd think we were with the Jews." The concierge pleated the sides of her mouth into a smirk. "I know the one you want. He's a Jew, the one you want, but I don't like to spread it around. A squatter boy, with another squatter, and now there's a third one, don't ask me why. It's a wonder he keeps them up there, he's an odd bird, Dr. Montalbano, who knows what they're up to —"

Garrulousness without plausibility. But what *was* plausible? Was it plausible that Julian had ascended from that other place to this place, the pauper to the palace? The woman was ready to jabber on, widening brownish lips in a know-it-all smile, while Bea escaped across the carpeted foyer toward the glint of a tiny elevator cage. It staggered shrilly upward, one, two, three, four, five, and at the sixth landing halted before a single door.

An ordinary button-bell.

It was cool here, and quiet. She stood and listened. Noiselessness behind the door, a ferocity of expectation — herself caught in a fixity, a movie-still excised from a scene of crisis, the frozen moment of her finger lifted, approaching the button, the button that was about to violate the silence behind the door (Iris's lifted finger seconds before it fell blindly on a violated key) . . . A muffled ring; then nothing; then still more nothing; and finally the sound of a staccato bark — but a bark with a human timbre. The heavy scrape of shoes, scrabbling with a kind of hobble, as if the laces were untied, and from a diminishing distance a growling American voice: "Fine, not again, just when I'm dropping off you people have to go and forget to take the goddamn key —"

A young man, flabby at the neck, a thin horizontal blond mustache, streaming eyes, a handkerchief over his mouth. Volcanic coughing followed by a river of French.

"English, please," Bea said.

"Oh, sorry, this stupid cold, so I thought it was . . . and when I saw it wasn't . . ." A smothered row of gasps. "He's away now, he's in Milan for the month—"

Bea said, "No, no," and then, as if catapulted: "I was here in July, I tried to look you up. Julian? Julian Nachtigall? I have your sister's letter—" She stopped and took him in; he was really no more than a boy. Even the mustache was undeveloped.

He stared back with—it struck her instantly—her own father's eyes: Tatar lids drawn low at the corners.

"My sister." Two spiteful grunts. He gave her his back—a rip at the collar—and shambled off into a large central room, out of which other rooms opened: impossible to tell how many. A palace, and too much furniture, a scattering of sofas and armchairs. Assorted articles of female clothing draped here and there, a stocking dangling from a lampshade, another thrown over a picture frame. A blanket on the floor. She shut the door after her—he didn't care, open or closed, stay or go, he was indifferent. She saw his shoelaces, straggling, undone. A wilderness, it was all provisional. It was incoherent. He picked up the blanket and tugged it around his shoulders and foundered into the cushions of a divan.

"You've got to be Iris's aunt," he said.

"Yours too."

His recognition—of who she was, of what she appeared to threaten—was almost too rapid to assimilate; he had unhesitatingly understood what he took to be the whole meaning of it. An instinctiveness arrogantly sure of itself. It hinted at intuitive stirrings. It hinted at an inner life. But oh, the outer one!

He said, "She told me she spent the night at your place. She came so you wouldn't. She told you to stay away." A rattling volley shook him; he wiped his eyes with an angry swipe. "My father sent you, didn't he? He made you come."

"I came because I wanted to."

"But *he* wanted you to, you can't deny it. Even if you think something's your own idea, he's behind it. That's how it goes with him, and don't say it doesn't. He always gets his way."

"Not with you. He's asked you to come back, and you won't."

"My mother thinks I've been abducted, I suppose you've heard. Little green Martians maybe." He let out a resentful groan and flung the blanket over his head. "My God, you walk in here, what are you, the company representative, the family spokesman? When in my life did I ever know you? Whatever you think I'm up to is none of your business. It's not my father's either." He reared up, shivering, from under the blanket. "Damn it, why aren't they back?"

She saw the dry swollen lips, the too pink nostril-wings, the fevered wretchedness of a sick and self-indulgent child. Sullen and stubborn. But she had surprised him, she was an eruption, an apparition — unfair and brutish. Standing there, tentative and stung, facing her nephew — Julian, the hard case — she had never so much as looked around, among all these little low tables and worn rugs and a bureau or two and a plethora of chairs, for a place to sit. The big room resembled a meeting hall, overused, abused, public, frayed. She had fallen into it no more than three minutes ago, and already a truculence was brewing. Had she crossed an ocean to be so quickly despised?

Deliberately, she made a space for herself at the far end of the divan, at his feet.

"Your father doesn't know I'm here. I never told him I was coming."

"Then what do you want?"

The question, even if soaked in phlegm, was pellucid. What did she want? It wasn't that she had taken pity on Marvin, inconceivable as this was — when had Marvin ever needed her pity? The boy was right: in the end, for one reason or another, inescapably, she was doing Marvin's bidding. Admittedly there was sanity in his bidding. The boy had somehow to be extricated. He reeked of chaos — it was an enveloping fume all around him. Chaos in his anger, chaos in this slovenly precarious abandoned flat. How did he keep himself alive? He was homeless, jobless, futureless. He was careless — he hadn't bothered to tie his shoelaces. And worse: he hadn't bothered to put on his socks: she discovered she was sitting on a dirty pair, with holes at the heels.

— The elevator's squeal, a commotion in the corridor, a treble female voice. Scratchings in the keyhole — the key hadn't been forgotten. A girl flew in — it was Iris — followed more soberly by the other one, Iris calling out, "Hey, sicko, we've brought you a cure-all, and a nice old-timey hot-water bottle for sick little old granny . . . Catch!"

A red rubber shape landed in Bea's lap. A faceless homunculus with a thick neck. And here was Iris's hand in midair, with her mouth startled into the beginning of a cry; but the cry came under instant guard, and slowly, coolly, Iris's pale look traveled from her aunt cradling the rubber thing to her brother scowling, his fleshy chin on fire, to her own gauzy stocking hanging from a framed print of a waterfall.

"Aunt Bea —" and let the syllables burn out.

The other one drew a cylindrical vial from its paper wrapper and set it down; then stood mutely.

"It makes no sense," Iris said. "It's gone beyond. It's pointless that you're here. There's nothing you can do, and it doesn't matter now."

But Julian, freeing himself from his swaddlings, got up and wound his arms around the other one. She was small and dark and thin and unbewildered. Scrawny, Bea saw, rather than slender, spiky at the shoulders. She was not young — or anyhow not young as Iris was young; she was a woman completed. Her collarbone protruded. With her cautious gaze fixed on Bea — Bea the intruder — she eased herself, familiarly but consciously, back into Julian's chest, drawing his hands down across the front of her shirt. It was a man's shirt, with long sleeves; her warm breasts were hidden there. She did not care how she dressed, or how she looked. Long sleeves in mild weather.

"Lili," Julian said, in a voice so growly and proprietary that Bea knew — it was as elusive and penetrating as an odor — that sex lurked behind it. Lubricious impulses. Surely his fingertips must be pressing into those twin nipples under the shirt. Bea imagined it, she imagined her own breasts under a man's urgent palms, pressing, kneading, the hard knuckles hurting the feeling flesh, the tender glands, she imagined her body as a floating vitrine, you could see into it, she imagined it as a movie, the movie music swirling upward, the camera trundling in for the close-ups, you could watch the heavings of the ovaries and the uterus contracting, and the shining slime of liver and spleen . . . spleen, one of the medieval humors, and what were the other three? This was her brother's son — her nephew. Inner life? The boy was no better than a savage. He was surprisingly plump, even his eyelids, swollen pink and fat as petals. A random drop hung from the tip of his broad nose. The stretched nostrils dripped mucus. And rasping, coughing between the words, he was intending to mock her. "Lili," he said, "since this is turning out to be a family reunion, you might as well meet my father's sister, come to save us all."

Spleen, he was full of spleen!

12

It developed, when Iris found him, that he and Lili were living in a clinic. A kind of clinic, with a capacious waiting room intimating certain therapeutic overtones — not that there was any of the expected equipment, or even an examining table, anywhere in sight. During the months Dr. Montalbano was away — he had other clinics in other cities to attend to — Julian, in exchange for the use of the apartment, was to inform anyone who inquired that the clinic was suspended until the doctor's return. The inquirers were likely to be new clients, since the old ones were familiar with the rhythms of his departures; nor would it be necessary for Julian to monitor the telephone. Dr. Montalbano's telephone was shut off in his absence, and anyhow all his clients, the old and the new, were treated in the most confidential and personal way, and were required to come to his door. A good number were responding to ads — Dr. Montalbano's ads were many and various, some posted conventionally in newspapers, some merely hand-printed and tacked up in local pharmacies. But many more (swarms, Julian said) were there through word of mouth.

Iris's suitcase lay propped against the leg of a chair. The noise of four-engine propellers still lingered in her ears. Julian was past the first surprise, half an hour ago — his sister out of place, his sister who ought to have been where his mind had planted her, at home in California, far away; but here she was, her arms around his neck, kissing him all over his captured head, grinning at him. Julian shocked, confused, glad, unhappy. Suspicious.

"It won't be just you, will it?"

"It *is* just me," Iris said.

"You mean so far. Dad'll be right behind you, hiding out at the Ritz or somewhere—he wouldn't've let you come alone."

"He didn't. He thinks I'm in New York with Aunt Bea. It was supposed to *be* Aunt Bea. A fussy old thing, what could you possibly do with her? So I came instead."

Julian said, "And what can I possibly do with you?"

"You can just let me look at you. At home we've been worrying that you've been starving in some attic, and well, you're absolutely fat!"

"If you wait on tables you get to see these outlanders grazing in one café after another all day—"

Outlanders. And wasn't he one himself?

"—and then," Julian said, "they leave half their dinners untouched. I guess I've licked too many platters clean."

"Oh my poor Julian, you've been going without regular meals—"

"Oh my poor Iris, you've just pronounced me too fat."

An offhand teasing parry, an echo of their childhood: it emboldened her. There were all those letters—he hadn't relinquished their old connection—yet she had sensed something veiled in them: a muffling of her brother's voice. Did he, after an immersion of three years, think himself grown into Europe?

"I've brought you some money anyway," she said, and instantly regretted it. She saw the beginning stir of a clutch of anger—it was in his neck. It bulged a little.

"A bribe from dad—"

"Nothing to do with dad. It's that I don't like to think of you needing things."

The bulge collapsed into a shrug. "I've got everything I need. Only gaze upon my vast holdings—"

"And what happens after this Dr. Montalbano gets back?"

"We're thrown out, I suppose, Lili and me. But in the meantime we've got the run of the place, and it doesn't cost us a penny."

"And afterward?"

"Afterward takes care of itself."

Iris said, "You talk as if you've suddenly got religion, everything's in God's hands. Wouldn't *that* surprise dad!"

"What's it to me what he thinks, I'm done with him. And I haven't got religion. I've got Lili."

He had led her to a pair of double doors and pulled them open. A narrow balcony with an iron railing, and a stretch of Paris below. She looked down on a scattering of pedestrians, the strolling ones, the intent ones; a bare-shouldered woman tugging at a whining child. The whine a universal language. Everything else oddly wrong: the width of the pavement, the snout-nosed cars (at home they had winglike fins, like big metal sharks), the very bricks of the building opposite, and the languid tallness of its windows. Even the light seemed out of kilter, as if the sun had started out that morning mistakenly angled, a ship in the hands of an erratic navigator. This light was different from California light: it fell out of a sky so much smaller, so much older: an old old sky, drooling wrinkled clouds.

Out there on the balcony — two scarred wooden chairs — he began to speak of Lili. In spite of everything (but what, Iris wondered, was "everything"?) she was the strongest person he'd ever known, not in that bullying, self-deluding way they'd suffered under all their lives — she was a small sturdy stem: you could bend it and it would arch and never break . . .

This was the familiar Julian, sidling into vapor. Iris felt she could put her finger all the way into such talk and never get hold of a single fact. His thinking wouldn't come clean, it ran around corners, it was all melting words, you couldn't pin it down — it was like those dirty street pigeons he'd made into glossy doves. Who was this Lili, where did she come from, what did he intend to make of her? Or she of him? He had always been excited about one thing or another. He was inconstant, subject to phases. He went from snarls to fustian. He didn't have his hands on the lever of life — this was how her father put it, but her father . . . well, he was what he was, a man who couldn't feel. Or see. He couldn't see Julian, the other meaning of him. What looked like volatility was absorption in the moment. Her brother, she knew, was born to feel. Listen to him now! He believed that a weed had a will. And this Lili, despite her name, was she a weed, one of those wandering European weeds? Those funny insertions in Julian's letters, in that strange curly handwriting, what language was that?

"Romanian," Julian said.

Distant, discordant, unreal. Waste and war, the weary guttural of one of those unimaginable hells. A place that wasn't in any of the history books — not in California, anyhow.

"What was the point of doing that, it might just as well have been Chinese —"

"I made her," Julian said. "It was telling without telling. Because nobody at home could read it."

"You could've written anything you wanted, they didn't have a clue when a letter came. I had a system, I told you."

"But if dad just happened to get a look —"

"He never did. And you know he wouldn't let mom see anything upsetting."

"It's not upsetting, it's miraculous. But it couldn't be told then, it wasn't decided — Lili wasn't decided. So I made her write it down that way, a sort of private code for herself, to convince her."

"Convince her of what?"

Julian laughed, almost a giggle, childishly.

"She was *supposed* to write 'We are going to be married' —"

"Julian! You didn't really, you aren't —"

"But what she actually wrote was 'He is a foolish American boy.' After the letter went off she admitted to it. She's like that. She says what she thinks."

"In a language nobody knows, so how can anyone tell what she thinks? Julian, you *didn't* do such a thing, you didn't go and get your-self married! To someone no one's ever heard of —"

"Two months ago, beginning of June."

"You *are* a foolish American boy."

His little blond mustache quivered: each sparse thread had its own wet glint. Were they tears, those droplets all at once stippling the hairs on his lip? Foolish, foolish, yes! What had he done, what had he let himself in for? A feckless boy with a wife. That straggly mustache a callow banner.

"Right you are. Foolish and happy."

But he was pulling a handkerchief out of the pocket of his shirt, and it was only that his nose was running, the start of a cold, he said, Lili had it first, he was bound to catch it, the people where she worked, refugees, DPs and such, half of them sickly, she was always bringing back the sniffles, or worse. They were mostly in trouble, those people, pleading and babbling in their worried old tongues, no use to them now, and dependent on a score of translators (Lili was one of them), and droves and armadas of letters, all with the same cracked cry: show me a way out, find me my niece, my lost second cousin, out, out! Lili took in these entreaties and hungers, she typed them soberly on white paper headed with an official logo. The life-throb was intense in her, he said, she had taught him everything. He had come to Paris like all those others, he'd gotten to know that crowd, he was at the far edge, he was nobody, but it was easy to get wind of where they partied, they'd begin at the Tabou at nine or ten at night and go on into the dawn, he'd tag along to the Monaco and the Napoléon, and always there was Alfred, this fellow from Brooklyn, bleached-out eyes nearly yellow, no lashes, bald as an apple, the squat middle of him round as Humpty Dumpty, short fluttery taffylike fingers, a yellow wig (no exaggeration!) wobbling on his shiny pate, Alfred knew them all, George Plimpton and Jimmy Baldwin and the rest of them, and once he'd actually made a pass at Julian, and offered to get some of his stuff into one of those magazines springing up all over Paris, poems and things — this was how he got into *Merlin* and *Botteghe Oscure*, and you remember how dad had fits — but when you came right down to it he wasn't the real thing, and most of the others weren't either, making it up for the sake of the parties, the whiskey, the local girls, the fake Beauvoirs, the girls from New York, the glamour, the fantasies of fame, it was all pretty exciting then, the kind of life he couldn't have imagined back home, the pointless hole he'd been cornered into, or pushed through, dad's clumsy ambitions for him, a ladder leading nowhere, the rungs at the top missing . . .

Nostrils streaming, red-faced, her brother rushed on, spilling the beans, though Iris could hardly string them together—it was and wasn't the old Julian. The old closeness, the old confidences, the old reckless Niagara drenching, but the beat was different, self-repudiation, he was telling her what he had relinquished, the stale simulacrum of himself he had come to despise. All that was finished . . . almost. There was, in a way, one leftover: Dr. Montalbano.

"The man who intends to throw you out," Iris said.

"*Us.* Lili and me, but only when he gets back. It won't matter, we'll be together—"

"Fine, and where do you go then?"

A grimace. "You asked that before. Stop sounding like dad."

She heard it herself: the spurt of impatience. Of exasperation. The money she had brought him would melt away in less than a month, and then what? And he had a wife. A foreign wife! If he had shed what he was, a footloose floater, what did he suppose he had become?

"He's an American anyhow," Julian said.

"Who?" She could not follow; he had jumped ahead, or behind.

"And he's not an MD, and it's not his real name either. He's from Pittsburgh."

"Julian—"

"The thing is," he pressed on, spitting it out, "they're practically all Americans, and they're all fakes."

"The one with the wig too?"

"The wig was real enough. He hated wearing it, so he killed himself finally. And by the way, all these cafés are unionized to the hilt. I got in through the cracks—Dr. Montalbano started me off. Poor old Alfred introduced us, I owe him a lot, he put me in touch with someone who got me jobs."

"But what is he, if he isn't a doctor—"

"An out-and-out scam for all I know, but he goes all over, he's got clients everywhere, there's a clinic in Milan and another one in Lyon, and it's made him rich. Lili doesn't like him, she's always wanting to get away. He cooks up potions out of turnips and onions."

It was comical and it was awful. Suicide, charlatanism, vegetables. And a wife, a wife! She had taught him everything, he said—good God, was this her everything? An aimless creature like himself, but worse, human debris discharged from the diseased bowel of Eastern Europe—*Romania,* where was it really, what did it signify—and wouldn't this, Iris recognized, have been her father's thought precisely? There was no way to escape her father: he lived inside her brain. She saw that Julian had chosen Europe. He meant to stay. He would never come home.

—No way to escape her father's brain? But Julian had done it, hadn't he?

13

Paris, September 5

Dear Marvin,

It's been more than a week since I got here, and I've left you in limbo, so I suppose I owe you some news. You wanted me here, and here I am, who knows why. It can't be what you call family feeling — mine, if I have any, goes backward toward mama and papa, especially papa, but turns blank concerning the next generation. Unlike you, I haven't g<u>ot</u> any next generation, and therefore nobody to grieve over. I see that you're grieving, and Margaret too. May I say that I regard these lamentations of yours as spurious and inappropriate? You carry on as if your children are dead, when they're very much alive, and in fact I've invited them to have dinner with me here at the hotel. The place is something of a disappointment, in spite of the expense, but there's a whiz of a chef in the kitchen, maybe the owner himself. I've been having my meals here nearly every evening, and always alone, not for want of trying — Iris keeps putting me off. I've felt anything but welcome since I arrived, and it's not likely that any good can come of my hanging on. They've been shying away from any overture from me, Julian in particular. At this point I hardly know why I made the effort (it <u>was</u> an effort, I had to impose on a colleague to take my classes). I imagine it's something to do with Iris — that one night she was with me in New York. The look of her, her hair, her California voice, the California way she was dressed. I was jealous — I suppose I was jealous, old lady that I am, and please don't ask me to explain.

As for Julian — your boy has his likes and dislikes, doesn't he? For one thing, he doesn't much like his father, and there's no chance of his getting to like his father's sister. It's not just obstinacy. From the little (the very little!) I've observed, he's resistant because he's fearful. He's afraid of you, it seems; I conclude you've made him afraid of me. Well, true, these are no more than intuitions — hints — so you don't have to take them as gospel. You've always scorned impressions in favor of proofs, or so you say. You'll be surprised to hear that I scorn them too, they're no solider than cloud shapes — Leo once accused me of wanting to compile a dictionary of clouds! Believe it or not, I'm as practical as you are, not that I could ever <u>think</u> like you. Even long ago you used to argue that people are no better than predictable formulas — chemical compounds. So if you want to apply any of that to your son, there may be a weightier element than you've known so far . . .

As if all she meant was that Julian was putting on pounds! And where, oh where, did *that* spring from, that incomprehensible specter of Leo?

She tore the sheet into strips (thin hotel paper, the ink bleeding into it). Not the kind of letter she ought to be writing to Marvin. Maundering. Verging on the precarious — she saw where her errant speculations were leading: to the woman wearing long sleeves in mild weather.

She began again:

It's been quite some time since I got here — exactly where you've wanted me to be! — so I suppose I owe you some news. The news isn't good. I've accomplished nothing, and it turns out there really is a girlfriend involved, as it happens not French . . .

Not French? Surely this would put Marvin in mind of one of those reckless flyaway New York girls nowadays flooding Paris — their pictures were always turning up in *Life* magazine, excitable girls in their purplish ankle-length postwar skirts; so she scratched out *not French* and went on to mix in, among the quotidian, a salting of fraudulence.

. . . and whether serious or a passing fancy it's hard to tell. Iris has moved in with the two of them in some sort of house-sitting arrangement, though who knows what they call it over here. The beauty of it is they're not liable for rent (anyhow the young woman seems well employed — I've met her only once). It's a spacious place in a building with a concierge, it's respectable enough, and Julian's given up waiting tables. But I'm not wanted, it's been a fool's errand, and there's not a smidgeon of hope I can do anything with either your son or your daughter — I can't even get Iris to agree to having dinner! There's no use my staying any longer, one week of trying is more than enough. Iris is a riddle, and your son won't budge.

What she'd left out! A risky reticence. Lili a passing fancy? And if this deceptiveness was so unsatisfactory as to be cruel, the truth might have been worse. She hadn't told Marvin that the woman Julian was living with was a foreigner (a foreigner even in foreign France) who undoubtedly spoke a clumsy English as harshly accented as their grandfather's, the greenhorn who peddled pots and pans. Though to be honest, so far she hadn't heard the woman utter a word.

The letter remained unfinished. How to go on with it?

14

Iris had put Julian to bed. His cold was worsening. He was fever-ish; he dozed, and woke, and dozed again. Bea had seen nothing of him.

"You should keep away," Iris told her. "He's so awfully irritable, he hates being sick. He was always just like this at home. No one could get near him."

"Shouldn't he have a doctor?"—the auntly thing.

"Lili knows what to do, she's very good at it. She makes him a sort of eggnog every night, for his cough—"

So Bea was flicked off, dismissed. The other one—Lili—was in-visible. She had her job, she was at work all day until evening. Her "job," her "work," as if this glittering metropolis with its home-grown impenetrability had a use for what she was! She belonged no-where, a stray, a drifter. Julian had attached himself to her, or she to him. He depended on her, she was his support. The case was even worse than what Marvin might think, his son living on a woman's wages, puny as they must be.

"Then I'll come back when he's a little better," Bea said. "In the morning?"

"The morning's too soon."

"But you'll let me know? I won't be staying much longer. And mostly I'll be sticking to my room."

"What a shame," Iris said. "You're here, it's Paris, why not go out and see things?"

Was this spite or indifference? Did the girl suppose she had come for another holiday? Bea had had her holiday. She was feeling her purpose less and less; it grew more and more remote.

"It's Julian I want to see," she said.

"Julian's all right."

"I'm all right," croaked a broken voice from a far room. "Tell her to go away, can't you?"

The brother and sister: *thick as thieves;* but that was long ago. There was something between them even now, a fresh cabal, an understanding to be kept, above all, from Bea.

It muddled her. She was disordered, she could not bear her room, and the afternoon had hardly begun. She was left with Paris, all of Paris, and what was the use of Paris now, and all that old history, and all these bright autumnal streets?

She asked the young hotel clerk where the nearest cinema was. He reached under his counter and spread out a wrinkled brochure.

— Which film does madame wish to see?

— Anything will do.

— An American film?

— It doesn't matter.

— *Whispering Winds,* very popular. Two locations, one in the rue Mouffetard, the other in the Marais. You don't want to go to the Marais, madame, it's not pleasant there.

Not pleasant? It suited her spirits, it suited her furies. She seized on it as if a horoscope had predicted the whip of recurrence: it was meant to be, Leo again driving her on, just as, in New York, he lashed her from neon marquee to neon marquee, in quest of his mood, his fakery. Her furies there, her furies here! She was repudiated, how they were gulling her, the brother and sister, thick as thieves, getting rid of her, spiting her! . . . Eyes sealed shut in yet another dirty cavern, the overhead lights not sufficiently dimmed, the projection booth growling, congestion, confined human sweat, wrappers crackling, garbled murmurs all around, restless, what were they saying? That foolish Technicolor ship burning at sea, the terrified lovers clinging to a splintered mast, ludicrous Gallic cries escaping their mouths seconds after their lips had shaped the words . . . in the rue Mouffetard the film hadn't been dubbed. Her eyelids sprang open, they would not obey, she could not beat off the flaming images, those gaudy scenes exploding before her, the music dissolving, evaporating into the make-believe hazards on the screen, those storming cymbals and horns and crashing drums, Leo's idiocies!

She turned to face the crowd, a laughing wave chewing, rocking, exhaling unhealthy odors, too worldly, too bruised for artificial dread, and saw, half a dozen rows behind her — or thought she saw — the woman from the Luxor, where last July the perfumed airy mannequin had floated by. Was it the same angry head of wild black twisting curls? Or were all these laughing outraged heads alike?

In the street she understood where she was. She had stumbled into the neighborhood of the displaced. They choked off the sidewalks, arguing, shrugging, laughing. Always this ironic laughter! They laughed at cheap films, they laughed at the weather, they laughed at grandeur, they laughed at the absence of grandeur. Here nothing was grand, everything was pinched and used up. It was half past five, the sun still glaring in the shop windows, an indoor café no bigger than a stall letting out a smell of sweet pastry mixed with the breath of the sleepless. The road was clogged with cars, those squat little domes, and not a taxi among them. She had come by taxi, how else to search out the errant corners of Paris? An eddying blur of languages, and no one to ask — but if she walked on, wouldn't there be a bus? Perverse to have run after Leo a second time in a single week, and in a faraway city! Perverse of Leo to have pursued her across an ocean! He had led her to this hallucinatory place, where the wiry-haired woman from the Luxor and her idling companions were multiplying like mad, spilling out of the shops, barricading the pavement in garrulous clusters. Pigeons flapped at their feet, pecking at the litter of peels and crusts, hopping fearlessly: not even the brisk stamp of a shoe could frighten them into flight. Homeless tramp birds, with eyes like the eyes of fish, feeding on scraps. *The doves of the Marais,* light-years distant from those tamed and overfed doves at Laura's wedding . . . Julian knew these streets, he had seen these human scavengers scurrying out of the shops with their meager pickings, a cabbage, a half loaf of bread, keeping themselves alive. He knew them, and what could it mean to a boy like that?

One of the shops as Bea approached it was not a shop at all. Blinds covered the windows, and over the door, painted in black letters on the transom, a sign, and out of the door in quickstep . . . could it be? If the woman from the Luxor was everywhere, why not the perfumed mannequin, with her long arms? And why not Lili? *Could* it be Lili, this one particular particle in the flow of urban humanity? Certainly it was Lili, and almost as certainly it was not, yet possibly . . . but the throng ahead, like quicksand, had swallowed her up.

Bea went scratching in the bottom of her bag for a pencil, and on the back of the stub of her movie ticket she copied the words on the transom: CENTRE DES ÉMIGRÉS. 24, RUE DES ROSIERS.

15

IT WAS A LONG narrow space, with the look of an ordinary office.
A double line of cubicles, and an alley between: tall makeshift partitions. Bea could not see over them, but the hidden voices ascended
in flocks, a fugue of indecipherable cadences, plea and despair, despair and plea. And then a sudden muteness, as if the entire crew
of a ship had stopped breathing all at once; and then, in the heart of
the silence, a sob like a breaker foaming. The place had the vestigial
smell of what it must once have been: a *boucherie,* say, with slaughtered carcasses hanging in bloody rows: a series of hooks at the rear
attested to these. Or were they only commonplace coat hooks? Or
did the smell steam out from living bodies in travail? A queue that
had earlier trailed from the vestibule into the street had diminished to
three or four. The cubicles were emptying out.

She had come by stealth, but not yet as a spy. A spy would lurk and
observe and vanish. Her idea was to waylay Lili at the close of the
day, to ambush her at an unclaimed hour . . . If this storefront bureau
should be Lili's lair (it smacked of a kind of public charitableness),
out springs Bea to seize her! And if not? Then yet another blunder
into Europe's wailing wall — she had caught sight of it in the cinema, among those wounded laughers, the victims, the refugees. Marvin's mandate, his ukase, to look the thing in its blooded eye, those
gypsy swarms his son had fallen hostage to . . . his son!

Iris had that morning again sent her away — Julian feeling a bit
better, the fever gone down, but no patience at all for a talk . . . She

71

had said nothing of what she had seen in the rue des Rosiers, and why should she? Iris would traduce it.

The squawk of a metal chair pushed back. The man in the farthest cubicle was taller than the height of the partition; for a moment his head reared above it, disembodied. When he emerged, Bea saw that he was wearing a frayed business suit, with a vest too big for him. He carried a cane and limped. But no, it wasn't a limp—an archaic little bow, rather, that engaged the shoulders and the knees: he was immensely dignified. He had the air of a judge or a senator. On second thought, it *was* a limp: one leg inches shorter than the other. He put out a ceremonious hand to the woman in the cubicle, murmuring in what must surely have been German—or was it Dutch? Or something else? Two fingers were missing: lopped off how, where, why?

He was the last to leave. Bea could not discern from his abruptly submissive back whether anything good had come of his time in this place. But judge or senator no more: his clothes were too shabby.

A rustle of papers; a lamp was switched off; the woman stepped out; and Bea sprang.

"Lili," she called.

She wondered if she would be recognized. Was it likely? To have been so put off, and in the first minutes of having set foot in that cavernous flat! Iris cold, Julian taunting. It hardly helped—it worsened things—that Iris had tossed out a promise: "Another time, when Julian's in better shape," while Lili in her man's shirt hadn't spoken at all; Lili had kept her recondite peace. Out of that silence she had fixed on Bea with those two watchful grooves drawn into a trench between her eyes. An unquiet track that seemed to gaze all on its own. But fleetingly.

And Julian's hands on her breasts.

Lili was answering calmly, "Iris sends you? But Julian is all right, yes? Already last night he was almost well."

How matter-of-fact she was; how formed and finished; how unperturbed and unsurprised. She was used to everything, and ready to expect anything. The world was as it was.

"How can I tell how he is? And nobody knows I've come looking for you, Iris has nothing to do with it. She won't let me see him. Not for days." She was breathless; open to quarrel. "If I don't get to see him, then I've wasted my time, there's no point to any of it—"

"Come," Lili said, "sit." Behind the partition she turned on the lamp. A typewriter, stacks of sheets, something resembling a ledger. A small ticking clock. "They are like excitable children, they hide their secrets." She tugged a little on the cuffs of her sleeves—as if her blouse didn't fit at the wrists—and looked steadily at Bea. "I hide nothing."

"What sort of place is this? I saw the sign, what do you do here?"

"It is to go out, only to go out. This man, you see how broken, in his home once a scholar of Goethe. *Das Land, wo die Zitronen blühn,* you know this? There they open willingly."

Bea said, "Then you speak German?"

"Whatever is needed we speak. So many laws in so many countries, it is not always possible they will permit. So many will not permit, and when one permits . . ." She wrinkled out a quick ephemeral frown. "Your nephew, he makes it romantic, he makes it noble—"

This was scarcely the conversation Bea had counted on; she did not entirely understand it. The furry accent, the too considered English—stiff, more than a bit off. And she thought again: tasteless, in mild weather those long sleeves.

"But if you have him living with stories of people like that, that man with the terrible fingers," she protested, and burst out: "Julian's too young to be made so sad."

"Julian sad, no! Theatrical, you saw how theatrical. Also his sister. He is like a boy in a play."

"A play? His family thinks it's time he became serious."

Marvin-ventriloquism. Or not: plain on the face of it, the boy was all anarchy.

"His sister is not so serious. A wildness, a wild bird."

"Don't you like her?" The instant it was out, Bea felt it as something only a tactless American would ask.

73

"She should not have come. She makes a complication. Also you should not have come."

"Especially if I can't get to talk to my nephew. Days and days gone by, and I've seen Julian for a quarter of an hour, if that. Not that I can blame him." An unforeseen glimmer of candor: how could she blame herself for an identical disregard? "We don't know each other," she admitted.

"A nephew who is for you a stranger. And still you speak of family."

Bea said lamely, "New York and California are a continent apart."

"Have you no husband, no son, no family of your own? If you do not know your nephew, why do you run to him, why have you an interest in him?"

"I'll ask you the same." And dared it: "What is it you want from Julian?"

Lili dipped her head. A few threads of gray at the crown. "I had once a husband. I had once a son." Up rose her chin, a warning, a wall. She would go no further with this. "Today I have Julian."

A husband, a son. People like that, one of those. There was no innocence in this woman.

"Next to Julian," Bea said, "you seem . . . old."

"I am already one hundred years, yes! But I am *for* him. I do him good, is this how you say it? I do him good."

"And what possible good can he do you? A boy in a play! The two of them, you call them children—"

"He becomes less and less a boy. At the same time he is a man."

"Oh, in *that* way—" It was her worst so far.

"In all ways. Do not mistake him. He is a man."

"A man," Bea repeated foolishly.

"You see now why you should not have come. Your niece tells you this. Also I tell you. And you see for yourself. It is done. It was not my wish, Julian wished it, he wished it and wished it. And so."

Unthinkable. Unconscionable. Done? Then the boy was in for it. He was beyond rescue, beyond even punishment. He was lost to fathomless incoherence.

Lili stood up; her hand went to the lamp. But it stopped midway, with a palm open to judgment — Bea made it out almost to be an appeal.

"You must believe me. I do him good," Lili said. "Now nothing is hidden, you see?"

It came to Bea then that the excitable children's secret was out. Lili had once had a husband. Now she had another.

16

Iris stood in the doorway: a sentry on the alert.

"*Tomorrow* evening? Is this about dinner again? We'll think about it. Can't you just put it off a bit longer? Julian needs another couple of nights to recuperate, at least — that awful cough, not that it's not on its way out, Lili's eggnogs maybe. He's really getting on, it's only that his mood's so bad. You won't want to come in," she persisted, "he hasn't had much of anything to eat, and he's cranky —"

Boorish, *piggish* to be packed off, time after time, day after day, like a peddler, like a beggar!

"We haven't once had a proper visit, or even talked a little. He snubs me —"

"Because you've got to give dad his report, that's why. Interrogation at headquarters, isn't that the idea? Look, Julian's fine, he can do without anyone's supervision, you can tell dad that."

"And what do I say about you?"

Iris rolled her eyes. Boorish, piggish! And something telltale, fumelike, on her breath.

"Don't you get it, that you're just another leash? We don't need it, we've been on a leash all our lives —"

"A leash? When for years I've had nothing to do with either of you —"

"Exactly. And then you show up here, and tug at the rope."

"It was you who came to me," Bea said.

"I was sent."

Mulish!—the two of them. These coddled Californians, with no inkling of endurance. They had lived without winter. And if anyone had Julian on a leash, hampering his future, stopping up his youth, wasn't it Lili? Oracular, too alien to comprehend. But unwilling to lie.

A blank day, then. Bea had it before her. An hour to change her return ticket, and afterward what? Another go at the Louvre, why not?—it was inexhaustible. A fake reprise of the summer, when she'd been no more implicated in these foreign intrigues than the usual tourist, a vacationing unmarried teacher (*have you no husband, no son?*), a triteness, and not . . . whatever she was now. A leash. A leech. They didn't want her, they were wary of her—possibly they would indulge her enough to let her pay for a meal, and good riddance. They were afraid of her: she was a messenger, an emissary. They took her to be Marvin's surrogate. They knew what Marvin was capable of.

The dazzling length of the Galerie d'Apollon, a gold-encrusted hall, and then on through the vastnesses of those brilliant corridors opening into still more brilliant rooms, Etruscans, Greeks, Romans alive in their marble veins and thick marble necks where pulses once throbbed, and on the old walls kings and warriors and highborn ladies in fluted silks, and pastoral riders shadowed by the weighty crowns of trees. A thousand resurrections, Magna Graecia becoming Naples, goddesses brought low, kitchen jugs venerated. Dust-unto-dust spited. She saw an embossed ebony cabinet, vines, leaves, fruits, beasts, niche within graven niche, every inch carved, curled, figured. She saw, in a small vitrine, a tiny polished lion, crouching, one paw extended: the gilded claws glittered. She looked and looked and looked—her eyes thirsted. In all this proliferation, paint dried centuries past, stone knees of dead monarchs, every object *made*, hard-won, it was humanity, it was civilization . . .

An empty bench; she sat down gladly, wearily, before a Flemish tapestry that stretched from one end of the gallery to the other. A million colored threads, faces, hands, topiary, minutely pebbled paths, a stream. Little fishes in the transparent water. She imagined Marvin beside her, gaping all around and seeing nothing. Belittling what he couldn't plumb. Amnesiac America, America the New. What's new is good, workable, efficient. Engineered.

But what he was capable of!

17

"THE LAST SUPPER," Iris said. "That's what Julian called it when I got him to come. For dad's sake, not that he cares."

The last minute, the eleventh hour. Bea had booked a midnight flight. In her odious room two floors above, her bags were packed and ready.

"He thinks you're going to crucify him," Iris said. "Fatten him up for the slaughter, serve his head on a platter."

Her ears had reddened; she was emptying glass after glass—it was soon evident that the three convivial bottles Bea had ordered wouldn't suffice. Julian, his mind on his meat, went on feeding as if he had been famished for months. The boy was a carnivore, the boy had an appetite! And beside him Lili, half screened by the heavy curtain that secluded this corner of the dining parlor and overhung the heaped-up bowls and bubbling sauces and tubs of dumplings and trays of tarts sent parading around them. Fragrances of what was yet to come flowed in from the kitchen. Bea had been extravagant!

But a fiasco, all of it. A futility from beginning to end. She was glad enough to be on her way. Goodbye to their mysteries, their entanglements, their concealments—she had been drawn in and kept out. In the subdued light Lili dwindled into a fragile little old woman in a shawl. Bea saw again that double crease etched in her forehead: two cut-off railroad tracks. She was picking at a lone lettuce leaf. Glancing over, Julian ladled out a large potato and set it on her plate.

Steam, and the honeyed scent of some unfamiliar herb, spiraled upward.

"Madame Bones," he said, "eat."

And to Bea, abruptly: "Do you know how my mother is?"

These were the first words he had spoken to her.

"Your father tells me she's in a rest home."

"A rest home? You mean a storage bin. An asylum."

Iris said, "She agreed to it, Julian, I told you. The place is absolutely posh, with all the amenities. She was perfectly happy to go."

"He *put* her there. Dumped her."

"She was sleeping all day, she didn't know what time it was. She was getting sort of . . . confused. You don't have to bring this up now—"

"Why not? He's the one who makes her crazy, isn't he?" And once more to Bea: "He'll make you crazy too. What're you going to tell him?"

"That his son is a stubborn loafer," Iris said.

"No, really," he pursued, "when he starts grilling you. You'll have to say *some*thing, right?"

"What would you like me to say?"

But Lili—disquiet in her quiet—intervened. "You should say what you know."

"What Bea knows," Iris said, "is that we got away, we're on the lam. Like Hansel and Gretel. Only we never intended to drop any idiot crumbs." Belligerent. Erratic. Erratic? The girl was smashed!

"Iris, you're having too much wine," Julian said.

"Julian, you're having too many cakes," she answered.

The nettling, the bickering, the ingrained impatient intimacy (Bea could hardly tell one from the other) went back and forth between them, while Lili sat gazing at the drenched potato in her dish like an augur reading a fate. She seemed as distant from these American offspring as that ebony cabinet in the Louvre, with all its little hidden compartments. Lili herself was obscurely recessed and crannied—and was it collusion, or else some mystical tie between them, that compelled the brother to lash out a charge as biting as his sister's? *Interrogation at headquarters.* And what *would* Bea tell Marvin, and what might come of it? Was this the incessant worry of the house almost from the hour Bea broke into their lives? Surely they murmured together, they turned it over, they pecked at the possibilities; what *would* she tell Marvin? They asked it uneasily, they asked it urgently, because Julian was homeless and jobless and reckless and rash. Did they hope, if only Bea could deliver a fitting story, that Marvin would soften and shower his capricious boy with money? Was some clandestine chance of it couched in the darkling groove between Lili's eyes?

Lili said sharply, "She knows."

"How, how?" — Iris's wine-dyed mouth a red hole. Julian staring, sweating in the folds of his neck.

"She knows," Lili said again.

When Bea left them there among the teacups, and went up to her room (good riddance too to the trough in the bed and the hose in the bath) to fetch her luggage, it was understood — though no one voiced it aloud — that Julian's lot was in Bea's hands. What the brother and sister had feared to disclose, Lili had laid open: the boy had a wife. His father took seriously the care of a wife; his own, even when ill, he had placed in the lap of luxury. Then it was at least thinkable, for the sake of the boy's having a wife, that the money would follow: it all depended on Bea. She should not have come, no — but since she had, and knew what she knew, it might be all to the good. Thus did Lili instruct the brother and sister.

In the plane, Bea put down her book — the cabin lights had dimmed — and played it out. It was probable, it was likely. The boy's naïveté, the pointless years away, how he dallied, how he looked for amusement, how easily he was beguiled . . . Doubtless Lili had taken his measure: he had no means of making a living, and no evident ambition either. But his father was rich. A boy with a wife was a man, and a man with a wife could not be left to drown. Accustomed in her cubicle to opening gates that were inclined to be shut, Lili had turned a key. The key was Bea. It was probable, it was likely. It accorded with Marvin's predictable suspicions: inexorable Marvin, who had logic on his side. It was in his nature, he had founded a business, he comprehended greed, he was steeped in the knowledge of bad faith.

Probable? Likely? But Bea did not believe it.

18

WHEN SHE WAS gone, they lingered awhile. The emptied bottles
lolled on their sides. Lili's uneaten potato lay cold and congealed on
her plate like a guillotined head. Where Julian had dribbled gravy,
an oily patch went on spreading through the cloth. Lifting her chin
over the debris, Iris said, "You think dad will make her crazy? She's
crazy already. When I was in New York — this tiny apartment she's
got — she offered me her own bed—"

"That's because she'd stuck a pea under the mattress," Julian said.

"—and just before that, I thought she wanted to kill me. There was
this enormous thing, with brass feet, *claws,* you'd expect to see a piano like that on a stage, and all I did was touch it, just one note really,
it was strange seeing it there, it took up nearly the whole room—"

"Wasn't she married once? To some sort of musician?"

"—one finger, I put one finger on it, and she froze up and looked
ferocious, I mean almost violent, with crazy eyes. As if I'd ruin it, or it
could fall apart, or if you hit a wrong key lightning would come out
of it. As if the thing was holy. — And then right after, as nicely as
could be, she said I should take her bed."

"The better to strangle you in the middle of the night," Julian said.
"So did you?"

"Did I what?"

"Take her bed."

"I did, why not? Instead of that ratty davenport. With those silly
claws practically under your nose."

Lili said, "In that house you made perhaps a sin."

"Because I let her sleep on her own ratty thing? What I really wanted was a decent hotel, but still, dad's sister, do the family honors, it was only for overnight and I was getting her to help—"

"Iris at her saintliest," Julian said.

But Lili said, "A sin to touch a holy thing, is it not?"

19

IN THE TERMINAL, waiting to board, Bea was attempting to finish the letter to Marvin, discarding one wary blunder after another. Either she was telling too much, or—this was certain—she was telling too little. The exertion strained her wrist; the flimsy hotel stationery went skittering over the flanks of her valise—a makeshift and unsteady surface—and she worried that her fountain pen might run dry. She surrendered finally to the old abandoned abruptness and left it at that: *There's no use my staying any longer. Iris is a riddle, and your son won't budge.* She dropped the envelope into a mail slot; they had begun to call her flight. The overseas stamp was big and showy. It would be postmarked Paris, as it must be. To take the letter with her, to send it from another city, was perilous.

She had exchanged her ticket for an earlier date—but also for a different destination. Marvin was not to know this; it was a recklessness. A whim. Or not a whim; it drove her. A handful of days remained before she was obliged to breathe the fetid airlessness of her classroom—Laura impatient, chafing, waiting to be freed from those hulking students with their long sideburns and beginning mustaches, how they must be hooting at Madame Defarge and her knitting, caterwauling in staccato falsettos *It is a far, far better thing that I do, than I have ever done,* swiping their necks, and how was Laura handling it?—Mrs. Bienenfeld, show us how it works, the guillotine, come on, show us, show us on Charlie! Poor Laura, was she pulling it off, staring down that mob of overgrown boys cavorting in their seats?

Paris had been hurtful; they had treated her badly. Their rebuffs and mystifications. But Bea knew now what Iris knew; they knew it together. A secret no more — Bea was carrying it with her. She had the power to divulge it or not to divulge it: either way, it was power.

The windows were black, the shades pulled down. Many of the passengers were asleep, their faces turned childlike under the dim cabin lights. The body of the plane vibrated like a tuning fork, obedient to the pulsing of the great engine quartet. In a matter of hours they would be escaping the night, outrunning it to cross into the ruddy seam of late afternoon. The shades would snap open, a dawdling finger of sun would wake the sleepers, and far beneath, as the plane's belly lowered, a famous ocean would rise toward them — not the homebound Atlantic, at whose lip lay New York. They were landing in California.

20

IT WAS ANOTHER country. Deep summer ruled autumn. Women strolled in the streets half dressed, in halters and shorts, with pearl-painted toenails peering from high-heeled sandals. The smell of frying things flooded out of eateries and greased the air. Streams of cars on ribbons of highways: Los Angeles haphazard and fragmented, as if an entire city had been dropped from the sky to be broken into shards and scatterings, the pieces flung miles apart. She had expected mountains, blue cones merging into a gray horizon. Instead, only these shards of towns with their Old World names and their New World obstreperousness.

The Suite Eyre Spa: an English manor set in an English garden. California!—where everything was a replica of somewhere else. The parking lot was hidden behind a stand of palm trees; abutting it a long lawn fenced by rose-mobbed trellises, its grass so shockingly green that it looked newly painted. Pools of flower beds wound artlessly through, as if a wild growth of peonies and zinnias had sprouted of themselves. Oak benches were dispersed among them, and these too pretended to have aged naturally in their soil. And beyond, the manor with its six white Georgian pillars and broad shadowy porch lined with cushioned wicker lounge chairs and urns overflowing with bougainvillea. But no one walked in the grounds or loitered on the benches or waited on the porch. A sanatorium in the hush of a communal indoor doze; or a flock of rich men's wives under a spell.

She passed a reception desk — no one was there, though a half-full coffee cup rested on its blotter — and then moved on through a corridor of doors, some shut, many open. Women sleeping. Medicated into torpor, self-lulled into immobility. The toxin of despair. Impulse may have brought her here; yet impulse was the frail carapace of what felt long calculated. Or if not calculated, then stored and readied. Her motive was shrouded even from herself.

Margaret's door was shut. On the doorpost a ceramic plaque: on it someone had crayoned MRS. M. NACHTIGALL. She turned the knob and looked in — and in and in, as into one of those mirrors that reflect other mirrors, far into infinitude. A suite of unfurling rooms, rows of windows, white curtains, brightness all around, bowls of unrecognizable flowers. An indefinable odor — medicinal, and foul, or else it was the flowers . . . the smell was repugnant. The flowers were silk, did silk breathe out so wormy a breath? A woman in a pleated dress — no, a nightgown or a long smock — sat in a straight chair in front of an easel. But her eyes were on the white wall behind it.

"Margaret," Bea said.

The eyes moved. The woman did not.

"It's Beatrice. From New York."

"New York?" That voice: the bodiless timbre, the light quick syllables. Drained, veiled, softened almost below the threshold of Bea's hearing. "Marvin's sister?"

She stood up then. Bea had forgotten how tall Marvin's wife was, but she could almost recover her face, mainly through the scrim of a snapshot or two, possibly decades old. It was one of those perfected faces, geometrically proportioned and aligned, that are beautiful on a girl of eighteen but wear badly: too much symmetry, like good manners early inculcated, turns flat. Margaret's face, Margaret's manners, were both perfected.

"How nice to see you again," Margaret said: a practiced chatelaine. As if they had met over cards only last week. Yet with the exception of a single perfunctory mumble and nod in a public corridor, they had never unaffectedly met. After his marriage — how many years ago!—Marvin had removed his new wife to the farthest end of the continent, and kept her sequestered there—because, he said, this was where the future of aircraft lay, and where he would make his fortune. The wedding itself, in a modest New England chapel, was all unhappy Breckinridges, and altogether bare of unhappy Nachtigalls. Bea's mother, and then her father, had gone to their graves without ever having heard their daughter-in-law's even-tempered vowels, or marveled at her rounded aristocratic forehead and its precisely placed horizontal eyebrows. Nor had they witnessed her as a bride, except in the serenely posed Bachrach photograph that acknowledged their awkward wedding gift—it had bypassed the designated registry and arrived woundedly in a thin envelope. Marvin journeyed alone to his parents' funerals. As for Bea, she was belatedly introduced to Margaret in New York, at the Princeton Club one afternoon, no more than an hour or so before Marvin hurried his wife and little daughter into a hired car to take them to that significant alumni reunion where Marvin would be honored as a lavishly philanthropic donor, and where he could not expect to greet his old classmate and brother-in-law. Margaret's brother had been killed the year before in the crash of a private plane after a drinking party; the woman in the passenger seat died with him. By then AMERICA'S HARDWARE EMPORIUM had expired, and all elderly Breckinridges and Nachtigalls, including Bea's three unmarried aunts, were dead. And by then Bea had long been Miss Nightingale. From Marvin's point of view, Bea guessed, she was the least likely of all known Nachtigalls to embarrass him. He had brought her on that one occasion—it was rooted in her mind with an indelible agelessness, like a movie still—to be offhandedly presented to Margaret and his child. The Margaret of the movie still was steadily smiling, and the child no more than an elusive flash of white-blond head.

But the Margaret who stood before Bea now was all flicker and twitch, an engine pumping mechanical civilities. "Are you staying at the house? Did Marvin manage it? He could be away, he's always on the run, but then the housekeeper's there until six—"

She broke off; the engine had failed.

"No, no," Bea reassured her, "it's you I've come to see. And I'm at a motel, I rented a car at the airport—"

"Marvin wouldn't like it. He'd be afraid of my getting upset, but I'm not upset at all. My husband has the idea that I'm unwell. I'm perfectly well, you can see for yourself."

Bea trailed after the painter's smock: it fell to Margaret's ankles and brushed her bare heels. She was leading Bea from one sunlit space to another, passing an unmade bed tumbled with pillows. They came to a room where two armchairs flanked an ornamental fireplace. The fireplace was fake, its useless hearth hidden behind a large unframed landscape. Settling into one of the chairs, mentally measuring, Bea speculated that this prodigal parade of invalid's accommodations could easily swallow her own apartment three or four times over.

She gestured toward the fireplace. "That painting, is it yours?"

"Oh, I don't do trees and things. The person who was here before me did it, I could never do anything like that. They say I could if I tried. They tell me I have some talent. They're expected to say things like that. It's therapy, you know."

With Margaret seated opposite and to the side, Bea could see only her profile, the thin nose pale as a wafer, the pale truncated eyelashes, the mouth drawn flat. In this place, a distance from where she had come in, the bad smell was not so strong. But she felt helplessly stymied—what had she supposed was to be gained from this dubious visit, these vapid courtesies of accepting and denying? The woman was flat through and through.

"Then you're satisfied here," Bea said.

It was meant as a question; it was not spoken as one. It received no answer. Instead Margaret said, "You won't believe me, will you? That I've always been interested in my husband's family—you'll say there's been no sign of it."

"Well, here I am, the family entire. The last of the Mohicans, there's no one else. But you've got a big enough clan of your own, don't you? There's always one or two mentioned in the magazines."

"It's only some cousins now. We're in touch at Christmas, though not lately—"

"The cousin in the Cabinet. The governor. The other governor. And the congressman who flew his own plane."

"My poor brother. It was horrible. So long ago, Iris was only a baby, and my son wasn't born, but he dreams it, Julian's always told me he dreams of falling in flames—"

She had turned to face Bea. Her voice had altered (was it because of that plane on fire, was it because of her son?); it coarsened to a rough noise, ragged as the work of a saw. "I'm satisfied, yes! The way Marvin sees it, his wife's run away, his son's run away, the only one who hasn't run away is his daughter. Why else do you think I came here? How else do you think I *got* here? And where else on earth could I go?" Her eyes were stretched wide, the lower lids lined with their narrow crescents of blood. "I—cannot—live—with my husband!"

The mild madwoman mildly incarcerated was all at once taking on a kind of sanity: it swept over Bea that it was the sanity of illumination. Clarity had stripped Margaret of the anodyne of manners. Her wild mouth, and the wilderness spitting out of it, impelled a tilt of her forehead and chin: she was becoming three-dimensionally alive.

Bea said slowly, "Do you mean you *wanted* to come? You chose to?"

"I got Marvin to agree to it. He thinks he got *me* to agree to it." She ground out a sour laugh. "Can you understand what he's made of me? Oh, but by now I can outthink him, I can think rings around him. I don't blame you if you can't see it. Why should you see it? Only I would imagine his sister . . . you lived with him once, you grew up with him, you had the same mother and father. I've always tried to imagine all of you, especially that mother of his, and if you're anything like my husband, I ought to hate you. That's what *he's* good at, hating. You know what he's hated since he was a boy, what he's hated more than anything in the world?"

"No," Bea said; though she thought she knew.

"That hardware store. That putrid hardware store. I never saw the place, I never *smelled* the place, he's told me how it smelled, paint, kerosene, insect spray, who knows, but I owe my whole life to it. My whole life, because he was ashamed. He said he was poisoned by it. A poison needs an antidote, doesn't it?"

She jumped up and bent her long body over Bea; her fingers forced pits into the velvet arms of the chair. The big gray short-lashed eyes came too near.

"You changed your name, didn't you?"

"When I was married I did for a while. But I went back afterward."

"You changed the name you were born with," Margaret insisted.

"I'm a teacher, no one could pronounce it —"

"It's German? Or I suppose it's that Yiddish. You don't think *I* could pronounce it? Or any of my own people? You'd have to gargle phlegm to get it right. Marvin changed everything else, just not his name. To torture himself, or maybe to impress my family with his so-called pride. He worshiped them, you know. Not that they took any notice of it —"

"It would be hard not to notice what a success he's made," Bea said. Was she defending Marvin, could it be? Or was it a hurt to her good-natured, modest father that she meant to rebuff, the memory of her father in the back room under an old-fashioned lamp, sunk in some novel, while her mother tended to business up front?

"Plastic airplane parts," Margaret spat out. "Advanced flatware, my brother called it — with Marvin, he said, the apple didn't fall far from the shop. My husband's good with money, it's the drop of Jew left in him. All the rest is mine." She pulled herself erect and stared down at Bea. "He's turned himself into what he thinks I am. That crest! All that research on the sacred family escutcheon! If Marvin could find a way to crawl inside my bloodstream, he'd do it."

Bea said, "Why don't you just take it for what it is? Flattery, or aspiration —"

92

"You're trying to pacify me, I recognize the tone. The therapists here talk like that. Can't you understand, my husband has no existence! He doesn't exist. He has no self."

Marvin the egotist: no self? Margaret, Bea saw, was intelligent. She had entered into a knowledge beyond the commonplace. She twisted up her face: the equidistant geometries crumpled.

"That green on the crest," she said, "stands for water. The water James Watt took from the Clyde — that's the boy who invented the steam engine just from watching a kettle boil, it's in all the schoolbooks. Breckinridges are descendants of Watt on the maternal side, did you know that?"

"No," Bea said.

"Well, my husband knows it! And he expects his children to live up to it, it's their *heritage,* noblesse oblige, they have to be worthy, they have to distinguish themselves. And he sees it in Iris — the chance of it. She's got the brain for it, he says, if she sticks to it. My poor daughter, he has her living in that lab night and day. But Julian . . . it's not only those nightmares, Marvin calls it an attraction to atrocity, he thinks Julian's in love with anything that's contaminated, can you believe such terrible words? Anything deformed, anything ruined, and he rushes to it — his own son!"

Then this was the moment — Margaret pacing to the make-believe fireplace and back, shoulders shrunken, clutching herself: the moment for telling. Bea stood up and took Margaret's hand — a hint of tremor in the fingers.

"He's afraid, Marvin's afraid, that's why! That thing Julian sent us, from some magazine they put out over there — about filthy birds in the streets. Ghetto stuff, Marvin said. He worries that Julian's some sort of throwback —"

"Margaret," Bea said. "I've seen him. In Paris."

"Julian? When, how?" Margaret's hand leaped free, as from an electric charge. "What's my son doing over there? Why doesn't he come home?"

"He didn't confide in me, you know. It was all so brief — he seems well enough, even a bit on the plump side. I had the impression that he's gotten fluent in French. Some people would call that polish."

Polish! Was it justifiable to lie to an invalid? The ruthlessness of honesty: it was impossible to be truthful to Margaret. Her neck was hunched; she had crossed her arms and thrust her fists into her armpits. She was attempting to curl herself into a ball; it was not passivity. She was a bullet, a cannon, a salvo. Little by little the shots erupted. "Marvin had this idea," she said, "a way to get him back. A capitulation, Marvin gave in, he actually gave in! Julian won't do science, he *can't* do science, he's not made for it, so all right, something else, as long as it gets him to come home . . ."

Margaret's eyes, the color of water, swam toward Bea like a pair of sharks. "He looked him up — that fellow. *That* fellow," she said.

"Who?"

"The one you used to be married to."

"Leo?" Bea cried. "What's Marvin got to do with Leo?"

"My husband knows everyone in L.A., don't ask me how, he has all these contacts, he gets in touch with people who get in touch with other people . . . he found out where that fellow lives, not far from *us,* in fact, Bel Air Circle, so he went to see him, it's only around the corner —"

"He saw Leo? Why? Why would he do that, what possible business could Marvin have with Leo?"

"It's the way Julian *is,* how he thinks — it's all unreal, Marvin says, it's dreaming —"

"What's that got to do with Leo Coopersmith, for God's sake!"

The invalid was in command. Bea had come to condole, to sympathize; or to test her daring, her restraint — was that why she had come? It was certain she had come in kindness. But the visit had turned topsy-turvy; Margaret's volleys were flying fast. Bea no longer felt kind.

"The movies. Hollywood. Marvin thought he could get Julian

some sort of job he'd fit into, something he'd really like, to lure him—"

"And did he mention me? Is that what you're saying? Was I his . . . his *reference?*"

"You were married to the fellow."

"And then I wasn't. Marvin went to Leo for *help*, is that it? He went begging to the oboe?"

"Oboe, what's that? He's in the movies, he's a famous movie composer, isn't he? And my husband doesn't beg. He never begs."

Bea said grimly, "Margaret, listen. Julian isn't about to come back, there's no sign of it. He's got himself married. To a displaced person—you know what that means, a displaced person? And your daughter isn't living in her lab, she's with your son and his wife. In Paris. Right now. I left them yesterday."

The water trembled; the sharks vanished. The tiny whitish eyelashes blinked.

"I don't believe you," Margaret said. "Marvin never told me anything like that."

"He doesn't know any of it. I'm the spy who was sent behind enemy lines to bring back the news. Fresh intelligence, Margaret."

"I don't believe you. Iris is in school. Julian's too young to be married. You should go away now."

"Yes," Bea said.

They walked, side by side, from cell to cell—the sun had moved lower, the windows were dull now—until they came to where the easel stood. Here the bad smell worsened.

"You should see my work," Margaret said. "My therapy."

She swiveled the easel to show Bea. Dark sky, dark hills, dark barren ground. A central smudge that appeared to approximate the figure of a woman, or was it a man? All of it dark and lavishly laid on.

Marvin's wife had mastered the art of human excrement.

21

FOR HIS TWENTY-THIRD birthday Julian received a check from his father, accompanied by a businesslike note explaining how to circumvent the bank's discount on foreign money, so as to change dollars into francs without a loss of value. His father was good at such shortcuts, but Julian was indifferent: he had no intention of beginning what was certain to become a quarrel with some factotum in a bank, and anyhow Marvin's instructions, thickened by numbers and percentages, were over his head. It was enough that the figure on the blue paper rectangle promised another installment on Mme. Duval's rent, and a whole week free of waiting on tables. Not that Julian despised shortcuts in general—it was Alfred who'd introduced him to a certain François who got him jobs under the table, or however they said this in French, and it was through Alfred that his little thing on the Marais had reached the Princess, and from the Princess had ascended to print. Print! It had happened twice, but now Alfred was dead, and he was on his own, without an intermediary, though he still kept a covetous eye on the *Paris Review*. Without Alfred, who was fearless and knew everyone, he had no chance there, he wasn't good enough, he wasn't diligent enough, or confident enough. He was what they called him at home, a *luftmentsh,* or at least his father called him that, his mother wouldn't have known such a word, it meant an inconsequential person, an impracticality made of air, she would have defended him . . .

He had read about those legendary writers who sat in a favorite café every morning, driving their pens, oblivious to everything around them, the clatter and chatter, the passersby, the street noises, the car horns. He had never witnessed anything like that, which didn't imply that it couldn't be done, and as a matter of fact he was doing it right now, not in the morning (he didn't get up early if he didn't have to) but at two o'clock in the afternoon, at Le Tisserand, where he had never worked and wasn't known and wouldn't be laughed at. About the check he was both happy and resentful — happy because he could loiter here, with a bottle of beer and his smooth new notebook with its margins marked in red, and resentful because he understood that the money was both a bribe and a threat. *One more month*, his father had written below the numbers and the percentages, *and then home*. Those six monosyllables pounded like gongs. A brief chirp from his mother: *Are you all right, Julian? We miss you*. Nothing from his sister — she had other means: she hid his letters, and answered them secretly.

He had already filled four pages: his idea was to invent a series of clever little fables, in style something between Aesop and La Roche-foucauld (Alfred had put him on to La Rochefoucauld), with morals at the end, only the morals wouldn't be morals — he'd call them *im-morals*, and they'd be the opposite of what his deceptively straight-faced tales appeared to prescribe or warn against. And the language would be simple and "transparent," a term he had learned from Al-fred; but Alfred was unhelpfully dead, and the *Paris Review* had al-ready sent back half a dozen of his fables. He thought he should find another name for them.

It had begun to rain, at first lightly, and a deadening of the air, and the smell of wet pavement drifting in from the outdoors, excited him a little: it was the smell of anticipation. Then it darkened, and a dim-ness settled over where he sat against a rear wall, with his feet on a chair belonging to a nearby table, and the rain hurtled down with a tropical force in dense gray curtains that flew in from the street. A rowdy party of three or four young girls dashed in, instantly soaked through, laughing and tugging at their backpacks: there was a lycée in the neighborhood. He liked looking at them—the rounded calves above their low socks, the rise of the small hillocks just under their collarbones, dripping hair falling to the middle of their backs. They were twelve or thirteen or even fourteen; and right behind them, a middle-aged woman. He presumed the woman was a teacher (she was carrying a briefcase), or else the mother of one of the girls, but she quickly separated herself from the group and left them standing in the doorway, giggling and squeezing the water from one another's hair and braiding it into pigtails. The woman spotted a vacant table and opened her briefcase: rain trickled from its sides. But Julian kept his eye on the girls—only one of them was really pretty. He wished she were older, eighteen, say; if she were eighteen, or twenty, he would get up and sidle close and tease her in his improving French. Or if she were one of those American girls (but no, she wasn't, the whole noisy bunch of them had erupted out of that lycée down the street), those American girls who were everywhere nowadays, in every corner of the city, he could start out as he always did with American girls: "So which one are you, Gertrude or Alice?"—which was of course a sort of test, to earn him either an ignorant retort or an invitation to say his name and where he was from and what he was doing in Paris, and after that who could tell what might follow? Especially if it turned out she was one of those French majors from Vassar or Smith or Bryn Mawr, who always knew who Gertrude and Alice were. And that was the joke of it: he'd learned from the photographs that Gertrude and Alice were ugly and old, in fact they looked like ugly old men, squat and (he guessed) pigeon-toed. The woman who had hurried in along with that gaggle of wild girls—the pretty one couldn't have been more than thirteen—wasn't exactly ugly, and not as old as he had at first imagined, but he'd had only a flash of her, she was no one he would ordinarily notice. He was noticing her now only because she was a distraction, more from the girls than from his pathetic cat fable, which was faltering anyhow: she was pulling a sheet of paper and a mechanical pencil (the kind his father kept in his breast pocket) out of that briefcase, cheap cardboard flaking off at the seams — it wasn't made to be rained on. She had arranged her things — a long-sleeved sweater and a bag with the oval end of a bread sticking out — two chairs away from where he sat (the one in between had his feet on it), and he could almost see what she was writing. It had the commonplace shape of a letter, and at once he lost interest: she wasn't a fellow inventor of fables, she wasn't pretty, she wasn't young, she wasn't a sort he would ever approach to ask about Gertrude or Alice. She was only a woman who had come in out of the wet.

A slash of sunlight cut into his eyes, reflected from a passing wind-shield: the storm was suddenly spent. The sea-salt aroma of after-rain hissed up from the sidewalk, and the girls with their pigtails and knapsacks tumbled out, shrieking, into the renewed afternoon. He tried to put his mind to his story: a free-spirited yet dutiful cat who always returns obediently home after a day of carousing in alleys. And what was the immoral of that? He couldn't think, he was impatient with it, it was stupid, he was bored. He didn't want to be the cat who comes submissively home, but he was homesick all the same; or at any rate sick. He felt sick, sick, partly in his stomach, partly he hardly knew how. He admitted to tedium, to looseness, to nothing-ness, it was all over with the crowd he'd been running with, that brilliant crowd Alfred was in the middle of, Alfred who could reel off a comic disquisition on a pubic hair held between thumb and forefinger (the rape of the lock, he said) — he'd run with them and drunk with them, but he wasn't of them, he didn't belong; he was always on the periphery. He tried and tried, he flattered them and scurried to catch up with them, he tried to *deserve* them, but finally they were sick of him or he was sick of them, he couldn't tell the difference. Either way it left him out. It was their brilliance he was sick of; it didn't stick, it was all mobility, it rolled here and there, aimlessly, quip after quip. His immorals too were no more than shallow quips. But the real trouble was the cat — he needed a bigger animal, one that would be capable of frightening the family when it returned. A bear; a fearsome grizzly bear. No: what household would keep a bear for a pet?

Besides, once let out, a bear would be a fool to come back to domestic life, where undoubtedly it would have to resume the chain.

"Damn, I can't do it," he said.

The woman glanced up, and he realized he had spoken aloud. He was embarrassed, but only a little—lately he sometimes talked to himself. It was anger that did it, lava foaming up out of a dried-up throat, he didn't care, he could do as he pleased, he could yell in the street if he liked. At three in the morning once, coming finely dizzily boisterously soused out of the Napoléon, Alfred three sheets to the wind, the pair of them yelling into the sky, yelling into the night, fat glorious American yells, and hey listen, Alfred said, which was the real wilderness anyway, the New World (it had aged substantially by now) or the Old? It felt marvelous, with Alfred's arms around his neck (but Alfred had killed himself, Alfred was dead), not to know whether he had or didn't have a body.

The woman said, "Then you must persist."

This old thing was answering him, as if he expected it, or needed it, or wanted it! The look she was giving him was both more and less than annoyance, the kind of look you turn on a child who throws a stone that seems about to strike you but doesn't. It made him believe even more than before that she must be a teacher from the lycée, some sour-tongued harridan that rough pack of girls had determined to snub. He took his feet off the chair. This small grudging feint toward propriety—she'd caught him out, she'd shamed him—made her laugh, she was laughing at him! From that first sound it was plain she wasn't French, she certainly wasn't American, what was she? Even a laugh can have a foreign chime in it, and this intrusive woman, with that elderly furrow between her eyebrows, was laughing at him!

22

THE BOY WAS absurd. The boy was contemptible. The self-con-sciousness of it, lord of the world, commandeering a flock of chairs as if he owned the planet earth, one of those know-nothing Ameri-cans besotted with old tattered visions of Sartre, that dolt, that foul Communist, that abettor of the worst. Paris was infested with these imitation baby Sartres and Gides sitting in cafés over their inky man-uscripts, an apéritif placed just so at the nearest knuckle to authenti-cate the parody, the foolish superannuated play-acting. And this one in romantic agony over some tragic flaw in his genius! A plaything, their Paris, a toy: they would wear it out, it would wear them out, one or the other would be discarded. And when they were done with it, away they'd go, how easy to fly off with their easy American pass-ports to those waiting rich cities and their movietone skyscrapers, their happy Clevelands and Chicagos and Bostons! They could come and they could go, ignorant that the ground was scorched, so oblivi-ously soft was it under their feet, and here was this raw entitled boy with his big dirty sandals up on a chair, showing dirty toenails . . .

So Lili laughed, and in her oddly arranged English snapped out her little mockery, and went back to writing to her uncle.

But the stupid boy didn't take it for the indifferent gibe it was, simple low sarcasm, or if he did, he was pitifully in want of conversa-tion, and would put out his tongue for any crumb of human warmth. She had no warmth to give him; she was cold, her warmth was for her poor lost mother's brother, far away where she had unearthed him;

it was her intention to go to him, in two months, in three. Lonely, then; the boy ought to be on his way, he had a family somewhere, why should he persist? Persist in what? In play-acting in a café? She had seen them everywhere, their drinking, their raucousness, their play-acting. Make-believe exile, an ephemeral game. The ground was scorched, the streets teemed with refugees, and these Americans were playing at fleeing! As if they had something to resent, to despise, to scorn, to run away from! As if they weren't the lords of the earth.

Yet this lord of the earth was looking at her unhappily, angrily — bitterly. His sorrows, whatever they were, were trivial, he was uneducated, his ignorance was no different from innocence; but she could smell the fume of bitterness.

"Am I a joke?" he said. Because she had laughed, and who wouldn't laugh at such a travesty?

"Oh yes," she said. "Exactly so. Because there are so many of you."

"So many what?" Only see how ready he is to be belligerent!

"So many purposeless. A carnival to pass the time. You come here and you do not know why."

He was being scolded; worse, he was being exposed. And by an imperious meddlesome woman who thought herself a clairvoyant. As if he had no right to be whatever he was. She was taking him to be part of a crowd, and he had given up the crowd; it wasn't fair. A pang of missing: only his sister was sympathetic. Well, his mother too, but she was so much under his father's thumb . . .

"You don't know me," he said, "so don't judge me."

In his own ears he sounded childish.

"You should go home," she said.

"I can't."

"And why is that?"

"I have no home."

Oh, portentous! This caricature, this scion of good fortune, claiming homelessness!

"No? Then where do you come from?"

He let it out like a worm: "California."

"So that is your home, is it not?"—though he might have said Antarctica, for all the reality it had.

"Getting born in a place," he retorted, "doesn't make it your home, not if they don't treat you like you're an actual person—"

She was drawing him in, he supposed, with the intention of drawing him out: why should he allow it, why should he tell her anything at all? Already he had said too much, again that childish speechifying. Now he examined her in earnest—how small she was, the jutting collarbone, the narrow well above the upper lip, the bitten flesh of the lip itself. White fingers still gripping that mechanical pencil.

And that laugh again! Scorn. A kind of hollowness in it. Was he a joke?

"You speak better than you know," she said.

He was mistaken, she wasn't old, thirty-five or so, it was only her voice that seemed aged. Such voices belonged to greenhorn immigrants in remote pockets of New York. He had seen the old films, the pushcarts, the shuffling old babushkas, the old men. He knew his father had had an immigrant grandfather (but not his mother, no!); it was a kind of family secret. His father had contempt for alien accents, he derided them, they offended him.

She saw how perplexed he was. Bitter, why bitter? A bewildered boy, he understood nothing. California, a fairyland, Deanna Durbin, Fred Astaire, singing dancing movies while the world burned.

And he—because of that voice, with its awkward foreign approximations overlaid by an unfamiliar cadence (it was too quick and also too slow, it was *wrong*), and the vibrating burr of her throaty *r*—he felt it, it stung him, he submitted to it: what she was. One of *them*, the ghosts of the Marais, those vagabond pigeons pecking at scraps underfoot. You were required, if you weren't repelled, to pity them, grungy things, a kind of litter in themselves. But if you pitied, even a little, they might brighten sleekly into doves, cosmopolitan knowers with hidden histories brought low by a wicked whirlwind. Doves were what he had named them, and when they landed, astoundingly, in the pages of *Merlin* (Alfred's doing!), doves they remained.

And she — observing just then in the darkening of those pale eyes some inescapable recognition, she took in the notebook with its red margins: suppose she was too hastily contemptuous, suppose there was a worthiness in that notebook, a boy in his twenties can think worthily, Eugen in his twenties was worthy, and even beautiful, not unlike this stretched-out boy with his big shoulders and sadly pointed chin above a softly plump neck, and the scraggle of mustache and the uncut hair and the broad nose with its curled lobes. But she did not wish to think of Eugen, and she did not wish to think of Mihail. She cast them away, Eugen and Mihail, she purged her eyes when they forced their way into them. A black purge, like a vomiting.

So they came together that afternoon, Lili and Julian, between ridicule and condescension, between vacuousness and uproar. He croaked out his California, the land of unknowing, no better than fabricated cats and bears. She bled out her Transnistria, where too much was known, and nothing he could imagine: she covered it over for him, the typhus, dysentery, starvation, shootings. The shootings and shootings. Mother, father, Eugen, Mihail. And then only Lili, Lili alone, with this ugly hole in her arm (she covered it over) from a failed shot, and the uncle lately uncovered in a far place. The black devil's Transnistria, and afterward the red devil's Bucharest, welter and waste. But she covered it over.

It came of pity: she pitied him because of his emptiness, he pitied her because she had been full and was stripped, and because of the hideous hole in her arm. She told him she intended to go to her uncle; her uncle was living in Bat Yam, a town on the sea, not far from Jaffa; her uncle was expecting her, and did Julian know Jaffa? He didn't. Where Jonah sailed from, she said; he barely knew Jonah, he had no religion. But in the end — it took more than a month — she went with him to carry his things away from Mme. Duval's. The two of them agreed (how difficult it had been to persuade her) to live for a while in Dr. Montalbano's unoccupied flat. She had much to teach him. He had nothing to give her but the miracle of his gratitude.

What she taught him was Europe. She thickened his mind. And he entered her body, gratefully. He forgot pity. She, who had less of it (because in truth he deserved less), forgot it too.

23

LEO WAS ANGRY, he was humiliated. He had met with the director that morning to discuss some newly added scenes — where the music would enter and where it would exit. The director was insisting on "hits," on "story points" — it wasn't the lingo Leo minded, it was the insult to his score. He wanted, for once, to have the thing flow from start to finish, seamlessly: so that, even though it coursed under and through the dialogue, even though it rose and swelled where there was terror or exhilaration, even though it galloped with the horses, even though it undulated evocatively at the moment of the lovers' climactic recognition, it would *live*, apart from this foolish drama, as the independent organism he meant it to be: it would be his.

"Leo! What in hell do you think you're doing," the director barked — it was Brackman, nasty arrogant Brackman — "a concert piece, we're in Carnegie Hall? You're giving me an opera? Look, I need to spot some sort of big noise right *here*, I don't care what, a drum maybe, a crash, you figure it out. Stick to the action, don't give me any fancy art music, you follow me?"

But the work had a trajectory, it knew its purpose, it was a living arrow, it had its own bloodstream. Schönberg, even Schönberg! Master, sublime inventor, and a failure in the movies; they'd thrown him out. Schönberg! They had no use for complex polyphony, for originality, for the higher imagination. If Brackman could have hired, say, Prokofiev instead of Leo Coopersmith, he would sneer just as he sneered at Leo Coopersmith — never mind that Eisenstein and

Prokofiev had collaborated like a pair of angels! Such a time would never come again. Yes, why not opera? Why not the empyrean, the sublime? What Brackman wanted was what he had heard before, in a hundred other films, reliable old sounds to fit reliable old images. Meandering tempos and saccharine strings.

Leo had long taken it for granted that he was no better than a factory hand. He was low man on the totem pole — far above him were the directors and the producers and whatever other resplendent figures hovered above *them* — but what a gilded pole it was! Here was this big house, and waiting in the circular driveway was his big car; a cook, big in the shoulders and wide in the waist, was in the kitchen. His wives were gone, both the first and the second. They had carried off his daughters, Lucinda with the first, Lenore with the second. Sometimes he remembered to correct the count: the first was actually the second, the second was the third. Commonplace enough in his circle, which had as many offspring from different wives as any Trobriand Islander. The true first was by now nearly a phantom — a buried episode (*episode*, an industry term), a whim so far in the past that it could hardly have happened. His half-forgotten marriage, and only a reckless fool would have abandoned a perfectly fine grand to a musical imbecile. The brother had made something of himself; at least he'd made money, or else married into it. In either case, a corporate mogul of sorts. The brother who had belittled him a hundred years ago, and then came groveling for a favor.

He was pacing before one of the tall front windows, tall enough to serve a cathedral. In this house everything was oversized, as if swollen by some disease. It had belonged to a deceased actor in silent films. In a locked cabinet (it had to be broken open) Leo found a collection of rubber swords and medieval-looking tunics. There were dog turds in the vestibule. The price of the house had plummeted when Leo bought it: with its ruddy Spanish roof tiles and its gaudy crenelated turrets, it had been on the market for four and a half years — the pool had been filled in after the deceased actor's German shepherd drowned in it. Carrie, Leo's first wife (but he meant the second), stuck it out for twenty-two months before decamping. Marie, the second (no, third) wife, lasted longer; but it was a house inhospitable to nuptial harmony. Or else the trouble was Leo; or else it was the custom of the country, that part of it facing the fickle Pacific.

Through the window he watched the little rented Ford maneuvering into the driveway behind his elongated Buick: look, she had learned to drive!—well, so had he, so distant was he from that antediluvian period of trolleys and buses and the pressing elbows of strangers in suffocating subway cars, and from the boy who boarded with his relations in the Bronx and was both confined to and prevented from practicing on his cousin's hideous out-of-tune old upright. He was distant from that boy, and a bit beat up from the unexpectedness of things since then, but the sounds in his brain were incorruptible, it was only that somehow, somehow . . .

She was approaching the door, his massive front door with its bell that gonged like the chimes of Big Ben (the silent actor, to compensate, had given the house a set of gargantuan vocal cords), and he considered whether he ought to go himself, or have Cora come out of the kitchen to relieve him of the first difficult look: would she be embarrassed, would he? Her voice on the telephone was unfamiliar: he remembered it differently, tentative, compliant. Are human beings made inconsistent by time? Oh, she seemed nervous enough—but deliberate. She wanted something. First the brother, then the sister. As for consistency, he was the same as that distant boy in the one way that mattered most: the incorruptibility, the sublime chorusing, of the sounds in his brain. Though, to tell the truth (he sometimes told it to himself), to the savvy eye what was he? A hack, another film industry hack, no more, no less.

But not to *her* eye! Over it, he knew, would shimmer the veil he was accustomed to seeing, that brilliantly colored silken membrane spun out by the national, the international, the galactic wizardry of movies. Movie magic: his public name that crept in wraithlike letters across the screens of the seven continents. He had seen it, that worshipful humility, inflaming the brother's broad powerful face, that flat hard mouth, those large lower teeth glinting with speechifying saliva: yet the man of force turned timid, fearful, ready to importune. Movie magic had him in thrall; it had every living being in thrall across the seven continents. The brother, the man of force, was impressed, daunted—though never by the grandeur of this house; no doubt his own was ten times bigger and better. It was likely that Bea too had left the tenements behind, if not very far behind—good grief, could she *still* be stuck in that festering school for toughs!—and when Cora led her through the acreage of vestibule and central hall to the blue lawn of carpet where he stood waiting among deep sofas (those were Carrie's) and marble-topped tables and too many fat-bellied Chinese vases (that was Marie) and framed stills from his films and the Instrument Itself, he believed he had the satisfaction of observing a woman cowed. A woman! How bizarre to have imagined she would look the same, or nearly the same. The girl had dissolved; here was another creature altogether.

He put out his hand to get through their hellos—what else was there to do? She took it almost sleepily: her palm was hot, the fingers lax.

"I hardly recognized you," he said, and since this was the main thing, why hide it? He didn't think she would mind; it was simple fact.

But she was searching past him into the lavishness of wainscoting and fluted draperies and, not to be overlooked, his reasonable hospitality—Cora's seed cakes. No trace here of the silent actor's vociferous choices: it was Carrie overlaid with Marie.

She was steadily staring. "You've got another piano."

"Another? I've had it for years, it's my prize," he said.

"It's a lot bigger than the other one."

"My cousin's tinny old box, oh come on, is that what you're thinking? Poor dim Laura, she must be out of your life by now—"

"She's filling in for me at school, it's how I could get away."

"So you're still at it," he said.

"No, not that one, not Laura's. The other one, the grand, I still have it, and yes, I'm still at it."

"Teaching," he said stupidly. He felt a perilous inquisition creeping toward him—he meant to deflect it. He was about to invite her to one of the sofas, but she had already settled into a chair with a rattan back and a tapestry seat. The tapestry was of an arched bridge. It matched the arched bridge on the fattest of the fat Chinese vases standing on the ormolu table at her elbow. He saw her turn to it, and it alarmed him that with some careless movement of her arm she might knock it off—he knew its worth. But her eye was on the other objects on this gilded surface: an ashtray (Marie was the smoker: the sofa cushions still held the latent fog of Camels), a snapshot of two children, crudely pasted onto a makeshift cardboard holder, and the book he had set down there at least half a dozen years ago.

"I see you're reading Mann," she said.

"*Doctor Faustus,* I haven't looked into it for a while. I just like to keep it in sight. A sort of talisman."

She picked up the photo and put it down again. "Who are they?"

"My girls. A birthday present, they made the frame themselves—"

Her look traveled all around, scanning corners, he supposed, for symptoms of little girls.

"They live away," he said.

She seemed indifferent. Her attention was again on the Instrument. What were his girls to her? She had no daughters. It amazed him that Beatrice Nachtigall, or whatever she called herself nowadays, was at this moment sitting across from him in his own house! It had no reality, it was a chimera. It was a visit from a fossil.

"Is this one a Steinway?" she asked. "You always wanted a Steinway."

"A Blüthner," he said. He was reluctant, but he went on with it. "Nineteenth-century concert grand, imported from Vienna. I'm told Mahler composed his Symphony Number Six on it, it's a treasure—"

"And do you compose on this one now? The way you used to on the other?"

So it was beginning: one of those naïve interrogations. Was it possible that she had come as a member of his awed little public, like her brother, blatant, intrusive—but if that was all, he could make do, he would surrender to it, as long as it wasn't personal. Yet how could it not be personal? Inconceivable that this unsmiling middle-aged woman could ever have been a wife, anyone's wife. Certainly not his! Her ankles, those shoes. Even her wrist bones. She was dry all over. Were there breasts under that wool jacket? She was dressed for New York weather.

She had mentioned the grand; it could not have been innocent that she mentioned the grand: *that* was personal. She had turned up for a purpose. He owed her nothing, it had been stipulated at the time that he owed her nothing—she'd been the one who was employed, he wasn't. Her leap into his ear the evening before: how his throat went out of control, how a wisp of a yelp escaped him, but she was dispassionate, she told him merely that she'd found herself in his neighborhood, would it be convenient if she dropped in? Better to say dropped out of the sky! A woman grown foreign to his life, erased from his history, obliterated; as if never. He hadn't given a thought to her for decades. He had no reason to speak her name.

"I remember how you used to do it," she persisted. "You would get into a sort of sweat."

"You don't know anything about it, you never did—"

"Leo, I've been listening to you for years. Years and years."

Ignorance steeped in flattery, was that why she was invading his house, his life?

"Look," he said, "is this something to do with your brother? Another go-round? You told him I could do something for his kid, now it's your turn? I can't do anything for his kid, no matter who asks."

It was startling to see how she reddened: it was as if he had struck her straight in the face.

"I heard about it," she said. "That Marvin came."

"For auld lang syne? Is that why?"

"I don't know why. I haven't spoken to him. I haven't seen him. It was his own idea—"

"If you haven't spoken to him, how did you know he was here?"

"His wife told me."

"Your brother, his wife, their kid. The whole blasted family. Find a spot for the kid in the movie business! You can't just show up asking for favors, Bea. You've got no claim on me."

He saw that he was shaming her; it surprised him that he was ashamed of her shame. She had always defended him against her brother, she had never taken Marvin's part. He had forgotten how much he had forgotten. It was the first time he had said her name in . . . he hardly knew how long.

"And supposing," he said, "I did have jobs to hand out, which the devil knows I don't—what does he imagine his kid could do in the movies? Sell gum in the lobby? Your brother thinks I'm famous, I've got influence, I can work miracles—"

"I haven't come for Marvin, I don't know what he thinks. I haven't come for his son. It's only because . . . because—"

"Because you think I'm famous," he broke in.

"I heard you in London, I heard you in Paris—"

Across the seven continents!

"Those were movies," he said. "They weren't me."

"Weren't they." It ought to have been a question, it was framed as a question; but it was a declaration. Or else she didn't believe it, and it was ridicule, a putdown. Or worse, she did believe it—this musical imbecile thought movie music equal to opera, to symphonies! She didn't know the industry, she didn't know music, she didn't know Mahler, she didn't know the truth of the Blüthner, she didn't know what it was to be blinded by the wilderness of the Sixth, the wound, the pain, the thud to the brain of the hammer . . . Yet she knew and she knew, and in his shame at her shame (he saw how she was ashamed of her brother, and maybe even of his son) he felt what she knew—she was there at its birth, she was its witness: it was his *will* she knew. His deeps, his passions, his abysses. She was the single mortal on earth who had expected him to write symphonies. Not Carrie, not Marie, and finally not even himself.

Cautiously he said, "London and Paris. You've been traveling then?"

"I don't usually. Only lately. In Paris I went to *Whispering Winds* twice, and in New York I've seen it half a dozen times. I told you, I've been listening."

"To contrivance. To mechanics and tricks. It can't be the real thing, it's not possible, they won't let you." He wanted to tell her *they didn't let Schönberg, not even Schönberg, they threw out Schönberg!*—but if she didn't know Mahler, how would she know Schönberg?

"No," she said. "It's you, Leo, I can tell."

"You can tell! You couldn't tell a piccolo from an oboe. That brother of yours—"

"Marvin's unhappy, he shouldn't have bothered you."

"Ambitious and a fool. I take it his kid's a nothing."

"He won't come home, that's all."

A silence opened between them. He had put her off her track, and what was her track?

He said, "Are you going to see him now?"

"I've seen him. In Paris."

"Your brother's in Paris?"

"His son is. I don't know where Marvin is, he was in Mexico a while ago. I don't know if I'll see him, I don't expect to. His wife is sick, she's in a rest home not far from here, so I thought of you—" She stopped. The redness had ebbed. She gave him a whitened look, like a blank page. "I think of you a whole lot. More than I ought to."

"A romantic. After all these years." Spiteful! Why was he drawn to spite? It wasn't Bea he was spiting.

"It's not that. Not that, Leo. It's that you made me think of you. You made me. Because you left it, you never came back for it."

"The grand," he said.

"The grand."

"You didn't have to keep it, what use is it to you?"

"It's in good condition. Nobody touches it. It's in tune, I have a piano tuner come in, I know that much."

"You could sell it. You could've sold it long ago."

A return of the reddish smudge, but only between her eyebrows. A Brahmin mark — recently he'd scored a thriller set in Calcutta.

She said, "It would have been selling your soul, wouldn't it?"

And now his spite overflowed. "Oh, I've done that myself, many times!"

"That's why I go to the movies. To listen to you do it."

He stood up. One leg was starting a cramp. The sofa was too deep, he had never liked it, it put pressure on his thighs.

"I couldn't have stayed, Bea. That place was a cell, I was afraid if I didn't jump I'd never get out. You wanted too much, you trusted too much. You didn't want anything for yourself, only for me."

"Then why didn't you come back for it, why did you leave it?"

"I bought myself a better one."

"Better? Because once upon a time somebody else composed a symphony on it?"

"Somebody else — as if . . . good God, you call Gustav Mahler somebody else!"

"But you didn't. You haven't."

"I haven't what, what are you talking about?"

"It's never happened." Her look was fierce and unfaltering; it was not the look he remembered. "There's no symphony."

"You're disappointed, is that it?"

"Not for me. For you, just as you said."

"You're seeing too many movies, Bea. Mine especially, and believe me that's where it's all tremolo faking —"

"You said you'd come for it, and you never did."

The cramp had turned vicious; his leg was hurting wildly, from calf to ankle. He watched her circle the room. His sofas, his Chinese vases, his fluted draperies, the spacious blue lawn of his carpet — he was certain she owned nothing like these. She earned a city teacher's wage, she lived in a city flat. She was nobody's wife: what had become of her breasts?

The lid of the Blüthner was shut. She lifted it and looked down at the keys. Did she fathom she was seeing history, seeing truth, seeing the mighty sublime? But she was too deaf to see. She was splaying the fingers of her left hand, the right she had curled into a knob. The left plunged like a lion's maw into the bass, the fist crashed down on the treble. The sound was tremendous, the sound was august, it was a thunder, a chorus of tragical gods, it was out of the deeps, it was out of the sky, it was hail, it was flung stones, it was majesty! It was the opening bars of the symphony he was yet to write. He stomped his foot to shake off the pain. The shame was his own.

24

THE AIR WAS thickening with early flower scents and intimations of rising heat. It was seven in the morning; Bea's flight was at eight. She had parked the Ford directly across from Marvin's place. His place! He had made a place for himself, and here it was — the size of it! In the Spanish style, more or less, bits of this and bits of that. Misguided geographies and scrambled histories: in some eyes it might be beautiful. She knew it was empty of wife and children — they had fled, all three. Possibly it was empty of Marvin, possibly the housekeeper came and went, and didn't live in; possibly it was empty altogether. Leo's mansion (from his uncle's couch to a mansion!) was no better than a cottage next to Marvin's — though you could hardly call it *next* to it. Here "around the corner" meant distance, streets that turned in circles and then turned again, grass down to the lip of the road, a dim click-click of gardeners clipping, half-hidden waver of a tennis net, driveways deep and deserted, garages set far back — miniature castles in themselves. And like a jewel laid down beside every great house, the glint of sun on water: pool after pool after pool. Each estate had nothing in common with the estate beyond it, except for the pool. Water has no past, or else it holds all pasts, and all-ness, say the philosophers of the East, is the same as nothingness. O California!

Bea was in stasis: her mind was rooted. Ordinariness had seeped out of it — she was filled with the heavy stillness, and with the shock of aftermath. The stillness of the day's first breath and the riot of those last foul minutes with Leo. The riot, the tempest! The violence that Iris had brought on with a finger, innocently, tentatively — that one high thin cry — *she* had discharged with the whole vengeful weight of her shoulders. She had put her body into it, sinews and spine and belly, the power burst out of her groin, the dinosaur crash, the rapturous meaninglessness of it! The sound was a horror. What had she done? What gave her the right to do it? But Leo had said only, "So that's it and that's it." He said it like a wind-up figure with a speaking mechanism inside. He had daughters, he was the father of daughters. She drowned them in that babel of noise, she swallowed them up with the smashing of her hands on those comatose keys; she smashed them alive, the black and the white.

Far across the grass she heard a chirp. Not a bird. A hinge. Someone was opening the door of Marvin's house. A young woman came out, wearing a cape that covered her torso. Her legs were bare. An older man followed, naked except for a pair of briefs. It was clear that she knew the way — she led him to a flagstone path that wound through a lattice of shrubbery, through which Bea could glimpse the rectangle of green water. They were headed for the pool. As she walked, the young woman plucked off her cape. Her waist was small, her hips narrow. Her hair was pinned behind her ears. Tiny earrings seized the sun. The carpet of curls on the man's chest was white, the hair on his head still black, but sparse. The black and the white. Bea had never imagined Marvin as balding. He looked fit and robust and not unhappy.

A shout — the woman's voice. A splash. And then another.

The spy in the Ford drove off.

25

Bea:

Why you didn't let on you were going over there after
all, I'll never for the life of me be able to figure out—and
after the hard time you gave me, how you couldn't leave your
grease monkeys, etc. Well, if you wanted to knock me over
with a feather, you've done it, and if you want to have me on
my knees, all right, I'm grateful. As far as it goes. Your airmail
arrived this morning—I suppose it means you're back home
by now. You mention you've put in a week or so there, but
where in hell is THERE? You haven't told me anything worth
a damn, so what's the point, what's the good of it, a building with a concierge, very nice, but you don't let on WHERE
he's living, not even that—NO ADDRESS, not a word about
when Iris is getting back to school, and then when it comes to
Julian—this girl, hasn't she got a name, who is she, what's
it all about? You were planning to take them out to dinner,
I suppose the so-called girlfriend too, is that all you have to
say about it? You can't tell whether some fly-by-night skirt is
roping him in, don't you have eyes? What was the use of the
whole business if you've come back empty-handed?

And there's something else. Margaret seems to be worse. I
went to see her yesterday, there's been some problem with her
therapy, they wouldn't say exactly what. I've always thought

all that healing-through-art business was a crock anyhow,
I don't pay them for trying to turn my wife into a female
Picasso, and now they've got her doing some sort of non-
sensical weaving — they tell me the painting got her over-
excited. The trouble is she's been hallucinating. She claims she
saw you — you, of all people, it's been years! — and that you
told her Julian's gotten fat and, believe it or not, married! It's
horrible, she insists on it, I imagine she's got marriage on the
brain because she's been so angry at me, I don't know why.
The thing is, never mind all that weaving crap and man-in-the-
white-coat voodoo, I feel she'd snap out of it for sure if she
could see Julian in the flesh. I'VE GOT TO HAVE MY SON
BACK, that's the bottom line. For Margaret's sake. I don't
care anymore what he wants to do with his life, let him tootle
on a whistle if that's what he wants. And Iris — my God,
you'd think Iris would at least write! What does she look like,
is she healthy? And what are the two of them living on over
there — air? Bea, I'm in agony, I'm losing my mind, I'm alone
in all this, what's happened, what's going on, tell me!

Marvin

26

PHILLIP PARSONS (his father insisted on the double-*l* before disappearing) was born in Pittsburgh, the fifth of five children (and the reason, he later learned, for his father's disappearance), graduated from the local high school, was drafted into the army, trained as a combat medic, and went through the fighting at Anzio. Muddied, bloodied, and depleted, his regiment passed through a rural village called Montalbano. The name seemed to him beautiful. A few old women came out of their low stone houses to give the Americans water in tin cups. It was well water, cold and pure; it was almost like swallowing clear light. And after that they went on to the Ardennes, where the carnage made a red mist in his eyes as he knelt in the dirt; and after that, a delirious triumphal week in a damaged but somehow hilarious Paris — raucous bullying American laughter in the midst of the debris. At the end of the war he endured a year of college on the GI Bill, but normality had descended so swiftly all around, and so bluntly and blandly, that he felt estranged — his family struck him now as helplessly stupid. What had he to do with any of them? His mother had remarried, his four older sisters were preoccupied with their tedious lives. He remembered Montalbano and the water that tasted of cold light.

And he remembered the giddy week in Paris — whatever Paris was, it wasn't Pittsburgh. He got a job as an orderly until he could earn enough to pay for a ticket and a little more. The hospital depressed him — not the diseases and the injuries and the dying, he was inured to those, but the terrible whiteness, the white walls and ceilings, the white sheets, the bedsteads painted white, the nurses' white caps and shoes, his own white trousers. Only the doctors in their suits and ties escaped the whiteness; only the doctors had authority. The orderlies were despised, the nurses were disregarded. The doctors were more than respected. They were trusted and revered.

On the ship across he shared one of the cheapest cabins below, no bigger than a box, with a French-Canadian student headed for the Sorbonne. It was a three-day voyage, without much conversation: he was miserably sick most of the time, and clung to his berth with a rubber pan beside him. When the student offered him a tug at his flask and asked his name, he refused the wine with a groan and could barely stutter out four syllables: Montalbano. On the evening of the second day he was better, except for the hiccups, and chatted freely. And when they docked at Le Havre, he was already Dr. Montalbano. In Paris he almost immediately befriended Alfred, or Alfred befriended him — it was hard to tell the difference, since Alfred befriended everyone and everything, including dogs and cats and their owners — which was why he had at first taken Dr. Montalbano for a veterinarian. For a very small fee he bandaged cut paws and saved kittens from choking on foolishly swallowed buttons and soothed mange with ointments cooked up on a two-burner stove and began to give lessons in dog training. The lessons, like the ointments, were invented, and of course it wasn't the dogs that were being trained, it was their masters. He was discovering a talent for persuasion, for instant intimacy — he felt it as a presence in some unnameable internal organ, an untried gland awaiting initiation, but he had never had a use for it, not at home with his mother and sisters, and certainly not in the war. When Alfred one night brought him a boy bleeding from a knifing, he stanched the flow and cleaned the wound and bound it up; it was easy enough, it was nothing to what he had seen in the Ardennes. The boy was afraid to go to a hospital, he was afraid they would report him to the police as a prostitute. "There were two of them," Alfred said, "and it was me they were fighting over, I couldn't decide which one I loved more, they're both so sweet." An astonishment: the boy had hundreds of francs hidden in a money belt, and before he departed, with a kiss for Alfred, he put down on the shelf over the two-burner stove the equivalent of fifty American dollars.

But Alfred was suddenly in tears. No one loved him really, he said, he was too ugly, people gravitated to him for what he could do for them, or because he was a figure of fun, a jester, a stupid clown, it came from the wig, from the childhood sickness that had left him hairless all over, his eyebrows, his eyelashes too — that joke about the pubic hair, it wasn't *his* hair, and if he took the wig off it was horrible, he could feel everyone's revulsion, his naked silly dome, his head like a doorknob, like a chess piece, he couldn't stand wearing the thing, but if he burned it wouldn't that be worse? Only the dogs didn't mind the look of him, the dogs didn't care. "You saw that kiss?" he said. "Didn't mean squat."

This may have been the moment when Phillip Parsons became Dr. Montalbano in earnest. Until then the name was fake, the ointments were fake, the dog training was fake: the man was fake. But he tore off a bit of the gauze he'd bandaged the boy with and reached out to dry Alfred's face. He patted the gauze against Alfred's cheek and under Alfred's nose. Not that it mattered: the weeping went on. "You've got the face of a baby," he said, "one of those babies with wings," and he let Alfred sob on his chest and wet his shirt through. Alfred was dead drunk, cranked up with booze, he was an alcohol rag, the scratch of a match could set him on fire; but it wasn't fakery to say that he resembled a cherub. He had the little rosy lips of a cherub, and little round ears, and round brown eyes, and a round white forehead wrinkling below the yellow wig. He was beautiful.

And Dr. Montalbano had found his method. His method was his calling. Who is not in need of a mirror? The healer becomes the mirror, and permits to be seen what is wished to be seen: the practice of shamans, who believe in themselves. But do they? Perhaps. Dr. Montalbano also saw, in the francs the boy had left on the shelf over the two-burner stove, that his calling might do for the improvement of his dinners. Alfred was beautiful, the world itself was beautiful, and innocent and ripe for persuasion—one had only to be a mirror, one had only to add a therapeutic nostrum or two. For such an elixir it would be simple enough to cook up the ingredients, though he would need a deeper pot and, while he was at it, a bigger place to receive clients. Alfred brought him his first clients, and soon these brought others, until it seemed necessary to advertise a set of proper credentials. This he did via the alphabet. It struck him as prescient now that his runaway father had doubled the *l* in his name as a herald of a future doubling of the *p*, so that (along with the flourish of a final francophile *e*), he became a kingly Phillippe. And to the majestic Phillippe Montalbano he attached a long serpent's tail of scientifically redolent acronyms, so that his card, and later his flyers, bespoke higher degrees and arcane laboratories:

Docteur Phillippe Montalbano, RFEAI,[1] ABN,[2] SFPA,[3]
PFO,[4] MBFES,[5] ADC,[6] LOH,[7] AVR,[8] etc.

  1 *Diplomate, Raw Food Equity Analysis Institute*
  2 *Chancellor, Academy of Botanical Nutritives*
  3 *Founder, Society for the Prevention of Aging*
  4 *Professor of Functional Organics, University*
    of Natural Healing (est. 1950, Pittsburgh, USA)
  5 *Consultant, Mind-Body Foundation for the Elevation*
    of the Spirit
  6 *Chairman of the Board, Anti-Dairy Commission*
  7 *Vice President, League of Oxidative Health*
  8 *Executive Secretary, Alliance for Vedic Respiration, etc.*

The list increased as his clientele grew, and his clinics in three cities swelled into suites of rooms at respectable addresses. And while his clients were restricted to bulghur wheat and carrot mash, Dr. Montalbano feasted on roast beef and heavy cream. Not every hedonist is a hypocrite, and Dr. Montalbano did not consider himself a charlatan. His work, as it spread south to Lyon and still farther south to

Milan, was notably charitable. His fees were reasonable, and he saw indigent clients for free. People swore by him, and some called him better than Lourdes, though no cripples threw away their crutches and the seriously ill went on dying—but with smiles of gratitude on their lips. And meanwhile the row of credentials was obliged to change shape and content from time to time, in order to satisfy the investigations of officials suspicious of unlicensed medical activity. Yet Dr. Montalbano never claimed to be a physician. He was, he said, a kind heart, a giver of commonsense advice, an ingenious cook above all. He was, in fact—what rings more Parisian than this?—a chef! His clinics were more kitchens than surgeries. On occasion, with a wink of make-believe complicity, he was even willing to name himself soothsayer. Not that he could see into the future—but certainly there is an inherent logic in things, you can tell in advance how an embattled marriage will turn out, you can predict a divorce, you can sniff out who will recover and who will not, and as for lovers: their fates are written in the stars, and Dr. Montalbano was at home with the proclivities of astral bodies. Venus was one of his specialties. He could stir up a potion for potency (this required a double boiler), though he never had a need of it himself: he was a magnet for girls. For this purpose he worked hard at his Italian, the northern dialect. His French too had become almost flawless, except for its Pittsburgh inflections, which he could never get rid of.

When Alfred brought Julian to him, Dr. Montalbano was preparing to leave for Milan, where a certain Adriana, a former client, was waiting for him. He had cured her of a wart on her breast by applying to it weekly an acidic salve of, as usual, his own concoction. The resulting scar was minor, and the breast, after this repair, was pinkly plump and appealing. Alfred listened sullenly; he wasn't interested in some wop broad's tit, he wanted to tell about his friend Julian, thinks he's a poet, something like that, he's got this strange old broad he's stuck on and needs a place to stay in until she drags him away to who knows where, Jerusalem or Constantinople maybe, some Bible heap like that . . .

"I wouldn't want my furniture broken up," Dr. Montalbano said. "Does he drink?"

"He's a kid from L.A., they drink sunshine and milk."

"And the woman?"

"Not a kid. Something funny with an arm. One of those."

Dr. Montalbano ruminated.

"I wouldn't mind a couple looking out for the place while I'm gone — that cockney witch of a concierge, lets herself in behind my back and gets her fill of snooping around, thinks I'm running a brothel. But I'd need to see the kid first, I don't want any of your hooligan pals throwing up on my rugs —"

Julian, who knew his soul was built on a last different from his father's (but did his father have a soul at all?), was nevertheless not without his father's judging eye. He saw at once that Dr. Montalbano was a bit of a fraud (all those letters after his name!), and Dr. Montalbano saw just as quickly that Julian was soft — he wasn't one of Alfred's hooligans, he was a marshmallow kid who believed he owned a soul. It seemed to Dr. Montalbano that his tables and chairs would be safe.

"But you didn't bring your girlfriend," he chided.

"She couldn't come. She's got a job."

This was even more reassuring.

"There's only one thing," Dr. Montalbano said, "when I get back the two of you will have to clear out — I mean right away. What do you say to that? Do you have somewhere to go?"

"It's fine," Julian said. "We'll figure it out."

So it was arranged.

27

AWAKENED BY CRIES, Iris thought at first of animal squeals. Then, as unsound sleepers ripped into sudden full consciousness are wont to do, she remembered where she was, and took in the unlikelihood of wild birds and street cats indoors in the middle of the night. The half-bottle of wine she had swallowed the evening before — it was intended to help her sleep — instead drew her to an insistent clarity. The wine was a discovery: it made her *see.* In this foreign city she had begun to comprehend everything that had gone before — those long strivings, the dogged classroom years and the noxious discipline of the laboratory, the solitary drive for perfection, for goodness, for her father's praise. She was perfect and she was good. She had earned prizes and fellowships. Whatever she did, she did diligently and well. But here — here she threw her stockings in the air and let them dangle for days from picture frames! Here it was normal to drink wine — people drank it daily with their meals, it was as ordinary as water on the table at home. And the wine found its own reasons: it was for pleasure, it was for digestion, it was for sleep, it was for . . . other things. For getting free of being good. For not caring what you said, or to whom. Like a cave, like a labyrinth, the wine had its secrets. You could step into its mouth and then, little by little, wind gingerly on; the deeper you went, the more wine-drenched the walls, painting themselves brighter and brighter — as when eyes shut against the sun are left gazing at their own red blood.

The noises were coming from two rooms away. It was not their lovemaking. She was familiar with their lovemaking, the murmurs and echoes that gained and slowed and gained again, and then broke with the crystal crack of an eggshell, and the orange yolk spilling blindingly out. Their lovemaking seemed incessant, and tragic, like some terrible thirst, more Lili's than her brother's — the wine told her so. The wine was a teacher. She was listening for the pangs and blows of their bodies. These high strained cries weren't the bleats of their lovemaking, no: they belonged to the dreams. Bad dreams: even in childhood Julian had cried out in his sleep: he was falling, falling out of some great vulnerable vessel into a fire. The falling and the fire and the smell and the burning frightened and woke him. But it wasn't the falling into the fire, it wasn't the lovemaking. It was Lili. Lili's bad dreams made a strange piping, and sometimes a harsh grim grunt, or even a metallic click, like the cocking of a trigger. Lili's dreams were deadly. Only Julian knew why. And while Lili would laugh in the morning at Julian's bad dream — "Poor Julian, papa Freud pulls him through the womb again" — there could be no mention of Lili's pipings and grunts and clicks. The wine begged Iris to inquire, but Julian forbade it. Lili's dreams were wounds. Sometimes they were terrifying resurrections: of her mother, her father. Her father had been a linguist, a professor at the university; he had begun teaching her German and Russian and French when she was very little, as a pedagogical experiment. In Lili's dreams her father was speaking in no known language — savage syllables and crazed chatterings. Her mother in the dreams was always on the point of disappearing, like a drawing faintly inked. Or the animal sounds were whimperings, and the whimperings were Mihail's last flailings after the last shot, or they would twist themselves up into words — Eugen's clear words called out across a gray field, from a distance; yet they could not be retrieved or remembered. And Iris was not to ask.

More and more, Iris was feeling the difference in Julian. The brotherly barbs and teasings were waning, and the mocking angers flew out only now and then. How he had scalded Aunt Bea! Iris too had stung her, mercilessly and meanly; but it was because of

Lili — because Aunt Bea had seen Lili huddled into Julian, and Aunt Bea would inform her father, and her father . . . what *would* her father do? It was weeks since Iris had come. She had come to succor and protect her brother, and had found Lili doing both. Lili was a nurse, a mother — but what was she really? Was she the protector or the protected? Julian was building a fence around Lili — there were silences Iris must never penetrate. She was not to ask about the dead husband and the dead child. Julian had given her all she was to know — that the husband was called Eugen, that the child, three years old, was called Mihail, and that was enough, that was all. As for Lili's arm inside her sleeve, it was always there, Iris had glimpsed it many times, its bulging depth and pucker, like a toothless mouth that has swallowed a bone. It meant what it meant. It told too much; there was nothing to say.

And Lili was always carefully kind. Her talk was careful and bookish and stilted and slow. She was often nervous. It was her work with those luckless people, Julian said, or living in a stranger's place: she distrusted Dr. Montalbano. But Iris thought, *Suppose it's me.* Was Lili wishing her away — was that why Lili was nervous? She went every day on the bus to sit in that old *boucherie* with the hooks for carcasses still on one wall, and those wretched importuners with their pleading eyes. *The doves of the Marais have pleading eyes* — Iris had read this in that Paris magazine Julian had sent home, the thing that had inflamed her father to boiling contempt. And what was her father thinking now? She hadn't so much as written him a note. It was too cruel, but she couldn't, she wouldn't! She was relying on her aunt (and how cruel she'd been to Bea!) to tell him his daughter was well, she was safe, she was with Julian. With Julian and Lili! What would her father say to *that?*

Meanwhile her money was running out. It wasn't an emergency, her ticket home was secure, and Lili's small earnings filled the larder uncomplainingly. But the money she had brought for Julian was gone. It horrified her: he had spent it nearly all at once, he was profligate, one day a dozen blouses for Lili (all of them, she saw, long-sleeved and frilly and awful, had he found them in a flea market?), then night after night flowers and fruit and puddings and cheeses and cakes and bottles of wine. First it was the wedding party they'd never had, and next it was a birthday marked but annulled — if the boy had been allowed to live, he would have been . . . Lili put a hand over his mouth. The number was a fortress, it was not to be broken into. The three of them lifted their glasses while Lili wept. Her tears fell into the wine; she left it untouched, and Iris drank it instead, the wine and the salt. It was the first true craving of her life: a danger was in it, things never before imagined. She had never before known anyone whose child was dead. Something of Lili was creeping into Julian. While Lili was away he brooded over a notebook. He declined to tell what was in it, but he was willing to say what wasn't. He had given up the immorals. It was plain to Iris that her brother was changed; little by little he was becoming another Julian. The old babyish drama was still there — look how he'd wasted all those dollars! But he had married a woman who was teaching him the knowledge of death.

28

Dear Beatrice,

Though I am repeatedly frustrated these days, your visit has left me angrier than ever. I am certainly not to blame if you arrived and departed unannounced, thanks to carelessness on the part of the staff here! These people are too frequently careless. For example, my easel has been missing for more than a week and they claim it cannot be found. (Do I suspect theft? Indeed. The chief therapist here is a devious creature.) Your visit was far from pleasant, and I have no wish to communicate with you further, yet circumstances demand it. It was difficult enough to persuade my husband to let me have your address. He insists it is futile, perhaps you will not reply. And also he believes it to be an impulse that I will soon forget. He is often right, even when he is not perceptive. My husband is not a perceptive man. It would not be an exaggeration to say that he considers me untruthful. A better way to say it is that he is convinced I am the dupe of my imagination.

This is why, despite my distaste for it, I must approach you. I write now with a request. Kindly inform my husband that you did in fact come into my rooms here, and that you did in fact give me news, impossible news, of my children. It may be that you lied. How can what you told me not be a lie, if my husband knows nothing of the sort about my son? I thought at the time that you were lying out of malice over my marriage to your brother, or out of some other motive. But lately it occurs to me it is likely my husband has all along known what Julian has done, and wishes to shield me because he believes I am ill. For some little while I have been aware that there is something deceptive in my husband's nature. This deception is not a kindness. When my son returns, I will greet him with joy no matter what he has done. As for my daughter, I have faith in her self-sufficiency. In this she is like her father. I take it to be one of the better Jewish traits.

I ask you now to be my witness that I am entirely in my right mind.

Sincerely,
Margaret B. Nachtigall

29

IRIS SAID FINALLY, "I'm thinking of leaving."

Julian looked up over the notebook's red margins. "All right. Where to?"

"I guess home. Where else? Back to the lab."

"Will you like it?"

"I don't know. It's not too bad. I left all those crystals growing, and sometimes it's exciting. If I could be really interested, it'd be exciting."

"Duty calls, you're doing it for dad—"

"I'm good at what I do."

"Chip off the old block. So's dad."

"He runs around."

"He's always been on the move, he goes where the money is—"

"No, I mean with . . . you know. Distractions."

"What, women? While mom's in storage?"

"Girls, sort of."

"It's nothing to me what he does. Only mom—" The swelling in the neck. "How come you've never said this before?"

"I haven't been thinking about it. It's just that going home, if I go home . . . I've got my own place anyhow, dad let me have it."

"So he could bring in girls after kicking mom out?"

"It's only once in a while, it's not a lot of the time. And maybe it's because she's been so mad at him."

"Marvin the philanderer, why not?"

"Don't say that, Julian, it's not right. Poor dad, it's just not like that. You don't know . . . before she got sick, or maybe it was part of being sick, a sign of it, how it started to show . . . mom would say things."

"What things?"

"Things." Iris struggled with it. "That . . . she'd married a Jew. And that on account of him you and I —"

"All that's old news, isn't it?"

"But the way she said it. It was the way she said it —"

"She took dad's name, didn't she? A long time ago. And gave up her own family."

"They gave *her* up. Maybe she feels it even now."

"Well, I don't. Especially since they're mostly all dead or got themselves killed and we never knew any of them anyhow."

"Or any of dad's. Except for Aunt Bea, and only because . . . I wonder how he's taking it. If she told him —"

"About Lili and me? Why should I care?"

Iris said cautiously, "Because you haven't any money. Because you haven't got a place to live. Or any way to make a living. You can't live on *that* —" Her eye was on the notebook.

"Go ahead, finish it," he said. "Say the rest of it, that I can't keep on living on Lili. But Lili can't keep it up either, she's just about worn out. All those miserable people day after day, it eats into her. She's thinking of trying for translating work —" His look wandered off a little. "Or something else. She talks of getting out of Nineveh."

"Out of what?"

"Out of Europe altogether. At least mom would know, they sent her to Sunday school. A rotten city in the Bible."

"Paris is beautiful," Iris said. "Europe is beautiful. And old. I love it that everything's old over here. I wish I could see every bit of it, places like Italy and Greece."

"It's all Nineveh to Lili. And anyhow we've got no choice, we've got to get out — I've had a letter. Phillip'll be back in two weeks."

"Julian! What will you do?"

"I suppose find a room somewhere and tread water for a while. I can always go back to waiting tables."

"Mr. Flotsam and Mrs. Jetsam, what a plan! What does Lili say to that?"

"My wife wants to get on a ship and sail to Jaffa and sit under some sort of gourd. I looked it up. Interesting book, that Bible."

It was the first time Iris had heard her brother utter "my wife." It jarred her, it baffled: how incongruous it was, Lily the stranger, no different from the people who were wearing her out.

"But what will you *do?*" she pressed.

"No idea. Sitting under gourds in the Middle East heat isn't for me, and Lili knows it. Even if I *am* half a Jew."

They ended it there. It was turning into a quarrel of cross purposes, the kind of quarrel Iris believed, from long habit, it was better to avoid—it was her practice to fend off such spats with her father. And then why leave now? Why not delay a little? Dr. Montalbano was returning, he was coming from Milan, from Italy! From Milan you could see the Alps! And meanwhile, in the notebook with the red margins, Julian was feverishly copying psalms. It made him feel close to his mother—he had lately discovered he was missing her terribly. By now he had got as far as number seventeen, and if Iris had looked into her brother's notebook, she would surely have judged him cracked.

30

"THANK GOODNESS you're back," Laura said. "How was the trip?"

"Complicated," Bea said. "How did you make out with my guys?"

"Well, they kept calling me Beanie, I suppose that was the worst of it. Not to mention the noise. Your crew is even tougher than mine, Bea, but you won't believe it — they actually *went* for *A Tale of Two Cities*, they liked it! And one day I found a pair of knitting needles on my desk. Look — "

She pulled out an elongated woolen mass from a canvas bag and displayed it. "A scarf, ready for winter. I started knitting it, five inches for every chapter, a race to the end, and they beat me, they won!"

Laura triumphant: comically, ingeniously.

And still it was the return to the quotidian; to the life before. Before what? Bea contemplated it. She had journeyed out as a kind of ambassador, she had turned into a spy against every ingrained expectation, and it was true: sometimes an ambassador serves as a spy, sometimes a spy is appointed ambassador. She had gone roving for Marvin, to begin with — for Marvin, yes, but was it only for Marvin? Something had altered. She had a stake in it, she was embroiled. It was no longer Marvin's need. The world was filled with need — wherever she looked, need!

She thought: *I will change my life*. Other lives were changing ("I do him good," said Lili), why not hers? Paris was the hinge. However uncongenial the visit had been—however spiteful the brother and sister—she had witnessed shiftings, mutiny, young rebels in flight. The crisis of the untried, the past defied. Turnings!

It was time to get rid of the grand.

31

DR. MONTALBANO'S TRAIN would arrive at two that afternoon. Lili refused to see him: he was not honest.

"But you never even got to meet him," Iris protested, "it was only Julian—"

"He is not honest," Lili said.

It was their final hours in Dr. Montalbano's flat.

The white cards they had found strewn on surfaces everywhere, with all those degrees, or whatever they were, marching across like rows of ants—that wasn't what she meant. Gibberish and nonsense can't hurt, and neither can water and ale, as long as you're thirsty enough. But once, searching in a kitchen drawer for a whisk for Julian's eggnog (he liked to lick off the froth, and he liked the funny name she gave to it too, *guggle-muggle*), Lili discovered a paper. It seemed to be a kind of formula, with three ingredients: water, ale, and an indecipherable third—in one instance it looked like "cascara," though she couldn't be certain. At the top of the paper was written, in clear capital letters, FOR DISEASES OF THE BLOOD, and under that, FOR CLEANSING OF THE LUNGS, and under that, FOR A HEADACHE, and under that, FOR FUNGUS BETWEEN THE TOES. The third ingredient was different under each heading.

She immediately showed the paper to Julian, who was wheezing on the divan.

"Your friend Dr. Montalbano is a magician," she said. "And this is a magician's place we stay in."

"He isn't my friend, not really. He was Alfred's friend, and Alfred swore Phillip would never harm a fly. He just shores people up when they need it."

"This Alfred is dead."

"Not from any of Phillip's recipes! Phillip's all right, Lili—look how he's helped us out all this while. Besides, it won't be much longer, we'll soon have to give up the key."

But the time to give up the key had come; and still Lili would not see Dr. Montalbano.

"Then why don't you both leave now," Iris offered. "I'll wait for him here and hand it over. I'll take care of it, I don't mind."

But Julian said, "You don't have to do this, Iris. He has another key for sure, he doesn't need this one. Put it under the little lamp. Or the concierge can let him in—"

"To find nothing and no one? After we've taken over his place and he's allowed it without a fuss? My flight isn't till six, I still haven't finished packing, and I've got nothing else to do. Someone should be here, someone should thank him, don't you think?"

"Fine," Julian said. "You're telling me nicely what a boor I am." Unexpectedly he patted her on the back. "Well, don't moon, will you?"

Was this the last time she would have her arms around him? Iris kissed him and kissed him, on his forehead, all over both cheeks, under his chin, exploding finally into his ears, until he laughed: she was excessive in everything. She made him feel he had a conscience. Her face was wet.

She watched them go, her tall brother with his unaccountably thickened neck, and small thin odd Lili. A childhood singsong jogged in her brain:

> Fat and Skinny had a race
> all around the pillowcase.
> Fat fell down and broke his face
> and Skinny won the race.

138

She would never see Julian again, it wasn't possible, Lili meant to take him far away: she claimed him, he belonged to her, he would do whatever she wished. Obstinate Lili! Why should she snub Dr. Montalbano? Those nightmare imaginings, a prescription for poison on a piece of paper in an ordinary kitchen drawer! Or else, if she didn't take him away, the two of them might stick to where they were, and when, after all, would his sister come again to this incandescent parcel of earth and its beckoning cities, unknown, sealed, glowing, never to be ventured? Great public statues pitted by age, spires, ancient bridges over ancient rivers, while ahead lay newborn Los Angeles boiling in its tropical glare, rawness cut greedily out of a wilderness of valleys periodically ravished by primitive fires. Her rightful destination, her chosen future—finish her courses, get her degree, and then . . . Imperative to finish her courses and flaunt that sheepskin! It was her life, and always had been. It was what she had always wanted. It was what her father wanted. Her father . . . she must somehow brave what was to be.

Her sweated hand was dutifully clenching the key. She set it down on one of the little tables—just in the middle of it, where Lili had placed the vial of cough syrup weeks ago (every gesture now had its ghost)—and wandered through the familiar spaces, here and there attempting to make order, straightening the picture frames, puffing up cushions. On the rug at the foot of the divan, a dark circumference in the shape of a spreading lake: wasn't this where Julian had carelessly spilled Lili's eggnog? Iris put a chair over it, to hide the guilty spot. The only presence was an absence. An empty clinic, awaiting clients.

On the other side of Paris, Julian was not surprised to learn that his old room was rented out. But Mme. Duval recommended her friend Mme. Bernard, who luckily had an opening—her most faithful tenant, a neat old man of ninety-five, had recently died quietly in bed. Not to worry: the mattress was turned over and the room was clean and well aired. Though Mme. Bernard's offerings were no more commodious than Mme. Duval's, there was the convenience of

139

a toilet on the same floor. (At Mme. Duval's, you had to go down to the landing below, and then to the end of a long corridor.) Mme. Bernard had one stricture only: no cats. She was allergic to cat fur.

"O.K.," Julian replied — this much American Mme. Bernard understood, though nothing beyond it — and hauled in his overloaded duffle bag; a nuisance, it held more books than shirts and socks. He would not let Lili lift its bulky tail. That other time, when they were still a little new to each other and he was leaving Mme. Duval's, she had begged to help carry the thing, and he yielded: it weighed like a ton of coal. But now she was his wife.

32

DR. MONTALBANO DIDN'T turn up until early the next morning.
He had missed his train: a last-minute skirmish, a genuine fight, fists
and teeth, her nails in his flesh, tearing the skin. Adriana when provoked (but how had he provoked her?) pounded and drew blood. He
slapped her hard, and his Italian operetta came to its noisy coda. He
couldn't say he regretted it. She was a woman without imagination;
she liked to see matters to their destined conclusion. He preferred im-
provisation. He spent the night prone on a bench in the train station
in Milan, with his shoes off and his feet sticking out.

The concierge was dozing at her desk; he passed her by. The elevator sang familiarly. The keys in his pocket, when he pulled them
out, were a confusion—Lyon, Milan, Paris, even the old Pittsburgh
set on a rusty ring—as if he'd ever go back! It was difficult to remember which was which, they all looked alike, but after one or two
resisted the lock, the door finally gave way and struck a bottle behind
it. It rolled off with a hollow clink and tipped over two others standing like ninepins. All three were empty. He noticed the suitcase lying
flat on the floor before he took in the rest: a head propped against it.
The head of a girl. An airline tag attached to a strap dangled above
it. His rooms smelled sourly of stale dregs, but inside the sourness a
different smell, darker, looser. Was she dead? Stupid, asinine, to have
trusted Alfred! Alfred had vouched for that marshmallow boy, and
Alfred could not even vouch for his own life. He had promised to

live; he broke his promise. And the boy was gone, leaving this corpse. Such things happened. There was violence all around—Adriana would have killed him if she could.

He scanned the deserted waiting room: it was not very tidy, but it did not seem abused. On one of the tables, under a lamp, he spotted the key he'd left with the boy—at least he hadn't run off with it. But this girl, abandoned, bullied, bludgeoned! He bent to examine the body. No marks anywhere. He lifted one arm, and the other. Nothing amiss with either . . . but hadn't Alfred said some bruise, some deformation? She was very young; she didn't look to be more than twenty, if that. And she was breathing! A bobbing pulse in the throat. He came to his senses: of course she was only drunk. Those bottles, why had he jumped to the most pernicious conclusion? Violence all around. She stirred into wakefulness.

"Lea' me be," she murmured. "Go 'way."

Now he shook her. "Hey you. Where's your boyfriend?"

"Go 'way."

"Where is he? Did he ditch you?"

"Go 'way."

Bending over her, he fingered the airline tag: IRIS MARY NACHTIGALL, 560 BEL AIR CIRCLE, LOS ANGELES, CALIFORNIA. And below this: *Flight 196, departing 6 P.M.* Ten hours from now? Tomorrow? Yesterday?

"Hey you," he said again. "Get up."

"Don' wanna. Lea' me 'lone."

He yelled, "Damn it, get up on your feet!"

It surprised him that she obeyed. She stood up and wobbled toward the door, then wobbled back and picked up her suitcase. And collapsed.

"Over there," she rasped, vaguely pointing. "Key—"

"Never mind. Just sit here, that's right. Where's that fellow was supposed to take care of the place?" He took out his wallet and searched for the slip he remembered putting there. "Here, I've got it.

Julian Nachtigall . . . Then you've got to be his . . . what? Don't tell me at your age—from the look of you—his wife?"

"Lili's his wife. He got married, that's why." The rasp splintered into a dry croak.

He brought her water in a cup. She swallowed it thirstily.

"Fine, you've been spared, so what the devil are you doing here?"

Her eyes swam in bewilderment. And then, gathering focus: "Home. Going home."

"Well," he said, "before you try that, maybe you should just sleep it off."

There was nothing to be done. He left her where she was. He was exhausted—that hard bench all night!—and hauled himself into his bed. He saw with distaste that the sheets hadn't been changed. A smelly blotch on the pillow. A half-full bottle on the bureau nearby. It was plain the girl had been living here. Goldilocks soused in his own bed. Alone, or with some lowlife from Alfred's crowd. Stupid, asinine, to have trusted Alfred! But the boy had appeared soft and safe and civilized . . .

When he woke to empty his bladder and came back he found her standing passively at the side of the bed, staring at the stained pillow.

"Dr. Montalbano?" she said.

So she knew him. He had slept for what felt like hours. He supposed she had too. But it still was not enough to stem the tiredness, and what was she jabbering now?

"I've behaved badly, I've behaved *so* badly—"

Yawning, he asked, "Did that Julian person let you in?"

"He's my brother."

"And did he invite in all his cousins by the dozens and the rest of his relations too?"

"It's been just me. I stayed on to say thank you, because Lili wouldn't, and I waited, but you didn't come—"

"You stayed to make a mess. When does your plane leave?"

"It went last night. Without me."

"So I see. You were delayed by Emily Post. By your nicely brought-up manners. To thank me for my invitation, which was somehow lost in the ether."

"Oh please, I didn't want to go home. I didn't want to, I couldn't, I was afraid."

"Of what?"

"Of going home."

Circles. What was he to do with her? Throw her out?

"Then go to your brother."

"I can't. He might be leaving pretty soon. Not to go home, his wife is taking him away —"

"None of my concern. I'll be having clients coming, you'd better find something."

"I'm practically out of money. I know I've behaved badly, I know it, but I thought . . . I thought maybe I could stay a little longer and finish cleaning up —"

"It's all right, I'll get the concierge to send up a crew."

"You don't understand!" she cried. "I'm not like Julian, he drifts with the tide, he follows this one and that one, I'm not like that! I *know* what I want!"

"Three empty liters," he said. "And one just started."

"Only because I was waiting for you, and you never came."

"Waiting to thank me. By getting drunk in my bed."

"I don't want to go home!"

What was he to do with her? He studied her face, her hair. Every strand of it was agitated. She was agitated all over. Was it the wine still? Or some innate force, a vortex of intent. An insidious will, the secret worm that burrows into the brain.

"Good point that," he said. "Neither do I." He hesitated. "I'll cook up something. You need to eat, don't you?"

"I'm too tired to eat. Oh, please, I know I've been bad, I know it!"

"Come lie down," he said.

"You won't mind? This was my bed, I'm used to it. Julian and Lili were down the hall. They were awfully private."

He felt her weight next to him. Long solid arms, intact. Hair shivering, the color of leaves in a Pittsburgh autumn. As if a wind were passing through. But there was no wind. They were enclosed in his clinic, and soon the clients would arrive.

They slept again, heavily, deeply. Dreamlessly; or so they believed.

33

A poor man came to a rabbi renowned for his sage counsel. "I live in a tiny hovel with my wife and seven children," he lamented, "and my wife is about to bear another child. We are so crowded that we scarcely have room to turn around, and I am too poor to change our dwelling for a better one."

The rabbi asked, "Do you have any chickens?"

"My wife keeps a few skinny birds for the eggs, which she sells for a few pennies."

"Then bring the chickens into the house."

The man did as he was told, but a week later he was back, more wretched than before. "Rabbi," he cried, "our lives are unbearable! The chickens scamper everywhere and squawk, the children scream and chase after them, and it becomes impossible to breathe."

"Do you have a cow?" asked the rabbi.

"My wife keeps a scrawny cow for the milk, which she sells for a penny or two."

"Then bring the cow into the house."

And so it went, week after week. In came the chickens, a horse borrowed from a neighbor, an ox lent by a farmer, a stray dog, and finally a sheep that had got lost from its flock.

"Rabbi!" the poor man pleaded. "Life is worse than ever. The new baby is here, and the children fight for elbow room, and my unhappy wife weeps day and night."

"I see," said the rabbi. "Then will you do what I tell you?"

"I will do anything you say," answered the desperate husband.

"Good. Send away the chickens, the cow, the horse, the ox, the dog, and the sheep. And when you have done all that, come back and let me know how you are faring."

The man went off and did as the wise rabbi had instructed.

"Well?" said the rabbi, when the man returned.

"Rabbi, all blessings upon you! Thanks to you, our house has become as vast and airy as a king's realm. You have transformed our little shack into an earthly Eden!"

Laura was reading aloud from a fat children's book, a long-ago gift from Leo Coopersmith's mother when Jeremy, the Bienenfelds' son, was born. It was called *A Treasury of Jewish Folktales,* and had been sent in gratitude (according to the inscription) for Laura's "cousinly kindness to Leo when he was boarding with your family and was studying music composition at Juilliard. Who knew then," Leo's mother wrote, "that so much success lay ahead!" Laura recalled solicitous awe rather than cousinly kindness, and certainly no reciprocal mildness from Leo — but what did all that matter now? Since then, a generation had gone into the earth: Leo's parents, Laura's, Bea's. And Jeremy was almost seventeen. Even as a little boy, he had never liked these moralizing old fables.

She had brought the book along, Laura explained, as a kind of celebratory joke; the tale she was reading from, with many interruptions from her husband, was titled "How to Make a Big House out of a Tiny House."

But Harold Bienenfeld pooh-poohed it. "Everybody knows that story, Laura, you didn't have to drag it out like that. And anyhow what the rabbi should've told the guy was go get some birth control."

"Folktales don't *have* birth control," Laura said.

Bea put in, "There's another version too, about a Bedouin who brings a camel into his tent."

"Sure, and maybe one about an Eskimo and an igloo," Harold said. "Some Jewish story!"

The evening's subject was the sale of the piano—how, with the monstrous thing gone, Bea's narrow habitat was suddenly magicked into an expanse as free and light as a prairie. All at once there was room for a broad dining table and four fine chairs, and Bea was inspired to give a jubilant little supper party; so here were Laura and noisy nosy insistent Harold. Jeremy had also been invited, but declined to tear himself away from what Laura called "the porthole," a brand-new television set with a small round screen and a two-pronged steel antenna on top. The Bienenfelds were, impressively, the first in their West 84th Street building to acquire one. "It attracts the neighborhood kids like fleas," Harold bragged.

The fumes of his cigar had begun to infiltrate Bea's ambitious dessert, an apple cake baked according to a complicated recipe on the flour bag. It was a ceremonial marker: the widening of a room can be the widening of a life.

Laura said, "And since we bought the set, Jeremy won't go near the piano. We had to let the piano teacher go. Not that she was ever satisfied either with Jeremy or my old piano."

"I wouldn't give two cents for that piece of junk," Harold said. "So how about it, Bea," he pressed, "this fancy white elephant you had in here, how much did you get for it?"

"Well, it did bring more than I expected," she said. "It's in pretty good shape, considering it wasn't new when we got it. The buyer seemed thrilled."

The vagrant "we" was an embarrassment. She rarely spoke of Leo even to his cousin Laura. And Laura herself usually avoided mentioning Leo, though it occurred to her, too late, that tonight she had been indiscreet: Bea must remember who had sent that storybook, and how it was inscribed.

"Sounds like you made a killing," Harold said.

If not a killing, then certainly a windfall. Leo knew how to pick his pianos! She had never suspected the real value of the grand, or that it would increase with time. And if Leo's abandoned instrument had fetched so much, what must his sacred Blüthner be worth? *My prize.*

A treasure. She understood it wasn't money he meant. And it wasn't money she meant either, in getting rid of the grand: it had usurped her wedding. A marriage without a wedding, and then no marriage at all. Worse yet: the heavy grand had weighted her years and pinched her orbit. Light! Lightness and scope! Lightness and amplitude, the lightness of infinity! She was a light-footed dancer on a stage as large as a tract, a fish in an unbounded sea!

But money was on Harold's mind: he was in pursuit of the price of things. The new television cost a fortune right now, he said, he was glad he and Laura could afford it with their two incomes, but when more people started getting their own sets, when every family got to own one the way today every household has a radio and a telephone, it was only a matter of time . . . though it had to be different with something like a piano, there's no technical stuff involved, nothing with vacuum tubes, it's more like furniture, so come on, Bea, don't hold out, how much did you really get for it?

Entertaining Harold was an affliction—but according to the rules of domestic hospitality one couldn't have Laura without the tedium of Harold. Bea seldom practiced those rules: where was she to have put a visitor? Even Iris, that one night, had seemed uneasy, and for Bea, stoically settling into the crevice of her worn old davenport adjacent to the grand, it had been a torment: the listless odors of stale grievance mixed with lemon-scented wax. She had summoned Laura this evening to be witness to the purging of these overfamiliar fumes—to the purging of Leo. Laura alone knew that the grand *was* Leo, and Laura too had endured her cousin's disparagements. Yet in that far-off time she had in a way welcomed Leo's acerbic swipes: artists are always granted leeway, aren't they? Leo was family on her father's side, the artistic branch—though Harold disputed the value of artistic branches.

"That ex of yours, Bea," he took up, "he's probably one of those Hollywood Reds out there. Dalton Trumbo types, McCarthy's got a job on his hands cleaning them out—"

"Just stop it, Harold," Laura said. "Bea hasn't been in touch with

Leo for ages, she wouldn't know anything about that. Besides, Leo isn't political. All he ever cared about was music."

"He might have turned. Those war movies we used to go to, with all that patriotic stuff, it was mostly Commies who made them. Soviet propaganda."

"But the Russians were our allies then, and what was so Soviet about Van Johnson? I'm still in love with Van Johnson, aren't you, Bea?" Laura shot her a rescuing glance. "And by the way," she said, "did you get that notice at school, the thing about next month?"

"No," Bea said.

"They put it in all the teachers' boxes."

"I haven't looked in mine since I got back."

"Oh Bea, you're getting so careless lately. Something about the teachers having to sign loyalty oaths—"

"Loyalty oaths," Harold scoffed. "What, all these pinkos don't know how to lie? You should've looked under the hood, Bea, before you let it get away from you."

"The hood?"

"The what d'you call it, the top. The lid, whatever. Of that oversized Tinkertoy you sold off. Maybe you'd find some sort of Russky spy map stashed away in there, y'never know—"

It was Harold's version of a witticism. He started to cut himself another slice of apple cake, but Laura picked up her purse and *A Treasury of Jewish Folktales* and began their goodnights. *When Harold leaves,* Bea thought, *so will the chickens, the cow, the horse, the ox, the dog, and the sheep.*

But Laura, loitering in the doorway, whispered: "That old thing did you no good, Bea. And you could give a ball in this place now—"

In the nearly denuded room the hairs of the carpet were ruthlessly indented where the grand's brass claws had long bitten down. A brownish discoloration lay there, as flat as a shadow, in the shape of a piano.

34

It was in his first year at Princeton that Marvin learned what it was to find oneself the object of contempt, a knowledge he hid under a skin of confidence, not always his own. His mother especially had confidence in him—he had, after all, passed the entrance exam for Townsend Harris High, and how many boys could do that? Marvin was bright. In high school it didn't count that he hated Latin and couldn't see the use of it, and sang out the resentful old hand-me-down jeers (*slippo, slippere, falli, bumpus*)—he was good at math and science. Unexpectedly—because his sister was the bookish one—he could write a passable school essay when he was in the mood for it, or when he saw that he could get something useful out of it. Approbation was useful. A few of his teachers were nineteenth-century relics; he liked to parrot (but only on paper) the high-flown style he picked up from the genteel-bachelor manners of these faded frail-boned elderly aesthetes. In Marvin it was all ingratiating artifice; otherwise he talked the tough New York talk of his peers. He was his mother's favorite—she prodded and blazed and egged him on. His father was more remote, and also more placid. He was untroubled by the worn wooden floors of the shop that had fallen to him as if through nature's edict, while Marvin's mother, on her knees with a bucket and a broad brush, was driven to lacquer over those scarred boards inch by inch, until every splinter was smoothed away under a honeyed gleam. Marvin was proud of her then (two years into Townsend Harris, and before modernity and his mother had risen to fluorescent lighting);

he had not yet been made to understand that a mother on her knees in an ill-lit hardware store is an embarrassment to be concealed, or at least suppressed; or that a spiritless father with a novel too often in hand is a disfigurement to be overcome.

If introspection is thought, Marvin was not introspective. He felt the contempt he lived under as raw sensation, as heat — heat in the ears, behind the eyes, in the tangled ganglia sheathed by the skull. And contempt, it seemed, was no different from fear. At Princeton he became afraid. It dawned on him that it was not enough to be bright (all Townsend Harris boys were bright): you had to be right. For the first time he was struck by the import of *birthright* — you slid out of the womb grasping it in your tiny fist, a certificate that guaranteed you would know how to speak and dress and scorn and brazenly intimidate everyone doomed to enter the world empty-handed. Not that Marvin was altogether empty-handed — he had his scholarship, and he had, most of all, the engine of his will and the grim burden of his hurt. He resisted humiliation by accepting it, sometimes almost appearing to invite it: it taught him what was suitable and what wasn't. He never repeated a misstep — he was meticulous and watchful. This meant that he was never free, as the others were, but it gave him an advantage — the advantage of the watcher over the watched; the advantage of strenuousness over ease. When a man intends to make himself over — the scion of a hardware store, say, into a blueblood under the spell of a birthright — he will shun arrogance and move softly. Marvin's program (he scarcely recognized it *as* a program, so organically did it evolve, an early tendril maturing out of the silent little seed of humiliation) was anything but self-refutation. He was still his mother's conscientious son, looking to aspire and ascend. He refuted, he repudiated, nothing: it was only that he was open to everything new. It was sympathy, it was yearning. In another kind of young man — in a young man less tethered than Marvin to the datum of the Bunsen burner and the doctrine of the formula — these stirrings might have been apprehended as imagination. But Marvin's science was earthbound, more boundary than boundless. He was made to be a maker of useful things. What he felt was neither dream nor desire, but feral appetite. What he felt was *wanting*: he wanted to have what he saw. The modish turn of Breckinridge's wrist when he plucked his watch from his vest pocket and dangled the loop of its slender chain. And Breckinridge's docile sister, with her perfect eyebrows and lightly rouged lower lip (a tender mauve-skinned grape, rounder and fatter than the upper) and small pale chin. And her voice!

She had driven down from Mount Holyoke on her way to New York to look at paintings, and stopped on impulse to visit her brother. She was studying art history, there was an exhibit of the Hudson River School at the Met this month . . . but where on earth was Peter?

"He's got a slew of classes this morning," Marvin told her.

"I never did let him know I was planning on coming down. Should I wait? What time do you think he'll be getting back?"

Each half-whispered syllable was tentative. Her tone was all hesitation. And yet she was a girl with a car of her own!

"He's off to football practice afterward." Marvin could account for Breckinridge's every move: an attentive valet.

"Then I'll miss him, won't I? Will you tell him—"

She left it unfinished; it was a trick of her voice, to let it hover, so that her meaning wafted vaguely, looking for direction.

"I'll tell him you came," he said. "Are the two of you twins?"

"Oh no, Peter's three years older. But only one inch taller—is it that I look like him? No one's ever said that before. Besides, we couldn't be identical even if we were twins, could we? Do I look mannish to you? I'd hate that—"

"You have the same mouth." That bottom lip—a predatory protrusion in the male, a pretty knoll in the female.

"Is that a good thing or a bad thing?"

He could not decide whether this was flirtation or taunt, so he said, "Depends what comes out of it."

"Well, I try—"

And again the rest of it hung unresolved. Tentative, hesitant—

docile. He was as much afraid of this docility as he was of Breck-inridge's sallies. He was unfamiliar with docility in a woman: his mother wasn't docile, the aunts weren't docile, and Bea could unleash rip tides of obstinacy—her infatuation, for instance, with that oboe boy.

But he was practiced at manipulating the little nub of his fear.

"I don't suppose," he said, "you'd want some lunch before you go."

"Don't you have classes too?"

"Sometimes I take a day off to catch up."

"Peter mentions you once in a while. He says you're awfully diligent."

He knew what this meant: at times they called him Dilijew. Not Breckinridge's invention, but also not foreign to his tongue.

"Walking distance," he said, when she pointed out her green coupe. He scouted a free table in a busy local coffee shop. She declined everything but water.

"They'll throw us out," he protested, "if you don't order at least a sandwich."

"You order. I'll watch you eat."

"Like the monkey in the zoo—"

"More like the lion in the jungle."

He understood then that there was no rift between what was flirtation and what might be ridicule. Had she really intended to find her brother, or was it curiosity about the rumored beast in her brother's house?

He said, "Then why did you come out with me?"

"For the company. I'm supposed to say that, aren't I? But if you absolutely must know—"

She paused to sip her water, and he saw how the rim of the glass slipped into the gap between her lips. He had never observed this action with so much suspense; it was punishing in its slow-motion efficiency.

"It's to annoy Peter," she said, "that's why."

"In that case," he said quickly, "I won't tell him you've been here."

"You promised you would. And I *want* him to be annoyed." She leaned toward him. A droplet glittered at the corner of her mouth. "Mostly I like what other people don't."

He did not question this. He hardly noticed the insult, and was it an insult at all? It was natural, it was the condition of his present life. He was passive before it, biding his time. And in Breckinridge's sister he sensed opportunity. She was pulling off her gloves—white gloves flecked with tiny stitched petals.

He dropped his hand over hers. She let him keep it there. "I think," he said (a new awareness, unlike the bruise of fear), "that when people say they want lunch they ought to *have* lunch."

"All right," she said. "Bacon and tomato. And you?"

He felt her small hard knuckles under his palm. A row of stones; but submissive, yielding. A mystery in that acquiescent lowering of her head. He could not read her look (in the absence of introspection, impossible to intuit another's thought), but her tall forehead, bowing, somehow spoke to him: that clear white wall, still uninscribed by anything more intricate than liking and disliking.

"The same," he said. To woo and to undo was his heart's program, formulated on the instant, and in the lightning glare of her white forehead. She was to be his America, his newfound land, the sloughing off of a skin too tight to breathe in.

35

Dear Aunt Bea,

I know you'll be surprised to be hearing from me after the way Julian and I carried on. I was a lot worse, I was the one who was really bad! The two of us, we've behaved so badly! You shouldn't blame Julian too much, though, his life is so jumbled, and who knows where he's at. I've been to see him twice, and the first time they were both there, but the second time they were gone. The hideous way we treated you! But we were afraid. I was afraid more than Julian—somehow Julian's let everything go, and it's only Lili he cares about, and the things he scribbles and keeps to himself. When you were here—it all went so speedily, four days, five, and we tried to hide it about Lili and Julian, but then Lili told anyhow, so you already knew on that last night when you had us all to dinner, and I suppose by now you've told dad everything, about Julian and Lili, and where we've been living, Phillip's place, I mean. I'm still here with Phillip, helping in the clinic, so I would know if dad had written, but what's so peculiar is that he hasn't. At first I worried about it, if he'd exploded in some horrible way—don't some men dad's age come down with a stroke when they've had a bad shock? That's what I was afraid of all along—that Julian with a wife would just about kill him, as if things with Julian before hadn't upset him enough.

But if you've got the idea that I'm writing now to ask how dad's been taking it—no, I'm not! There are three reasons why.

1. I'm no longer afraid.
2. What dad thinks doesn't matter.
3. I've stopped caring.

These may sound like all the same reason, but they're all a bit different. I guess if I had to face him I'd still be afraid, but he's in L.A. and I'm in Paris! And I'm <u>staying</u>, as long as I please. Not always in Paris exactly, or rather in Paris just for now, but there'll be other places too, and there's not a thing dad can do about it. In six weeks or so I'll be looking at an Alp! It's because I saw—really <u>saw</u>—or Julian made me see—how easy it is to slip out of a harness. You just slip out of it, that's all. And now that I'm out of it, I can think back to how scared I was in those few winks of time when you were here and Julian and I thought you were snooping around to please dad—well, you <u>were</u>, weren't you? Remember how Alice in Wonderland nibbles at the mushroom and then shrinks so quickly that her chin hits her shoe? That's how fast you were—in and out, you came and went, and didn't even stop to inhale the Paris air! Our fault, I admit, the way we rushed you out of sight—but at the last minute, when I was feeling a little tipsy, it seemed it was <u>you</u> who wanted to be rid of <u>us</u>. When we were children dad hated seeing me with Alice and make-believe books like that, or Julian either. Julian used to be stuck on The Yellow Fairy Book especially, I never understood why, but dad would take it away from him and give him something like How Electricity Works, and make some joke about how only cowards love yellow, and then Julian cried, and dad would say, See? I told you so. That's dad's mean streak, and I've got one of my own, or I wouldn't have been so rotten, even behind your back. I've been rotten all around, maybe to Lili too. I could never warm to her or get close, not that I didn't mostly try — she's like nobody we've ever known. It's just so weird about Julian, he fusses over her, he watches out for her. And she watches out for him, they're like a secret society together, not that it does either of them any good! When I went over there — the rooming house they moved into when Phillip got back — it was around 6 PM or so and Lili was bunched up on the bed — the place had only the one bed and a chest of drawers and a wardrobe with its doors hanging loose off their hinges, and nothing more — and you could almost smell the gloom. I'd expected Julian to be pretty much flummoxed that I hadn't left Paris after all, but he was so wrapped up in Lili that he shooed me out, even when I told him I was staying on with Phillip. I couldn't tell from the way he explained it whether Lili had quit her job or for some reason they'd let her go. She was lying there not saying a word, with her face all brownish and scrunched up and old-looking, so I just turned around and walked out — what else could I do? — and Julian never tried to stop me. Afterward some funny little man showed up at the clinic asking for her, he might have been one of Lili's people from that place, but I never did find out what the trouble was. I went right back the next day — Phillip came with me — and they were gone. The landlady began screeching that if she'd known they were going to be a pair of irresponsible truants (Phillip's French is first-rate, so he got it all) she would've rented to someone more reliable. Phillip asked if she knew where they were headed, and she said the devil take them wherever they are, but then he asked again and she said she hoped they went where swindlers like that belong, le pays des Juifs. So we couldn't figure out from that if it was a curse or what, if it meant they were really intending to go to Lili's uncle — he's supposed to be living somewhere or other, I don't know, not far from Tel Aviv. Of course they hadn't damaged that woman at all, it's just that she has to wait for another tenant to come along.

You notice I keep calling him Phillip. After the first day or so it seemed silly to go on saying Dr. Montalbano! I was a little bit sick when we met, but he had me rest and then he fixed me up right away, some sort of powder in milk, with cinnamon in it. It peps you up pretty quick, and he showed me how to mix it myself. He says I have good lab hands, which almost sounds like something dad would say. He's taken me on as his official assistant (that "official" is a sort of joke), but I'm not getting an actual salary because — well, because. I don't need or want anything when I'm with Phillip, I'm completely happy for the first time in my whole life! I've honestly never felt so filled with a sense of the future, of the world as open, instead of that stale old trap waiting to snap me up back home. Phillip is a marvel, you couldn't ever predict or dream him up, the sweetest combination of businessman (dad would like that part!) and gypsy — the part I like best. He's going to show me all of Europe, not just where he has his other clinics, but places thick with history and legend and myth. If that makes him sound like a kind of poet, that's exactly what he is. But a poet who can make a living! (Dad's definition, I remember, of an empirical impossibility.) We're going to see the Colosseum, where the lions ate the Christians, and Phillip thinks he knows the precise spot where the Delphic Oracle used to be — I know he makes things up, but what fun! Lili was always suspicious of Phillip, but Lili is suspicious of everyone and everything, and I'm afraid she's twisted Julian to be the same, she's crawling with preconceptions — Julian once told me she hates Europe, even Paris! — so who knows where they've gone to?

Which brings me to the point of this long letter — I do believe it's too long, in view of what a thug I've been! Two points, really. So the first has to be regret and apology — we

159

chased you away. Or you felt you needed to run away from us, and there's hardly a difference, is there? And the second is to ask a favor, the last I'll ever again trouble you with, I promise. I recognize that dad's silence must mean something terrible. He's already had the big blow — you've been the postman who delivered it, and I for one am grateful for that. Julian would never on his own have given dad the awful news about Lili. And now there's me. I can't write dad myself — to tell the truth, Aunt Bea, I won't, I'm free of him! There's no way I can comfort him or get him reconciled, so will you let him know that I'm staying on, and that I'm in wonderfully good hands, and will you tell him that I'm wildly happy?

It's very early in the morning now, and I'm out on the balcony, with a notepad on my knees. There's a pinkish-bluish dawn in one half of the sky, and a wintry sun peeping out from the other half. I can just see well enough to write, though it's brightening pretty fast. And cold! I've got my new coat on, the nicest present I've had from Phillip — he's inside in the kitchen, getting our coffee ready and working on his special poultices, and I'm about to go in and start stirring. It doesn't bother me in the least that some of the people who come are under the impression that Phillip's a medical doctor — in an important way he's so much more, and does so much good. I've watched him hold their hands, and he speaks to them so sympathetically and seriously, but always with a kind of lightness too, and he gets to the heart of things. I've felt it too — how he knew right away that I had to stay on, that it would be the mistake of my life to go back now — he says I'm not supposed to be responsible for my brother's troubles or my mother's or my father's. This should tell you that he's practical (this coat!) and not at all syrupy, he's built up my spine, he's made me brave. I've never been brave, I've always been afraid, and it was cowardice that had me acting so nastily, I see that now.

My new coat, by the way, has a gray fur collar, something no one's ever had much use for in L.A.! When I got here the weather was warm and I didn't ever imagine I'd be sitting on this same narrow balcony in the middle of November, with its two old chairs left out in every season, where Julian and I first talked — all that seems so long ago. I think I realized almost from the start that he'd never go back home. And now I won't either, even if I'm not sure about the "never." Phillip says he hasn't ever wanted to go back, but I noticed once that he still keeps his old Pittsburgh key in his pocket. He laughs at it, though — he says it's to remind him of why he left. — So for now I belong here, and in the next hour and a half the waiting room will fill up with Phillip's clients, and the day will begin. In Paris it always begins so beautifully!

Iris

36

BEA GRIPPED THE half dozen sheets in a surge of anger—clearly there was a crime in progress, but whose? She had read the girl's letter over and over, seven times, eight. It sickened her. How like Iris to evade confrontation with her father, and to thrust it all—again!—on Bea's shoulders. Aunt Bea the postman: but the postman hadn't yet emptied his pack, and its burden was undelivered. The crime was Bea's own: all these weeks she had told Marvin nothing. She was letting him dangle unslaked and ignorant in his suffering. To put off the blow was only to increase its force; and still she deferred. Marvin's outcry, the edges of its envelope damp and curled up, languished on her bedside table in the drying puddle of a spill from a glass of water in the night. The hard blow, the bitter poison: Marvin's disappointment, his pain. His ego, his bristling amour-propre. His proud expectations denied—as if he were a god who, having sent forth his seed, could mold his creatures as he pleased. The wayward immature son, and now the daughter, still half a child, who imagined herself in love with a charlatan, a seducer, even a kind of kidnapper—*there* was the real criminal! Taking the girl on as a servant without wages, an adoring little slavey, a sex slave in fact, dragging her all over Europe until she bored him and he dropped her, alone in some faraway city, unprotected. And wasn't it protection she was searching for? The letter was speckled with *dad, dad, dad*. She was invoking Marvin even as she reviled and repudiated him. Only see how it is a blessing to have no children! Or an affliction to have them. Leo and his daughters:

They live away. Marvin's children too lived away. They could not live with their father—he had driven them off. The girl was inflamed. She had inserted herself into the unstable lives of her brother and his wife, a couple entangled nightly in sex. *He is a man*—so had Lili, old in the ways of bodily congress, spoken of the boy she had aroused; and there lay the girl in a nearby room, listening, inflamed, alert to hints of hidden erotic longings, ripened and open to the charlatan, the false doctor who fed her potions and enlisted her in the stirring of cauldrons, turning her cold to the brother she had come to solace. Julian had disappeared into the nowhere, exactly as Margaret envisioned it. Margaret, who emptied her body of its malodorous fruits to daub smudged fecal fields . . .

It was senseless to be scandalized—sickened—by this childish letter; childish; cynical; importuning. And Marvin: she'd been keeping him too long in the dark. She could hardly influence him, and even if she could—influence him how, influence him to do what?

This burning in the throat, this grinding under the heart. It wasn't the letter, Iris wasn't to blame! She had been sick and irritable for days—in her classroom with the biggest boys and their antics, and with Laura in the teachers' lounge, where they had gone one afternoon to protest the imposition of loyalty oaths, but in the end had signed them anyway, hectored by the principal's threats. On the question of loyalty oaths he was not so easygoing. They are designed to shield our soldiers from internal espionage, he announced, we must be vigilant, in Korea it already looks as if the Communists are winning . . .

All that morning, in a fit of futile aspiration, she had been force-feeding Shakespeare to her seniors. It was *Macbeth:* since they'd liked the guillotine so much, perhaps they'd like the gore.

— The little rise of nausea, just below the breastbone, inching upward. The stale canapés in the teachers' lounge, some sort of fish paste left over from a party for a shop supervisor soon to retire, a Mr. Elkins, who would have preferred beer and pretzels. Was it the fish turned bad, or was it the guilty roil of her own dereliction? The dereliction had long preceded the fish. She owed Marvin what she knew, and what she knew was an unholiness—how vile a butchery it is, to be the one who wields the knife fated to eviscerate a brother's bowel. Cain and Abel, tossed out to Iris in the Broadway dawn. But Marvin was no peaceable Abel, and Bea was no butchering Cain. What she was obliged to convey was a commonplace, children gone wrong, life gone wrong, love traduced, hope rotted, how ordinary, how banal, how easy to get it said. *They live away. It is their intention to live away.* It could be recited in a telephone call, in a neutral word or two, without the Sturm und Drang of primal sin. And why not the telephone, after all? Writing was safer—a hiatus mercifully intervenes before the answering explosion. But phoning was quicker, and the cost of a long-distance call all the way to California would keep it short. Marvin would insist that she reverse the charges, he would insinuate some nastiness about her pathetic schoolteacher's salary, he would offer to call right back at his own expense—anything to press and press, to have it out, to finger the suppurating wound. She would resist, she would be adamant: let it be short and quick, get it over with! *If it were done when 'tis done, then 'twere well it were done quickly.* The tomfoolery of her boys groaning over *Macbeth*, undone by all of it, cackling at the bloody hand and hooting at the creeping greenery. *Hey, Birdie, that's like camouflage uniforms, ain't it?* Soon many of them would be in Korea as mechanics and drivers, and what was she to say when they argued that Lady Macbeth was useless to men under fire?

The telephone stood on a small square table across the room, under a window—where, in different weather, a carafe of iced tea had awaited an unknown niece. It was an indulgence to walk barefoot over the carpet, one of the comforts of living alone and unseen. A clovery softness under her toes—crooked embarrassing things they were, a hammertoe among them. Leo, attempting once to pluck the discordant digit into conformity, had gleefully named it a *diabolus in musica*. In the Middle Ages, he told her, the offending foot with its dissonant tritone would have been excommunicated as the work of the devil. Well, so much for that. A fresh lurch of the stomach, and the return of the crinkle of acid. The grand was gone, and wasn't the last of Leo and his hurtful dazzlements out of her life?

The carpet had originally been an autumnal beige, now grown many shades paler from years of afternoon bleachings by a lazily lingering western sun. It had been installed wall-to-wall, a postwar fashion, and Bea's one concession to what in her hemmed-in rooms could pass for luxury; it traveled consolingly through the tiny vestibule and on toward the windows. She pushed into its warm grassiness and went to fetch the little book of reminders she kept in her purse, where she'd left it on the bedroom dresser. Of course she had never learned Marvin's number by heart; in that long silence between them, what need of it? Marvin's voice on the telephone, could she endure it? The fury and the sneers.

Halfway to the bedroom, she stopped and looked down. Here, *here* was the sickness! She had been treading on it day after day, a darkness before her eyes. Not Iris, not Marvin, not the fish paste, not those prancing howling boys—the sickness, the lurch and the acid, was here. Her naked toes were swamped by it. The blemish, the shape, the muddy dark. A brown estuary flooding the threads of beige. Where Leo's piano had planted its legs, under its broad black belly where the sun hadn't reached to drain out the color, the grand's bleeding silhouette persisted. It persisted, it bled, its edges were as undefined as a cloud of brown dust. In the dictionary of clouds, it was the sickest.

She lifted the telephone, and early the next morning—out, damned spot!—three burly men, wearing jackets with the company logo stitched into the pockets, arrived to rip up the carpet and scrape and varnish the wood floor beneath.

But she hadn't phoned Marvin, and on second thought what would be the good of it? To hear him rail? Or was it because, for the pity of it, she could not bear to hear him rail?

37

BARON GUILLAUME de Saghan, a distant cousin of Marcel Proust (unfortunately on the Weil, or maternal, side), had founded the Centre des Émigrés out of conscience, and on the understanding that it was to be a temporary service: when its task was completed, it was destined to dissolve. He had set the place up out of conscience certainly, though out of something else as well. It was perhaps true that he had had some unsavory connection with Vichy — or perhaps not. Such a rumor was difficult to verify, and what difference did it make in the present circumstance, since he was clearly doing good? Besides, if even so much as an atom of fact adhered to the charge, then it could be said that the establishment of this charitable office was a felicitous act of atonement. At the same time, it was true (or was not) that he was overly conscious of his relation, however remote, to Mme. Proust, the daughter of a Jewish stockbroker, and was thereby, as his critics put it, "taking care of his own." Taking care of their own was what all those other agencies and relief organizations, pouring in from New York after the war, had done, harrying the displaced willy-nilly onto ships headed for Haifa and whatever other dingy ports lay along the newly Hebraized Levantine littoral. He didn't know, or wish to know, the geography of La Terre Sacrée: he had been made to learn it as a boy, and remembered only Golgotha, a hill in Jerusalem, and the river Jordan, which roared in his imagination as a rushing cataract — never mind that nowadays it was described as only a shallow narrow stream. Yet might it not have dried up in the long centuries between the appearance of the Saviour on earth and our own time?

Such properly Christian ruminations reassured him. He was doing good. The unseemly remnants of these persecuted tribes had not all been carried off — he saw every day how Paris still teemed with them and their polyglot garble and the melancholy hungers in their alien faces and their strange fits of inquisitive exuberance, as if they would not be denied. Denied what? Normality, he supposed, everything they had been deprived of. But here they were not normal; they could never become normal, like those old-line Sephardim, French nearly to the bone, who had been sojourning in France since the fifteenth century, and were by now as acceptable as anyone else. He had put his money into the Centre solely that it might disintegrate itself: in five years there should not be a foreign Jew left in Paris. And he had situated it in the Marais because that is where the foreigners lingered.

He rarely visited the place. He had an active distaste for it: he fancied that it kept its old smell of ritually slaughtered meat, though he acknowledged to himself that this was a foolishness, and even a prejudice, unworthy of his generosity and his public compassion. The running of the Centre he left to his manager, a Pole named Kleinman, himself one of the displaced, who hired and trained the staff, which consisted of five men and two women. It was Kleinman who had devised the plan of the cubicles, so that each interviewer might provide privacy to each woeful applicant. There were often sobs behind the partitions. The more these people wailed, the sooner they were likely to vanish. The difficulty, of course, was not so much in getting them out of Paris as it was in getting them in somewhere else. La Terre Sacrée, the part of it in the hands of the Jews, had open doors and welcoming arms; yet it was beyond reason why any normal person (these people were *not* normal!) would want to live under a withered Golgotha and beside a dried-up Jordan. Still, many had swarmed there as to a benison bestowed by their worn and half-forgotten god. Many, but not all: the most stiff-necked among them were also the most given to hallucinations of sentimental reunions with ghostly kin scattered all over the resisting earth. They stood patiently in the long queues and entered the cubicles grasping torn bits of paper, somehow preserved though decades old, inscribed with superannuated far-off addresses of obscure family relations faintly recalled from childhood. Did these dreamlike relatives actually exist? It happened on occasion that some putative cousin, or the cousin's offspring, could be excavated out of Buenos Aires, or Cincinnati, or Stockholm, or Melbourne, or Santo Domingo, or who knew where. Kleinman, as obstinate as these hopeful seekers, had had his few successes. And if not, there was always Palestine, the part held by the Jews, to fall back on. The main thing was to hack through the babble of the queues; to achieve this, Kleinman had found, in the mottled streets of the Marais, his many-tongued crew. He could not keep them long — they too had their hearts set on elsewhere. Kleinman himself had already given notice, and was soon off to, of all queer places, San Antonio, which ought to have been in Spain, but was, absurdly, in the American State of Texas.

At half past five this Monday afternoon, the Baron had come for the latest figures. Kleinman tallied them: in the last week alone, twenty-three to Rio de Janeiro, eighteen to Rome (but only as a steppingstone), fifty-one to Israel. And to New York how many? The usual lot.

It was the end of the workday; the staff had departed. Kleinman put on his hat. He had stayed on to sweep away the fragments of crumpled paper that littered the floors, thrown down in despair — too many of those ancient street names were dead ends. The Baron surveyed the gaunt man in the hat: it made him look like an ordinary citizen. It was awkward that his employee was as tall as he, if several inches more slender at the waist, and that his eyes were as gray as any Frenchman's, and that his hat had the temerity of looking nearly new, and on the Baron's francs, no doubt. In fact, sir, Kleinman reported, the queues were beginning to thin out, and Lipkinoff, his valued Russian and Georgian speaker — remarkably, he also knew

Kivruli—was one of those lucky ones headed for New York. That left six to man the cubicles when, truth be told, five would surely be enough, at least for now.

"Then let one go," the Baron ordered. "I won't have my payroll fattened to no purpose."

"It would be a pity," Kleinman said in his Polish-accented French. "They are all so needful." He pronounced the r of *pauvre* with a machinelike trilling of the tongue against the palate. The Baron was disgusted—that repulsive Slavic noise was one of the several reasons the Centre des Émigrés had been brought into being: to clean out all such offenses. Generations, he believed, were required to produce the purity of French, and Paris, let alone France itself, was being sullied by these ugly frictions and betrayals.

Out of one of the darkened cubicles came a low sound, something between a purr and a hiccup.

The Baron moved his feet to make an irritated little circle. "I thought," he said peevishly, "your people were released for the day."

"They were," Kleinman said.

"Are you sure? I hear something."

They both listened. The Baron's gaze seemed to penetrate the fragile partitions that marched in geometric rows all the way down to the rear wall, where the rusted butcher hooks protruded like scythes.

"A straggler perhaps," Kleinman said. "Sometimes—" But the sudden flush of his employer's face stopped him.

"What do you mean, a straggler? The property is to be cleared for the night, that is your responsibility."

Kleinman struggled: but in five weeks he would be greeted by a certain Mrs. Davis, the elderly sister-in-law of a newly discovered great-aunt, long deceased. Mrs. Davis had signed a paper on his behalf, and never again would he be accountable to the Baron. He said, "Sometimes, sir, when they are newly arrived in the city, when they are adrift and have no bed to sleep in . . . I do keep a blanket to soften the floor, and what harm if —"

"So you are running a hotel in my Centre?"

"No, no, only sometimes to offer a roof, which hardly contradicts the purpose—"

"This is not a mission house for vagrants!" the Baron bawled, and turned again in the ring his feet were following, and saw the woman standing in the opening of the farthermost cubicle, weeping.

"Lili," Kleinman cried, "did something happen, are you all right? What is it, are you sick? Tell me!"

But the Baron began, "If this is one of your people—"

She said nothing. She was wearing her coat. The collar was wet.

"Then this is the one you will let go," the Baron pronounced.

"Sir, she is excellent in every respect—"

"This woman was hiding. What normal woman hides? And blubbering. We don't want a weeper, she will incite the queues, and then comes a flood"—here the Baron smiled—"and no Noah. I am not anyone's Noah, Kleinman, and this place is not an ark, n'est-ce pas?"

Kleinman thought, no, not an ark. A chute. A siphon. Before the war, before the onslaught, he had been a statistician for a well-known insurance firm, with a wife and two daughters. Now he was alone. Mrs. Davis had promised him the position of bookkeeper in her grandson's dental office. In his youth, before his marriage, before the war, before the onslaught, he had relished all those cowboy movies, the cattle, the cactus, the horses, the sky. Already he knew the possibilities of Texas.

38

LILI SWITCHED OFF the lamp and got into her coat. November at
the close of the day was bringing on a northern chill. All around,
the chattering of goodbyes, the shufflings, the hurryings, a sneeze or
two (the usual contagions in progress), momentary whiffs of street
air. And now the whooshing of Kleinman's broom. They were all
gone, all but Kleinman and his broom. Still she could not leave; she
would not. She fell back into her chair and pressed her cheek flat on
the desk, unwilling to stir. Her head felt as fixed as waxworks, or
stone, or some fallen meteorite. She thought to call out: she feared
Kleinman would lock the place up and trap her inside. Yet what if
he did? She knew where he kept the blanket—a tattered old *perene*,
really, a down quilt leaking its feathers. There were worse ways to
live through a night; she had lived through far worse, when a *perene*
would have been paradise. But to go home . . . where was home? The
rundown room Julian had found for them? Julian—a boy, only a
boy, homeless, helpless!

The sweeping had stopped. Voices, the native one with its syllables sliding like oil down the gullet of a glass jar, and Kleinman's
deferential murmur; and then, though she fought to resist it, a stinging behind the eyes, half suppressed, as if something volcanic was
about to erupt. A heaving sea brooded in her head. She lifted it, and a
thicket of tears swam into her mouth, and a latch gave way, she could
not force it shut again, and a noise sprang from her, and she knew she
was discovered.

She had never before seen the Baron, but she understood at once who he was—the man Kleinman called their benefactor, the man who had pledged to pay, one by one, the passage out of Nineveh. He was large all over, Kleinman's height but so much vaster, a continent next to Kleinman's slim peninsula. He flicked at the floor with an ornamented walking stick; he wore green leather gloves. He was smiling even as he was ordering her never to return—an ingratiating smile, more kindly than sardonic. And how could he not be kind, the Centre's founder, the befriender of the displaced? She hadn't caught what the two of them, the Baron and his manager, were saying; her little booth under the hooks was too far back to hear, but it had to be, it had to be, otherwise why was the Baron sending her away? She had come to the Centre hours late this day, many dreadful hours, she had come in her unwellness, but able somehow to conceal it all, it was numbly concealed, no one could tell, Kleinman could not know, he knew only that instead of commencing at nine with the others, she had arrived at two in the afternoon, and surely she recognized, Kleinman said, what an infraction it was, the rules weren't his, they were the Baron's, and of course he would never expose her, it was only that he was himself afraid of exposure, there was no way to predict, morning or night, when the Baron, who guarded his francs against waste, would burst in to inspect . . . *But he is one of us*, Lili thought, *Kleinman is one of us, why should he betray me? It has never happened before, only this once.* This terrible once. And she thought again: *Because he has become careless, he no longer minds, he is on his way, already in his feelings he is gone, he is free, and how are we to live, where will we go?* A mistake! She had supposed it was possible to seize the living moment for its own sake, as if past and future were no more substantial than mist. As if this life, this boy, were all there was to be grasped in the doom of having been born. As if birth were a thing of no value.

She stood in the street and breathed in the small cold wind of dusk. She had Julian to face, after all. Turning away—she was still in pain — she could not hear the last of the colloquy behind the Centre's door.

"That woman," Kleinman was saying, "is maimed." In the summer, when she was alone in her cubicle examining papers, he had looked in to see the sleeves of her blouse rolled up from the heat.

"I did not maim her," the Baron retorted.

"Intolerable, sir," Kleinman began again, and frowned under his hat. He had taken it off, but now he put it on again. Also, he had intended to omit the "sir," a habit he hoped to erase. "To sack her for no reason —"

"No reason? You saw what I saw. Hysteria. Breakdown, no self-control. Given what our aims are here, to succor the unfortunate, to place the morally discontented in more favorable circumstances elsewhere . . ."

The Baron was assuming his public tone, the fluently memorized phrases that so often earned him communal admiration — and, on one brilliant occasion, a framed commendation and a medal from an important city official. But he could sense how ridiculous he sounded — he glimpsed it in Kleinman's look, Kleinman who dared to judge him! Why trouble to scatter these pearls before this foreigner, who either did or did not take them seriously? So, still smiling and teasing, he planted his stick against the manager's chest, and said, "You will see, M'sieur Kleinman, how they will deal with you in Spain!"

39

BUT JULIAN WAS not there. The room was almost dark, only a rib-bon of white on the wall from a streetlight; the window had no cur-tain. Lili threw herself on the bed—her groin ached still, she was hollowed out, an iron comb had hollowed her out, she was too weary to stand or walk or even cry. And again the tears broke from her, why should she not cry for the old man who had died in this very bed? She cried for the old man, and for herself, and for what she had made hap-pen that day, and she cried with a deep relentless anger because Julian was not there, because she had permitted him to go—it was sense-less, she had argued against it only weakly. He had gone in search of François, who could always get him employment in the cafés, he didn't care if it looked a bit shady, François the friend of that Alfred who was dead, as dead as the old man, and she cried for the old man, and for Alfred, and for herself, and for what she had made happen that day. Senseless and useless, that hand-to-mouth life of the cafés, how would it help them now? How were they to get on? They had parted in the morning, Julian to seek out François—but unnerved, distracted, she had argued against it only weakly; her thought was on what she would make happen that day.

She lay on the bed, shoeless and curled up with folded knees to as-suage the ache in her groin, waiting for Julian.

In less than an hour he returned, carrying a paper bag.

"Supper," he said. Two rolls and some uneven lumps of hard cheese—his old trick, he'd cadged them from leavings on plates.

He hadn't found François. He'd looked in one café after another, the Napoléon, the Monaco, all the usual places. No one had heard from François, he hadn't been seen in weeks. One of the fellows at the Deux Magots (but he was new and unreliable) guessed that François had been in trouble with the police — drugs, or drink, or a boy prostitute, how could anyone know?

She could not eat. She could not swallow. There was nothing to drink.

Julian said he would ask the landlady for a pitcher of water.

"Don't go," she said. But he left her.

"She hasn't got anything like a pitcher," he reported. "She says she'll look for something else. I gave her some money."

"Today," Lili said, "I am sent away."

She saw that he was half alarmed and half bewildered: tenuous under the solidity of his young man's flesh. Yet she must injure him.

"Finished," she said. "No more. There is nothing now."

"Finished?" he echoed. How stupid he sounded!

"Dismissed."

"It's all right," he said. "Really, Lili, I promise. I'll find something right away, even tomorrow, there's got to be something —"

"There is nothing," she said again, and stared at his mouth. A young man's moist and writhing mouth, with its leaping tongue. She hated it then, the mouth, the tongue. She hated his body, all of it, the long thighs, their treacherous male grip.

Wearily she lifted the burden of what she must tell him, of what he must know. The clinic, she told him, was very clean, she was treated kindly, how sympathetic they were, it was not an ordeal at all, it was only that her groin still hurt, already the hurt was ebbing, they had hollowed her out, her body was empty now.

"I asked to look at it," she said. "It was nothing. A little bloody bud. A bloody little head, no more. Not a human head. Not human. A little fish."

She had injured him, yes — she had never before seen him with such clarity: how he felt for her, how little he knew, how feeling

175

could be so improbably distant from knowing, and what did it matter that he felt for her if he understood nothing, nothing at all? How perversely untouched, how whole! The tiny fishlike thing they had wrested out of the sea of blood . . .

His breathing was too close. He took her hand. She let him take it; her impulse was to recoil. He made a shelter for her head against his chest, and the buttons of his shirt cut sharply into her cheek. Her ear pressed down on a seashell roar: his calamitous heartbeat.

"Why," he said, "why, why?"

"Why do you ask why? Stupid, stupid!" she cried, and pulled away from him.

"But it was alive," he said, "it was alive, it could make up for—"

He halted. *Make up for.* He had learned that certain ordinary idioms she could not fathom.

Guardedly, in fear of her, he began again: "It might have been instead, instead of —"

Her palm shot up against his mouth.

"Stupid! There is no instead!"

She was flinging death at him, and he was failing her. And why shouldn't there be an instead of? Why shouldn't there be renewal? Why else had he fled to Paris in the first place, if not for renewal? Not to be his father's son; to be made over. He had read in the Psalms about deliverance. He felt chastened, ashamed. She was sobbing beside him, long heaving gasps. The worn old mattress shook with the labor of it, and he remembered the Sixth, how slowly, carefully, taking it in, he had copied out *I am weary with my groaning, all the night I make my bed to swim, I water my couch with my tears,* copying like a medieval scribe in the notebook with the red margins.

A noise on the stairs. Mme. Bernard, bringing water—he'd left the door open for her. She had made him pay for the water, she was suspicious of him, one of these American loafers, and that little brown woman, a Jewess probably, a pair of vagrants, were they good for the rent? Her narrowed look fixed on his battered sandals. *Une cruche?* Her precious crystal pitcher, a thirty-year-old wedding present, she kept it for proper company. For money she would search for an empty bottle.

But it was his sister who stood in the doorway.

"Julian? It's so dark in here, is something the matter —"

"You didn't go," he said.

"Julian, what's wrong, is it Lili, what is it?"

"She's out of a job, and what's wrong with *you?*" he barked back. "What are you doing here, why haven't you left?"

"I came to tell you. I wanted to tell you —"

"You were going to go back!"

"I'm staying, that's all. I decided to stay, Phillip said I could stay. I'll be helping him, he wants me to, and then —"

"Stay, go," he shouted, "only go away! Can't you leave us in peace, can't you *see?*"

He was running her off, driving her out — that downward clatter on the stairs. His sister, an intruder, a witness, he was stricken, and how could she not see how their lives were shaken? Lili rocked by unholy spasms. He wished that God could be real; only in the Psalms was God real, nowhere else. He wished that the fishlike thing with the bloody head had lived.

"Lili," he said, "Lili."

"Finished," she answered. "Enough."

How old she looked to him now: raw eyelids, swollen nose and lips. The corners of the mouth cracked from dryness. Haggard. The tumbled hair. The weeping was done; in an instant of self-mastery she was declaring it done.

She said, "It is time you go home now."

"Because of your uncle? You want to go to your uncle, is this what you're telling me?"

"That place is not your place."

"Don't leave me, Lili, don't," he pleaded, but he knew his force, it seized him at the shoulders and in his straining calves. "Don't, don't," he said, and with his man's body and his boy's fear he bore down on her, pleading, and she yielded, she opened to him, dry-eyed, dry-mouthed, surprised and unsurprised, hurting in the place where they had combed her that day with an iron comb, he hurt her, he hurt her, until they lay breathing, breast to breast.

40

A BIG-CITY COMEDY, snatches of jazz among the skyscrapers, a swoop of cello when the elevator breaks down between floors, the usual strings for the lovers: it could be scored in under a month. Leo was indifferent to it. Another B movie, Brackman getting stale, getting pushed down the pole, Leo Coopersmith with him.

But something had happened. He woke into it, it was inescapable, it had taken root in what he presumed were the wrinkly lobes of his brain, though too often it flashed down to inflame the tender secret testicles that lurked like darkened planets between his legs. He *felt* it more than he heard it, or so he at times believed. He felt it in his sexual parts, even in the stiffened tips of his nipples, as a woman might feel it. Yet mainly — there was no denying it — he heard it, the elusive horrible noise of it, and he could occasionally smell it, too, a smell like earth turned under a spade. How had she done it, how exactly had those polyphonic antiphons, if that's what they were, come into being, and from no recognizable system — what could you call that sound? When he tried to imagine it (he was always trying), it was scarcely stable, it was a fleeting exultation, or else a hideous hollow, like an anus, or a growly scrabbling of animal claws. Or — this was unbearable — a perpetual crazed crescendo. He struggled to remember the position of her hands: the left hand with the fingers spread, of that he was nearly certain, the long thumb reaching beyond an octave; but the right? It made no sense that she had rolled it into a fist. A fist could not account for the shudder of beauty between his legs.

It was the exultation he was after. He sat at the Blüthner hour after hour, hunting it down. Now and again, by gently throbbing the pedal, he could almost catch hold of a single legato thread of it, in B-minor, in the bass, sighing like a leaf-tremor; but of course she had been stolidly standing in those middle-aged homely shoes of hers, and what did she know of pedaling? He understood it had been fortuitous, a kind of mystical miracle — in plain words, nothing more than an accident. She was a musical nonentity, it was a lucky hit; yet it had *happened,* and if it happened once, it could be replicated, it could be found. No such chimera in the world as a lost chord, that silly old song by a fool who aspired to grand opera, and got famous through jiggling tunes for jingles. The lucky hit, the accident, the mystery, was *there,* shut up in the Blüthner, undisclosed; he had only to seek out the operative combination. It existed, it was alive in the keys . . . it was there.

41

Dear Mrs. [this was crossed out]
Dear Miss Nachtigall [this was crossed out]
Dear Miss Beatrice Nightingale,

Please forgive me that I write suddenly this letter. My husband does not wish me to write it, but from many difficulties he agrees. English I read with more skill than I can write or speak, but such is the way with language that is not one's mother tongue. Please forgive my errors, and also my penmanship on this poor paper. I no longer am permitted the typewriter, being dismissed from my former employment. Some small wages I received without expectation on my dismissal, they are already gone.

I write now because I have been told that you are a teacher in an American school, and I believe I too own the quality to be a teacher in an American school. I have diploma (is this a correct expression?) in Modern Language from my university in Bucharest, but unfortunately all document evidence for unhappy reasons is no more.

I can teach French, Italian, Spanish, and (if necessary) German. (I think there is no use of Romanian in an American school!) I request humbly whether it is your opinion such a position can be available, in your own school or elsewhere. I can also translate, though perhaps not in America so usefully.

Here in Paris in recent weeks I am translating literary works from Romanian into French language. My husband has no employment.

From many difficulties (I acknowledge I say this twice, it is unhappily truthful) we do not live in a good way here. We are deciding to go to America. From my work of translating, which is not very much, nevertheless we have already billets for the voyage. My husband being a citizen of USA, we are assured of my entry without great impediment. I ask humbly and gratefully, can you accept us in your home for a short while? We come to New York nine days from today. Please reply par avion to Poste Restante 51, Paris.

Yours sincerely,
Lili Nachtigall

Perhaps you are thinking, what will my husband do in America? He will return to be a student.

So the scheme was under way—Marvin's wily mean thinking, invading, pressing. His suspicions, his clever convoluted cynicism. His crafty distrust. Lili's plot, and what else could it be, if not a plot? *My husband, my husband,* and Julian nowhere in sight, neither in name nor in volition. A boy with a wife is a man, and a man with a wife cannot be left to drown. She had cajoled him to retrieve what was his: his America, and thereby his father, and thereby his father's overflowing dollars. Life-stricken and impoverished, she was a canny woman who had maneuvered a rich American boy into marriage for the sake of his family's money, if only he would be compliant: one of the oldest stories in the world. She was cautious, she was intelligent, she would take it step by step, pretense by pretense. The pretense of looking to be independent—laughable anyhow, a foreign-born would-be teacher from an Eastern European country lately turned Communist, at a time (and who should feel this more than Bea?) when principals everywhere were pushing for loyalty oaths, how likely was *that?*

And the even more improbable pretense of Julian's easy surrender to his father's design: *he will return to be a student,* what guile, what calculation!

And the whole of it resting on Bea. On Bea's opening her door to the wanderers, a respite before the great transcontinental charge to golden California. On Bea's having paved the way with Marvin, and readied him for conciliation — oh, but she hadn't, and surely Lili had counted on it! How deliberate, how explicit, were those sly preparations for the pounce, those shrewd old urgings: *you should say what you know . . . now nothing is hidden, you see?* And the most cunning of all: *I do him good.*

Marvin's thinking, Marvin's mania. How it worms its way into your brain, how it works its way into whatever you believe!

But it was the last that made Bea hesitate. Was it really a ruse, was it really a plot? *I do him good* — words that, despite every doubt, carried the sound of a widening world.

42

The Suite Eyre Spa
Suite 312

Dear Margaret,

I believe you will be pleased to hear that there is good news
from Paris. Julian is on his way home. He will be accompanied
by Lili, his wife.

I hope you are continuing well.

Yours with good wishes,
Beatrice

•

November 25

Marvin:

Some time ago I very nearly risked phoning you, but
dreaded the uproar and thought better of it. There is something pacific (if surely not pacifist!) in silence, especially a long
silence—I acknowledge that the fault is mine. As you've no
doubt suspected, I've been withholding information (I don't
call it knowledge, as you'll soon see), and not without cost
to my conscience. In all brevity, then: Julian is ready to come
back. My short-lived visit—I always felt I was representing
you as a kind of plenipotentiary!—was a diplomatic failure in
the extreme. Your son repudiated me from the first instant. He

was, in fact, painfully derisive, and I can finally report to you that he was keen enough, and resentful enough, to see me as nothing more substantial than your shadow. What moves him to return appears to be his attachment to the young woman you already know of — it won't do anymore to say "girl-friend," and I discovered belatedly that it was never the right word to begin with. I have had two or three rather scanty en-counters with this person. My impression is one of uncommon gravity and endurance — nothing lighthearted or frivolous. I have learned very little of her background, beyond that she is the daughter of an educated Bucharest family, and apparently has some literary skills in several European languages, though her English is stilted and in certain aspects insufficient. She is older than Julian, I would think somewhere between eight and a dozen years. She is a widow and has lost a child — I gather she was interned with her family during the war and somehow ended in Paris with hundreds of other such uprooted people.

I hope I have said enough to make you understand in what mode Julian returns. He returns as a husband. My apartment is small, but because it has lately undergone some convenient changes, I will be able to accommodate the two of them for a reasonable time. They will arrive on December 3rd.

Yours,
Bea

43

IRIS WAS NOT the first of Dr. Montalbano's assistants. He had enlisted ("employed" didn't exactly fit the case) a lively roster of others, particularly in Milan, where he had had the advantage of a series of dark-eyed, dark-haired enthusiasts. He lost them one by one; the most vengeful had the habit of reporting certain aspects of his practice to the authorities. No matter: he kept what he called his Christmas kitty, local Pittsburgh lingo for a bank account set aside for a specific use — it forestalled anything more dire than a fine by paying off the relevant officials. Italy was lenient in this respect, unlike Paris and especially Lyon, where a stricter atmosphere reigned. But Iris was his first American, and as blond as Patsy and Mary Alice, the two sisters just above him, with this critical difference: she gave off an air of indulgence, of high expectation; even of just deserts, as if she had accomplished something worthy of reward. It surprised him that she was a virgin — she wasn't a baby, she was past twenty and more. He judged it to be a purely American prudery, distinct from the European type, which was grounded more in duplicity than in principle. He had seen this restrained unrestraint in Patsy and Mary Alice before their marriages — so far and no further, maddening their boyfriends, who departed at three in the morning with bulging flies, while the girls went off to bed laughing, their teeth lipstick-smeared, their mouths swollen.

No laughter in Iris — she wasn't a tease, at least not with him: gratitude made her tractable. She took him up, instead, with full seriousness, like a difficult course in school, wanting to do well. She was as stiff as a corpse (and hadn't he mistaken her for a corpse at first sight?); he came too soon, it made him angry. It was as if she had no instincts, and had to be taught—or as if she was listening, in her head, to a different set of lessons. At such times she spoke of her brother and her brother's wife; she asked whether everyone made love in the same way. — Jeez, he said, what d'you think human anatomy's *for?*—No, she said, I mean if someone's been injured, if someone's body got mangled forever, a missing piece, a hole in the wrong place, wouldn't that change how you'd feel? — Listen, kid, he told her, there's only one hole that matters, and it's in the usual spot . . . but even then she didn't laugh. He could talk dirty to her and she didn't laugh. He had gone with her to that horror of a rooming house, with that shrieking landlady and her curses; by then her brother had disappeared.

In bed (she still considered it *her* bed) she rattled him from moment to moment. He had mistaken her for one of those well-off American girls who grow their hair to their waists and follow whichever import is currently popular, sometimes an African singer, sometimes a Greek filmmaker: Paris has its fads. Until now he had stayed away from American girls—a man with four sisters at home in Pittsburgh knows better. But this one had turned up drunk on the other side of his door; he couldn't avoid her and he couldn't throw her out. The smell disgusted him. All his life his mother had reeked of the stuff: when his father left, she got herself work in one of those bar-restaurants that are more bar than restaurant. Her cotton dresses came out of the wash smelling of beer. A steamy mist rose up from the ironing board smelling of beer. It astonished him that when he took the girl in, on the condition there'd be no more bottles, she stopped—stopped on the instant, just like that. It was beyond his understanding, and beyond his experience too. He had never been able to get Alfred to stop, or, as a matter of fact, anyone else: a drunk is a drunk.

He figured it out the day they went to look for her brother.

"It's over," she said.

He asked, "What's over?"

"What I tried."

"What was it you tried?"

"To love him. The way we used to be at home. I came to make him feel better — not just with money. He didn't want me, he didn't need me. He had Lili."

She was a woman of projects. She gave herself assignments, she had a program. She thought like a scientist; she hinted that her father had something to do with chemistry, with plastics. The wine, he concluded, was deliberate: like Freud with cocaine, say. The brother was a failed project, and then came the wine, plumbed for its sensation, for its effects, but when she got to the bottom of it, after the flowery burst, after the descent, there was nothing. Stupor, blackout, sleep. Prone like a cadaver on the other side of his door. He had told her to give it up; she gave it up. This was her stubbornness. Her brother; the wine; and now she must open her legs to please him. He saw that she meant to satisfy him. She worked at it with diligence, as something to pass through, a test demanding success. She had the idea — but how would she have acquired such a notion? — that there ought to be noises, small moans, gasps. Even outcries.

In the clinic she was useful and enterprising. A pair of gendarmes had turned up, asking to examine his business cards, the usual first step: he knew what might follow. He suspected the concierge, though it could easily have been some disgruntled client. His concoctions were generally innocuous, yet it stood to reason that now and then someone would break out in a rash, or worse. He was prepared to treat the reaction, whatever it was, but there were times when he couldn't subdue the resentment. The gendarmes came again, more threateningly. He was a despiser of laws; he concealed himself, while Iris, gesticulating in the doorway with her fragments of school French (he scarcely heard two words of it) charmed them away. They went off grinning, and the visit was never repeated.

He asked how she had managed it.

"Just as you would," she said. "Mumbo jumbo."

Her term of admiration, of trust. She admired and trusted his way with the clients. It wasn't what he gave them to chew or swallow or rub on their skins or between their toes; it was how he got their imaginations to work. Mostly it was his own imagination at work. His mumbo jumbo (she'd begun to call it that almost from the start) was no more spurious than nature itself. Nature was the true shaman; she saw this, she understood it, she had witnessed such transmutations in beakers and vials, liquids into solids, solids into gases, gases back into liquids, lifeless molds in petri dishes burgeoning overnight, crystals growing. Not one of the others was so clever—those chirping girls who had come aboard in this or that city, a whole row of them, all sexually pliant, not one of them given to listening for ghostly groanings. Mumbo jumbo, she said, and he caught what she meant and was flattered: nature, intuition, inventiveness. And sometimes scam—what harm in it, if it brought in francs and lire, and dispensed a bit of transient joy? He hadn't expected that she would show so practiced an interest in those francs and lire—he still thought of her as California-rich—until he remembered that apart from him she was destitute. She kept her ticket home in a kitchen drawer, among his spatulas and sticky ladles; he supposed the thing was well past its expiration. She had this in common with him—those half-rusted keys to burned-out Pittsburgh pads that daily jangled on a ring in his pocket. She never wrote to her father, though she mentioned him often enough. He took it for granted that she was, like everything else, transient, passing through. She wouldn't last.

In the meantime she trusted him; he trusted himself. He trusted that his urgings would soon melt her. She trusted that before long they would stand together on the frozen peak of some mighty Alp, or at the lip of Como. She did not refuse the invasion of her mouth. She wound her hair, a slippery manacle, around his wrist. But the rest of her was enigma: naked under his nakedness, she lay like an inert

Pompeiian cast in the bed that had been hers alone while those yawps and mewls and solemn lowings came drifting to her ears from her brother's lovemaking, or from his wife's horrific dreams. And when at night the blind blows of the soothsayer's member struck and struck at the root of her flesh, she could not tell one cry from the other.

44

LATE ON THE WEDNESDAY afternoon before Thanksgiving, Bea sat at her desk in her deserted classroom, red pencil biting down. A rainy dusk blurred the big windows, and the rows of empty seats exhaled the mingled malodors of young males. Under her hand were her class's Shakespeare reports: misperceptions, misspellings, verbs and commas running wild, wrong turnings everywhere. A starvation of words. Still, she detected in this thicket of blots and brambles a subterranean mindfulness: at home they knew Iago and Goneril and Edmund and Lear, they knew their simulacra, they knew fear, they knew rage. They had seen into the tragic, and she was not ashamed of their errors. Their errors were short-lived paper phantoms; but they were skilled and manly boys, and they would not live paper lives. Her red pencil could not demean them.

Four days free, the longest weekend of the year. Laura had asked Bea to Thanksgiving dinner: they were going to do the works, from the stuffing right down to the candied yams and cranberry sauce. And apple cake! Harold had loved Bea's apple cake. Jeremy, believe it or not, had volunteered to make the fruit salad. Besides, Laura said, there'd be a special lure for Bea—live drama on their television.

Live drama? The new machine was giving birth to new expressions.

"Real *plays*," Laura explained. "Like going to the movies without leaving the house. It's not just Sid Caesar and wrestling anymore. And anyhow you don't want to be alone on Thanksgiving—"

"I don't mind," Bea said. "I picked up something from the library to keep me company."

"Oh you," Laura said. "Missing out on all the fixings for a book——"

It was *Doctor Faustus*. In that stale and enervated room stinking of the ghosts of snuffed cigarettes, Leo's venerated old Modern Library copy at her elbow . . . and she hadn't touched it. She had been bold enough, but not so brazen as to lay a finger on that impalpable part of him haunting a book. Instead, the pitiable photo of those little girls. The grand was banished, its shadow erased——but still there remained this galling bedeviling invisible specter: Leo's brain. Unexpectedly, it continued to take up space in her own. How to be quit of it? The days of quiet to come, undistracted: then let there be one last solitary exorcism.

Someone had placed a foil-wrapped chocolate turkey on the corner of her desk. Around its neck, confined by a rubber band, a labored note: A BERD FOR MISS BERDY. It made Bea smile; she hadn't noticed it before. She thought she could identify the giver, a boy who never wore socks and had the habit of solemnly staring. She shoved the heap of papers into a drawer and dropped her red pencil in after it. Done, a relief, she was her own woman until Monday. She picked up her raincoat and shut the lights and went out into the silent hall.

A man was walking toward her, hesitatingly, looking into the open doors of the darkened classrooms. She clutched her purse and stood nervously. This was no ordinary weekday afternoon, when the corridors would have been alive with scufflings, hoarse muddles of reluctant tutoring floating along the walls, thuds and yells pounding upward from the gym. She was aware of an emptiness, an abandonment——everyone, boys and teachers, had rushed away to begin the holiday. But plainly not everyone: in the dimness, a single bulb over the stairwell, she saw that the man was large and hatless and balding. Mr. Elkins then, delayed like herself, searching for who knew what he'd left untended. Bea had heard him boast in the teachers' lounge how he never departed the premises without properly tidying up, a lesson for the slovenly.

The man came nearer. It was not Mr. Elkins. An intruder: he had no business here. He seemed perturbed, waving and calling out, his shouts flying apart into echoes and shards. She caught fragments of it: "—told me in the office this was your floor—were all leaving—said you'd left—weren't home, tried there first—"

With each step his shoes were printing wet ovals behind him, until he halted just in front of her, so close she could hear his breathing. "Raining cats and dogs," he said, and Bea felt her mood strain toward these old schoolyard words, as if for this one instant he and she were children again. But he had no other greeting.

"Helluva job tracking you down. How d'you live with it, place smells like puke—"

"It's only the disinfectant they use on the floors," Bea said.

"Stinks anyhow, let's get out of here pronto. Goddamn stairs, is there an elevator somewhere?"

There was no elevator. She led him down five flights. His body, the hurtling panting bulk of it, sent out a heaving strenuousness: he was well past middle age.

In the street, under a nearby awning funneling a watery spew at either end, she asked, "Where are you staying?" A courtesy one would put to a visiting foreigner.

"The Waldorf. Good business location."

"So it's work that's brought you—"

"No," he said. "It's you."

Bea considered. "Come back with me then."

"Back where?"

"My apartment. There's a bus, it's not far."

"Nothing doing. I've been there, got myself soaked. No doorman, one pile of bricks same as any other, helluva way to live—"

"It's not your way, no," she said. "Will you come?"

"Listen, I didn't fly out here ten hours three thousand miles and changing planes twice to have a goddamn cup of tea—"

193

"Then why did you?"

"The point is there's something you need to understand, and right away, that's the point, you follow what I'm saying? Fine, your place, when it comes down to it what do I care—"

He had turned indifference into a command. He lifted an autocratic finger. A cab slid to the curb, splashing their shins.

Bea's place—here he was then, improbably, inconceivably: a monarch at the dining table that had usurped the space where the grand once reigned. Where she had never imagined him. He was loosening his tie; he had already undone the top button of his shirt. A fat neck—she saw in the father at least this much of the son. She had hung his dripping coat on the shower rail.

"It's not so bad," he said, looking around. "Two and a half rooms, you'd think it'd be a lot more crowded."

"It used to be."

"Is this where you . . . your husband and you . . ."

Bea said drily, "Where we cohabited? No, that was long ago and far away."

"Well, how would I know? For years you didn't keep in touch."

"Nor you," Bea said.

"I've had a business going, there's the difference. And a family, what do you know about having a family? And then when you finally get around to writing, you don't answer, it's start and stop, it's nothing and then it's bits and pieces, and hints and hidings, and then it's nothing again. That last letter, it was goddamn cold. Cold as ice, and believe me, it won't stand, over my dead body it's going to stand, you follow me?"

"Marvin," Bea said, "what's this about, why didn't you let me know—"

"Let you know! And have you throw some sort of cockeyed excuse at me, when it's got to be stopped, I mean stopped right now, *corked*, why can't you understand this, are you so dense . . ." But he broke off, and again Bea saw his look travel from corner to corner, from the window to the door, and across the newly naked floorboards. "Don't tell me you were actually planning to put my boy up in this rabbit hutch —"

"I intend to give the two of them my bedroom, same as when Iris was here, that was only the one night, but Julian's coming with his wife, so —"

"His wife! His wife! Are you out of your mind? To send me a crazy letter like that, and to think I'd let it happen? It won't happen, Bea, *it is not going to happen,* can't you get this into your head?"

"They'll be here in six days," Bea said, and stood up and walked away.

"Where the hell do you think you're going?" he called after her.

"To get me some supper."

"I need to talk to you! Considering I left everything in the middle, canceled a meeting, didn't even stop to look in on m-Margaret . . ." She heard him falter; it was almost a stammer, but he was quick to recover. "Bring me some coffee while you're at it, will you? And make sure it's good and hot."

In her little kitchen — and how miniature it all at once seemed, a rabbit hutch of a kitchen — Bea put up the coffee, scrambled half a dozen eggs, toasted four slices of bread, and carried it all out on a tray.

"What's this?"

"Thanksgiving dinner," she said.

"Listen, there's a swanky restaurant over at my hotel, what do I want with this stuff?" But he ate hungrily.

She did not know what to make of him. He was unshaven, and the stubble aged and roughened and hollowed his face. His nose was broader than she remembered. His mouth had thinned to a dry line. Flecks of white dotted his eyebrows; two or three hairs, blacker and longer than the rest, curled upward like insect antennae. She thought he was even balder than when she had seen him weeks ago, on his way to the pool behind the hedge — but that had been at a distance, and from across the road.

"I don't see why you're objecting," she said — she was careful to be direct, to avoid any shade now of vitriol. "It's exactly what you wished for, isn't it? What you wanted, what you wanted from me, what you asked me to do."

A crumb of toast hung scornfully on his lip. "What d'*you* know about what I want?"

"You wanted Julian back. He's coming back."

"Good God, not like this! I never wanted this!"

"He's very young," she admitted.

"Young's got nothing to do with it, Margaret and I weren't a whole lot older, and Margaret—Margaret was Margaret, that's the point. Margaret couldn't take a thing like this, she wasn't made for it—"

"She took *you*," Bea said.

"And I put an end to it, didn't I? I finished it off, it wasn't supposed to get into the next generation, and it never did, I stopped it right from the start. You saw Iris—"

"I did. Right off the Mayflower."

"Cut it out, Bea, you're not the one to talk. I've kept my name just the way it came from pop, which is more than you've done, and I'm not about to have some little old grandma with broken English creep into my family. I'm sick over it, I won't allow it, the boy's a goddamn fool, I can't sleep, I can't think, I'm only half alive—a fool, you had a look at him and you made a secret of the thing, and now you think you're going to sneak him past me . . . well, you can't, I'm here to stand in your way, and I know how to do it . . ."

Marvin in full rant. Her throat heated up; she was embarrassed for him, and for herself, for her petty retaliations—that Thanksgiving dinner remark, the silly Mayflower jab, why so sardonic, wasn't he suffering, even from his own awful contradictions? He made her more tired than angry.

Tiredly, heavily, she said, "Why not just wait and meet her?" But she could hear how simple-minded this was.

"*You've* met her, one's enough. I don't want to set eyes on the woman. I know what's coming, I've seen the films like everybody else, and I can't have one of those, not in my own family. All that's blood under the bridge, it's not my business, and I don't intend to invite it in. And don't think I don't know what you're thinking—"

"You wanted him back," Bea said, "you wanted him back at least for Margaret—"

"Callous, that's what you're thinking, I'm callous, I don't have a drop of what d'you call it—*compassion*, wouldn't that be the word you'd like? Not to mention that I've got my own little war medal and earned it at forty-four, if that counts for anything, and look, I'll contribute all they want to those organizations, whatever they are, same as I give to the Red Cross and such, and more if they think I owe it to 'em for solidarity's sake . . . solidarity! But I don't want any of those people in my house, I was done with all that a long time ago, and look at you, you're no different from me, in fact you're worse, you haven't got the means for the type of donations I can swing, so what good is all your fancy feeling without the money to back it up? I don't want to see her—I don't want to smell her—and I don't want to see my son, the damn fool . . . Bucharest, where the hell is that, Romania, Bulgaria, who cares? He's gone back three generations into the past, the boy's digging up skeletons—"

Bea said narrowly, "But you went to the oboe, nothing stopped you from that."

His eyes jumped: two quick beasts in a cage.

"What are you talking about?"

"Leo Coopersmith."

"How do you know that? Who told you?"

"He did."

"What, are you in touch with him?"

"No. But I saw him. I saw his house. I saw his . . . instrument. It isn't an oboe, it never was an oboe."

"My God, Bea, a stale old quip, the way you can hold a grudge—"

"Someone you've had contempt for your whole life, and then you go looking to him for influence—"

"He didn't come through anyhow. Julian's got the idea he's a bit of a scribbler, they could've made something of a boy like that in the movie business, why not?"

"You thought you could use me to get to Leo."

"It didn't harm you, did it, and damn it, I'd do anything for my son, can't you see that? Even now, even now . . ."

Bea watched him pull up from his chair, bisonlike, with his shoulders humped and his chin thickened, reconnoitering as if measuring the distance from one wall to another, or impatiently inspecting whatever his nostrils drew him to: an agitated ruminant sniffing for fodder. After another turn or two he came back to her and tossed a paper on the table, among the sticky plates.

"That," he said, "is a whole lot of money. A tremendous lot of it. You could say it's enough to live on decently for fifteen, maybe twenty years, depending, and this is *not* the way it's done, I've got lawyers, I've got bankers, it's got to be done with trusts, the whole paraphernalia, I know damn well how it ought to go. But hell, I don't want any goddamn lawyers, not yet, the complications I can take care of later, I want it the way I want it, and right now this is how I want it—plain and simple, never mind what's behind it, the kid has no more idea than a two-year-old how anything works in the real world. I want it the way the boy can understand it."

His neck and forehead had dampened; his breath was coming fast.

"Now listen to me, what you're going to do is get this check to my son pronto, air mail special delivery, you follow? Before he has a chance to put a foot out the door, wherever he is. And tell him to stay put. Stay where he is. Keep away. He fell into some muck over there, let him stay there."

Bea went on staring: the big chest under its moistened shirt was bobbing dangerously. "You really want to do this?" she said. "When he's finally ready to come home?"

"He'll see I've made it worth his while, I guarantee it."

"But what about Margaret," Bea pursued, "you said it was for Margaret he had to come back, her health depends on it—"

"It doesn't matter, not anymore. She's too far gone, in the last few weeks she's stopped making sense. I told you, she hallucinates, she has visions, you'd think she knows things before they happen . . . My God, Bea, I'm a man without a wife, I live like a monk."

"Do you?" Bea said. The leafy path, the girl in the cape, the pool; but she let the lie pass. "And what if Julian won't accept your money?"

"He's not that much of a fool, and if he is, *she* can't be. People who've gone through all that over there have to be practical, they take what they can get."

"You think she's a user—" She held up the word like a mirror.

"What else could she be? Why else would she hang on to a boy like Julian?"

"And despite what you think you're willing to provide for this woman?"

He threw up his arms and wailed, "He *married* the creature, didn't he?"—and sent out a broken rattle that Bea at first could not recognize for what it was: the start of a spurt of short high laughs, giggles almost: a paroxysm of grieving hilarity. She comprehended him then—her blunt brother was capable of a hideous irony. She was moved to embrace him, to hold his head against the safety of her body while he vomited out those cackling convulsions; yet she did nothing; and if he had wept, possibly she might have wept with him, for the pity of it (she pitied him unresistingly now), but he had no tears, not one, and what was she to do with his laughter?

When he left her, she remembered that he had scarcely mentioned his daughter at all. Nor had she confessed her clandestine visit to his wife—a deceiver's lie of omission yet again.

45

SHE COLLECTED the dishes and carried them away to be washed, and when she was done she looked fleetingly at Marvin's check inert on the table where he had hurled it, and with the long evening still before her went to fetch the book Leo Coopersmith had declared to be his talisman—had declared it defiantly, or defensively, in that gaudy grand house reeking of old butts. But when she passed by a second time, with *Doctor Faustus* in hand, the check, as thin and light as a leaf, fluttered from one spot to another, seeking escape—so she plucked it up and stuck it into the body of the book to prevent it from flying off again. How thin it was, this check, and how light: but the sum on its face was weighty. An unfathomable fortune, a treasure, a king's ransom: in this sum Bea could count a hundred times more than the two decades of her wages; of her life. Marvin, she saw, was willingly surrendering to his son—to his son and his son's wife—a royal inheritance. But the conditions for it! An inheritance intended to punish with the lash and sting of exile, and an iron door inexorably shut. He could not imagine Julian's refusing it. And surely Lili . . . *people who've gone through all that over there have to be practical, they take what they can get.* Whatever else Marvin was, he was worldly, he was sharp, he was a virtuoso of self-interest.

The tail of the check, a translucent wisp, hung out from the middle pages of *Doctor Faustus*. She had inserted it there unthinkingly, randomly. But now it flickered before her that she might, for the whim of the thing, attempt a divination, after the practice of those believers who open a Bible and blindly point with a finger to any passage the finger may alight on. From this passage a fate will be determined; and so it would be with Leo's talisman. It was Leo's fate she was after—his present fate, not his future, not what was still to become of him; rather, his situation at precisely this instant, or, if this were not forthcoming, then the subterranean germ that had brought him to where he was now, alone with his sacred Blüthner, bereft of his little girls. It was a game and it was not a game; it was a willed superstition and it was the opposite, a disgorgement, an ultimate cleansing—the vatic link between divination and exorcism. To find Leo out, to parse him, finally to see him, to see *into* him . . . to cast him out. And then the maggot that crawled along her nerves would die. The emperor Titus had a gnat in his ear, maddening him with its incessant buzz. How Titus got free of his gnat Bea could not tell, and legends are not often guides for the perplexed; but it was a certainty that through Leo's talisman she would drive Leo out. And what else was there to occupy the melting hours of this wild night, when Marvin had burst in on her without warning, in the fanatical storm of his scheming?

Hurriedly, as if what she was doing was shameful and likely to be discovered too soon, she leafed through the pages until she came to the crack in the spine where Marvin's check clung, humbly hiding, half through the force of static electricity, half of its own volition. And over this same page (it was 379) she whirled her index finger once; she whirled it twice; she whirled it a third time, and, eyes shut, allowed it to descend to the noiseless syllables it dizzily fell upon.

She saw:

and the same fear, the same shrinking and misgiving awkwardness I feel at this gehennan gaudium, sweeping through fifty bars, beginning with the chuckle of a single voice and rapidly gaining ground, embracing choir and orchestra, frightfully swelling in rhythmic upheavals and contrary motions to a fortissimo tutti, an overwhelming, sardonically yelling, screeching, bawling, bleating, howling, piping, whinnying salvo, the mocking, exulting laughter of the Pit.

Gehennan gaudium, hell's jubilation, the laughter of the Pit. Yes yes yes, Leo to the life, derided and undone. The man who longs to become, and is too fearful to become. To become what? The Mahler of the Sixth Symphony, where the hammer pounds down, the Beethoven of the Allegretto of the Seventh Symphony, as the trooping winds die into secret melancholia, Hindemith with his jagged staggerings . . . Never mind, she hears nothing, fifty bars, one hundred bars, all are lost to her, she is shut out from those yearning yammering notes—nevertheless she is seeing Leo plain, Leo's terror, Leo's not-becoming. She imagines a red, red pear ripe on its bough; but soon, in horror of crashing to the ground, it yields to the stupor of an internal rot, breeding its own devouring wormless worm.

It was not a game. It was not a superstition. What now was Leo Coopersmith to Bea?

She knew immediately what she must do. She went back into the kitchen and dropped Marvin's check into the sink. Then she struck a match and watched the leaflike paper flare up until it shriveled into black ash. Then she let the water run it into the drain.

46

SOUTHERN CALIFORNIA, even in late November, keeps its summer smile: the sun is always in its accustomed place, shedding maroon shadows alongside a sometimes unbearably blinding sparkle shot from windows and windshields and watch faces. The brightness made Margaret squint as she looked out over the far-flung grounds, pocked by red-and-pink flowerbeds, of the Suite Eyre Spa. On this very day she was determined to go home. Many of her neighbors had already been fetched away for the holiday by dutifully vigilant families carrying the Spa's distinctive orange drawstring sacks; these things bulged with odorous vials. Marvin on his last visit—when could it have been? here timelessness reigned—had himself proposed what he called a holiday furlough, an outing to such-and-such a fine restaurant for Thanksgiving dinner; but she had demurred. As long as Julian is gone . . . when Julian comes back . . . "Same old palaver," Marvin grumbled, and went off as uneasily as he had arrived, leaving her money for treats. She understood he meant bribes for the lower echelons of the staff. The therapists could not be bribed.

The therapists too had vanished for the day; and also (or so it seemed) more than half the rest of the staff. A somnolence deeper than the usual torpor. The lobby a marble shell, cold under her feet. A pair of china figurines on the receptionist's desk: a Pilgrim couple, he in his broad hat with its buckle, she in her bonnet and apron, and propped between them a big square cardboard announcing OUR SPECIAL THANKSGIVING MENU, 3:30 P.M. Out of a back corridor, two or three laughing voices. The woman who ought to have been at the desk was nowhere in sight—who could blame her, with nothing to do and no one to oversee? Margaret passed unnoticed to the porch with its white columns and sleepy cushioned chairs; the oak benches that grew up out of the grass were unoccupied. The only evident path wound, mazelike, among the flowerbeds, and brought her back to the porch; so she set out again, this time directly across the long lawn, heading for the gate that abutted the freeway. The brief sizzle of a bee hurtling too close to her ear momentarily obscured the steadier hum of distant cars. She remembered a bus stop right there at the gate—she had heard the lower echelons speak of it. Plenty of change in the pocket of her smock—they had stolen away her easel, but never her painter's smock. The thieves, whoever they were, had been too stupid to covet the smock. She wore it now for its capaciousness: it kept her hidden, invisible, no one could judge her, no one could grasp the joyfulness sequestered in its bottomless pocket—the *other* pocket, not where those dimes and quarters weighed and jangled . . . how often, from the minute it came to her, had she unfolded and folded the joyfulness, so that its creases opened all on their own! And to think that the joyfulness had been sent by her husband's sister, of all dislikable people, the sister he had never had anything to do with for years and years . . . and yet it was her husband's sister who had turned up out of nowhere with the first inkling of the joyfulness! *Displaced person,* how else could it be? The war and its upheavals, and kings and dukes and countesses and such deprived of their thrones, deposed and displaced, driven from their lands, still clinging in foreign cities to their rightful titles . . . was it possible that Julian had married one of *those,* though it wouldn't surprise, there was her cousin Roseanna, a family legend, who had gone to Cracow in the twenties and converted to Roman Catholicism in order to marry a Polish count, or someone everybody said was a count, he didn't have a penny, but he did live with his mother the countess and five sisters on the remnant of a grandly decaying old estate that had once boasted a dozen stables for thoroughbreds . . . the joyfulness twice joyful, Julian back at last, Julian *home,* Julian in the embrace of an aristocratic wife! And there they all were—and on Thanksgiving Day to boot—Iris—and well, Marvin, it had to be—and oh— Julian and his princess bride—and very soon, after the half-hour's ride in the bus, she would see them all together, feasting, and how they would greet her, Julian with his shining childlike look when she strode in with coins bouncing in one pocket and Marvin's sister's letter in the other! Ever since the joyfulness had flown into her hands, that incessant unfolding and folding, until the creases knew on their own how to go . . .

By now she had come to the gate. The bus stop was not there. She put up her hand to shut out the sun's glare (a passerby might have supposed that the woman in the unwieldy garment and the bare feet, costumed like some impoverished angel, was in the act of saluting) and realized she had been mistaken. The bus stop was on the other side of the freeway. Surely there must be some way to cross? A traffic light to halt the ruthless flow of cars—and there it logically was, a distance of one or two city blocks to her left, though in this secluded place no trace of city life, only this relentlessly rushing road connecting suburban cluster to suburban cluster . . . A burning and stinging in the soles of her feet. Somehow she had forgotten to put on her shoes . . . or no, not forgotten, it was on account of the joyfulness that she was at one with the air, skimming an inch above the ground, or hovering like a hummingbird! Then why this burning, why this stinging? She lifted her foot to see. A pebble embedded in the heel. She lifted the other foot. A cut under the toes, bleeding, and how painfully out of reach the traffic light now seemed! Car after car screeched past, louder as it loomed, one screech instantly dying, instantly reborn in the next screech, and the next, and the next. The crazed procession of screeches dizzied her a little, but look—again and again a gap appeared in the two parallel columns of cars charging in opposite directions, a gap in the near lane and a gap in the far lane; and every so often the two gaps miraculously coincided, opening a clean swath like the parting of the Red Sea, and how easy it would be to pass through the double gap, straight across to the other side of the road! And fortuitously just now, among the maddening screeches, a grinding vibrating growl: the bus itself, at first no more distinct than a blue blur, flashing multi-windowed flanks as it approached, and scarcely slowing as it shuddered toward its appointed stop. Margaret saw her chance: burning and stinging, she fled through the near gap, and was halfway through the far gap, when her heel, the one with the pebble stuck in it, slipped on a flat smear of grease, or oil, or unidentifiable spill, and she tumbled forward on her face while a new screech, louder than any other, howled in her head, and the gap closed over a crushing of bones and living flesh.

When the police and the ambulance arrived, the bus was long gone (there were no passengers to pick up, it had never stopped), and Margaret, her sister-in-law's letter bloodied but still legible in her pocket, was dead.

47

December 2

Dear Aunt Bea,

When your cablegram came I wrote to dad right away to tell
him I'll be coming home to be with him. You know better than
anyone how bad I've been — this was the first he'd had a peep
out of me since I got here, but he answered in an airmail and
said he's glad to hear finally where exactly I've been staying all
this time. He didn't even sound angry — more like all broken
up, it's so grim and horrible, and nobody seems to have figured out why it happened or where mom was going. Dad said
the only way they could tell it was mom was from an envelope
they found on her, with a note in it from you. I never knew
you and mom were corresponding, I don't think I ever heard
her mention your name. And poor dad, he's really all alone
now, so I've got to leave here as soon as I can. My old return
ticket's no good anymore — I learned this just today — which
means I have to wait till Phillip gets back to pay for a new one.
Dad would send the money for sure, but I'd rather not let on
that I've been depending on Phillip for everything. Actually
I'm here by myself now, and I guess that's a good thing, otherwise I might have been in Greece seeing the Parthenon or at
the Uffizi in Florence, and I would've missed getting your
cable. So it's all worked out — well, I can't say for the best,
can I, when everything's so awfully sad and shocking. Greece

didn't pan out anyhow, and neither did Florence, Phillip was called back to Milan practically overnight, some sort of emergency, an old client of his—he'd done some minor surgery on her a while ago (he really does do surgery!), and he asked me to hold the fort here, the way Julian used to, just in case it took him a week or so to fix up whatever the problem is. So you see we still haven't had a chance to go on any of the trips we've talked about, the clinic's been so busy here, though Phillip did promise that when it was time to move over to the Milan clinic I'd be going with him, and then we'd run down on the weekend to the Uffizi, where they've got a Madonna by Michelangelo and other amazing things, but when this emergency came up with this Adriana person, it's some cranky old lady who gives him a lot of trouble, he thought it would be better for me to stay put. So here I am! I keep thinking of mom every minute, I just can't stop crying. Julian's always been closer to mom than I ever was—she sort of played favorites, maybe because even when we were small Julian kept waking up from scary dreams. It's hard to know whether mom liked being married to dad as much as dad liked being married to her. It's funny about marriage, isn't it, and please forgive me if I'm being too personal, but you were married once, and I imagine you didn't like it very much either, since you ended up getting divorced. I'm pretty certain I'll never want to be married, there are parts of it I'm sure I wouldn't like, and I might even have it in my blood not to like it, I mean I've heard about those three old maid aunts in dad's family. If I can work up the nerve to say this outright, Aunt Bea, I can't help thinking how you've lived most of your life on your own, and that's exactly what I intend to do. And if there's one thing I hope won't ever happen to me it's that be fruitful and multiply business, which is some sarcastic Bible quote mom used to throw at me whenever I got her really annoyed. Mostly she said it when I had to spend a lot of time in the lab, sometimes pretty late at night. I guess she decided long ago I was too much like dad, who's always been consumed by whatever's going on with his company, but she wouldn't think it anymore if she knew what I've been up to in Paris! Only now she won't ever know. And Julian, wherever he is, it'll kill him when he finds out about mom. Or maybe not, that weird secret way he is with Lili and with everything else. I never told him, I never told Phillip either, but the night before Julian and Lili moved out, and I was supposed to leave too — they were asleep and all packed except for Julian's notebook — I sneaked a look, and he's got religion on the brain, can you believe it? I figure by now he's over there in the desert sitting under a crazy gourd or whatever. Which is something he said he wasn't absolutely keen on, but who can tell, when he's so bound up with Lili?

I've written again to dad to warn him that there'll be a delay before I can get a flight home. I had to fudge it a bit, I couldn't say my airfare has to wait for Phillip to come back — he seemed awfully concerned about this particular client — he said he wants to make it up to her for what went wrong. Well, I expect now I'll never see the Uffizi or the Alps or the Parthenon or Lake Como or anything like that. And I'll be giving up my own little studio place too, to stay with dad and try to make him happy. He'll be pleased if I go back to the lab and get my degree, and I guess that's what I'll have to do. Maybe someday when I'm old I'll take one of those tours, with a guidebook and a map. — Aunt Bea, would you mind if I keep on writing to you now and then when I'm back in L.A.? Not just to make amends for all those bad things from before, but to find out what it's like to be on one's own for the rest of one's life. To be honest, I never realized it until only a while ago, but I think you're terrifically brave!

Iris

48

IN AMERICA on Thanksgiving Day it is always easy to travel, especially on trains and planes. Everyone heading home for a family reunion or to a festive gathering of far-off friends has already arrived, and will hardly be ready to depart until two or three days after the holiday. This in-between time found Marvin the sole passenger in the curtained first-class forward section of his Pan Am flight to Los Angeles, anticipating an enforced two-hour wait in Dallas. The blasting roar of the four propellers brought on a muted but constant shrieking in his ears, the familiar sensation of internal sirens that he knew was bound to outlast the trip, hanging on long afterward like the whistlings of angry spirits. He had picked up a news magazine in the terminal at LaGuardia and thumbed through it desultorily: in Korea this battle and that, Eisenhower defeats Taft for the GOP nomination, cave paintings of Irish elk discovered in the south of France, Mau Mau depredations in Kenya, Soviet Jewish poets doomed . . . He waved the stewardess and her tray of drinks away, though he had ordered his usual pair of gin and tonics not three minutes before. He had slept badly in the doughy softness of his hotel bed. Between yawns, and between the two rivalrous coasts of the continent, it felt as if he had not slept at all. And still he was aware of a habitual swell of potency, an expenditure of elation, as after a hard-driven round of negotiations leading to triumph over a competitor, or the not infrequent pleasure he took in outthinking his teams of chemists and engineers. His brain was good in a crisis: he could resolve the intractable.

As always, there was a lesson in it for the vanquished. Marvin's science—that meager aspect of it nearest to the psychological—was rooted (so he might have put it himself) in Mendelian genetics. He was the son of a strong mother, which clearly accounted for his own energies—but he was also the offspring of a weak father, the shop-keeping son of a shopkeeper, an unaspiring pushover given to reclining during business hours on an antiquated settee wearing his eyes out in heaps of unrealistic bookish claptrap; and this unforgiving heritable wastefulness had unhappily shown up in Julian. Surely there was a lesson in it—not for his boy, the luckless carrier of a predetermined deficiency, but for his daughter. What precisely was the lesson for his daughter, he could not be certain—it hung before him, but dimly, behind a veil. She had sought out her brother; she had, in inscrutable fact, decamped to live with him and the woman, and what did it mean, what could it portend? A better head on her shoulders than her brother, thanks to Mendel and his sweet peas, and thanks also to that ancestral tea kettle; Margaret too had a part in it. Iris had grown into a sound young woman. Tender pragmatist that she was, her motive in bolting after Julian may well have been to denounce without renouncing, as if old intimacy could keep its influence. A job markedly different from Marvin's rush to New York: the quick clean cut. A lesson not for the boy, no! (the boy was ruined beyond repair), but for this industrious bright girl, a steadfast mind like his own. Iris would see the justice of what he had done—the calculated business-like balance of it—repudiation without abandonment. There was a lesson in it, a lesson for his daughter, but it was slipping away, he nearly caught hold of it and then again it eluded him . . .

He rang for the stewardess.

"Where's my gin and tonic?"

"I brought it, you said you didn't want it—"

"Well I want it now. And bring me some eyeshades, will you?"

He drank, and the thickness of his neck became overwarmed, the fatty nape and the fat all around his Adam's apple, and the sirens in his ears diminished (but only a little, ghostlike); he could not sleep.

What was the lesson, and if he could retrieve it—it drifted almost, almost at the penumbra of his thought—would the girl recognize it, would she embrace it, would she live up to it? What were his children's grievances, how had he offended them? His son and his son's wife were the offense! While Iris, a steadfast mind like his own if a trifle more yielding . . . he had lost one, had he lost the other?

Many hours later, as Marvin labored up the path to his house in the depleted fatigue of sleeplessness, he was surprised to see the heavy door with its stained-glass fanlight wide open, and the white-haired housekeeper standing there in her street clothes gripping her washing bag—she had long ago acquiesced to Margaret's insistence on a maid's uniform, and commonly carried it away for a twice-weekly laundering. A much younger man—a motorist asking directions?—was displaying what appeared to be a dirty scrap of paper. The housekeeper cried out and tapped the man on the elbow to get him to turn to her approaching employer.

"I was just this minute leaving for the day," she called, "and God help us it's from the police."

Afterward Marvin recollected, however pointlessly, that the officer too was in street clothes.

49

MARVIN ON THE PHONE the morning after Thanksgiving, hoarse, haranguing, accusing, what on earth was he telling her? A confusion of elements, impossible to sort out. A lawsuit, he said, he'd sue them out of their imbecile brains, out of their last cent, a dereliction of duty if he ever saw one, he'd found out anyhow this wasn't the idiot's first time falling down on the job, she'd been warned before, supposed to monitor people's comings and goings, sign in visitors, et cetera, they'd fired the woman on the spot what good was that now? And no shoes, her feet were bleeding, it was ghastly, the goddamn driver, sue the bus company won't let them get away with it, murder pure and simple, and that letter they took out of her pocket, soaked in blood, out of your mind to send a sick woman a letter like that, rile her up and barefoot, my God, barefoot in the middle of the freeway, murder pure and simple!

Marvin, suffering. The scraped voice, the headlong anguished fury. "You'll have to tell my kids, you're the one to do it, I can't do it myself, I can't, I'm not up to it, even if I knew how to reach them, not a line from Iris all this time, and my son — well, it's all over with Julian. But he has to be told, Margaret would want it—"

And Margaret: sick or sane? A little of each. Sanity it surely was to resist Marvin, to see into him, even to deny him; and to see into him was inevitably to deny him. But what did it matter now if Margaret had seen, resisted, denied? A broken body on a California road.

"And how is it your business to be sending my wife that inane little note, Julian's got himself married, he's on his way home, exactly the things it so happens she's been babbling about in these lunatic delusions she's been having, you never knew Margaret anyhow, you've never had a thing in common with her, how would you, you've lived practically your whole life like a goddamn nun, and if you ask me it's you and your goddamn little note that's killed her—"

Bea said feebly, contritely, "I thought it would make her happy."

"Happy! Bea, she's dead, my wife is dead."

And then the electric silence of the miles between them.

But again he had left her with one of his inescapable imperatives: it fell to her—again!—to be emissary to Marvin's children. Inescapable? She was already a master of betrayal—what Marvin didn't know, what she'd concealed from him! He didn't know she'd been to see Margaret, he didn't know she'd spied on that girl in the cape, he didn't know she'd burned up his check. He didn't know his daughter was in thrall to a crook! Bea counted it up, she turned it over, she weighed the consequences of confession—suppose she were to confess these things to Marvin—in the end it would all amount to the same. Margaret was dead. Dead, whether exonerated of delusion or not. Marvin a likely adulterer. Julian exiled by his father; there would be no reprieve. And Iris . . . In all this Bea saw herself as blameless: she had come to side with the party of the far horizon. As for the ashes in the sink, she had thwarted Marvin's unreason with sanity: sanity it was to thwart Marvin! Money frees, yes—she might have freed Julian altogether, she might have given the son his inheritance without revealing the father's stipulation. But money is also bondage—if Julian were tempted to take it, or could be persuaded to take it (by whom? by Lili?), the money would always and forever burn with his father's imperium, his father's contempt. In the logic of her betrayal, she had released Julian from the vise of Marvin's spite. Freedom! In order to liberate, expunge! No last vestige of attachment, no last link . . .

The exorcism of Leo Coopersmith. The exorcism of the ashes in the sink. Merged in a single night.

On the other hand—oh, the torment of that eternal other hand—hadn't she expunged Julian's chance to choose, to take the money if he dared? To take it even if he were made to understand the condition of his taking it? In the absence of choice, where is liberty? And Marvin's horrendous indictment—was it true? Was there the faintest breath of truth in it? It couldn't be true! Grief is nightmare, grief is gargoyle: the shock of fresh bereavement must be stirring up such grotesqueries of criminality. Out of a highway accident! Or, God forbid, a suicide. In that sumptuous vacuous mausoleum for the living, how harshly she'd spoken to Margaret—yet how was it possible for a little bit of paper, sent in recompense and remorse, to kill?

50

BECAUSE THE BARON had jabbed the foot of his stick against his breastbone — that patch of outraged manhood where his most unspoken intuitions were stored — Kleinman knew he must go to Lili tonight. The fault (the sin!) was the Baron's; he felt defiled by that humiliating poke. But Kleinman too was culpable; he had been servile, a bystander to Lili's maltreatment. He had allowed the Baron to harangue him, to jab him with his stick, to mock him, and through it all he stood servile and afraid. Afraid to call Lili back — he had let her go, he hadn't so much as called her back, even for the half week's wages that were rightfully hers. And Lili was ill, it was plain she was ill. Ill and driven out, like Hagar, into some uncharted trouble of her own — but Hagar had the consolation of Ishmael her son, and poor Lili was childless. Or perhaps . . . Kleinman had once seen her with a boy who seemed to have come expressly to meet her, a tall plump boy in American-looking sandals, unlike anyone in the queues. Kleinman didn't pry into the hurtful lives of his staff. Their stories were bound to be melancholy.

In his record book — he kept it admirably, the figures scrupulously ordered (the Baron would not have been able to dispute a line of it) — he discovered where Lili lived. The neighborhood was unfamiliar, and took him by surprise. His people, Lipkinoff, for instance, and Kleinman himself, took rooms in one or another of the overcrowded crannies of the Marais. But *this* — the stone façade of a fortress, these tall windows with rounded tops, the heavy doors and their carvings—this was an edifice! He had brought with him a thin packet: the handful of francs owed to Lili, and a rush of sentences he had hastily set down, remorse and regret, shame and apology (he was complicit, he had let her go with no more than the feeblest cowardly protest), he meant her to know how his inmost faith, his faithfulness, was *with* her, he had not ever intended to shunt her off like some discarded Hagar, the sin was the Baron's, not his! He had no power to console, he was childless himself, and wifeless besides, but if ever she was in need . . .

The sentences stretched on and on, and he understood that sentences such as these had been written thousands of times in the history of the world, and in truth carried no redeemable coin, and would be blown like vapor into nothingness. The wilderness of Texas lay before him (*bamidbar*, the desert, he too had Hagar's destiny), and for Lili, what, where? Their journeys diverged, he to the west, she to the east . . . she had spoken of an uncle, would she go now to that uncle? And in the meantime, how was it possible that these few francs could permit an establishment of this grandeur, the luxuriantly carpeted foyer, a gilded cage of an elevator, a sour-faced concierge whose accent was as uncongenial as his own?

From behind a marble barrier the woman held up a hand to halt him.

"What do you want here?"

"I've come to see a friend." How else should he say it?

"You're one of those, aren't you?"

She had already appraised him; she knew instantly what he was. All over Paris they knew. They could tell it even from a corner of the eye. Would it be the same in Texas? Why not, it was the same everywhere.

"Not that he's open for business yet, as far as I can see," the concierge said. "He's just back, there's only the one girl up there now. And that squatter boy's gone too, not that I could ever figure out was he a Jew or not, never mind he had the name."

Kleinman blanched. Was he being taken for a visitor to a brothel?

"*Sixième étage,* it's that chap Montalbano you want. As long as I get my tips it's none of my affair —"

Ascending in the elevator, he thought: No, not Lili, it cannot be Lili . . . yet the world was filled with contradictions. He pressed the button and waited; a fit of shame seized him, shame for Lili, shame for what he was being taken for. The door opened and a young woman, only half dressed, appeared before him — he saw at once that she was an American: there is something different in the faces of Americans. A look of — how to name it? — exemption. He had glimpsed that same look in the boy who had come to meet Lili, the boy who did not resemble anyone in the queues. In America, a population of cowboys and gangsters.

He tried out his new English. (How diligently he had been studying!) "Excuse me," he said. The phrase rang right, exactly as he had practiced it. But it fell from his tongue submissively, like a cringe. That she should be standing there so boldly, so unselfconsciously, in such dishabille!

The American young woman said in a businesslike American voice, "Sorry, these aren't our regular hours, no clients until after the weekend."

"I wish to see Lili," he pleaded.

"Lili? She's gone —"

"I must see her, I must. Please, tell me how to find where is Lili."

"You should keep away, she's sick, she doesn't want anyone."

"Sick, yes!" he cried. "I have money to give, so now I must see her —"

What misshapen words were these? As if he was in search not of the Lili he knew, but of some . . . whore.

"Please," he said again. His head, his chest, flooded with the stain of it. "I beg you, tell me where is Lili."

So Iris told him, and shut the door behind him, and called out to Phillip, who was already naked in her bed, "There! I hope I did that well. My first official act," she said brightly, "for the clinic." Then she bethought herself; she hadn't spoken truthfully. "Not really for the clinic," she amended. "Someone from Lili's job, one of those — the way he carried on you'd think the world was coming to an end. But I knew right away he wasn't a client."

In the foyer below, under the concierge's contemptuous eye, Kleinman took out his fountain pen — the important one he used for the Baron's bookkeeping — and carefully added three words to the last of his heartfelt hurried sentences.

"Whatever your circumstances," he wrote.

It was past seven o'clock when he arrived at the rooming house. A mean address in a shabby outpost. He had blundered into the wrong neighborhood after taking the wrong bus, and had retraced his route and started out again. The evening had deepened. There was only one streetlight — the others were shattered and dark. He nearly tripped on a crack in the threshold, and when he righted himself he found that the door had been left unlocked. The hallway smelled of something foul, an unpleasant sweetness covering a stench; but in a moment he recognized it as a woman's unclean breath. She had stolen out of the dimness (an overhead bulb was missing) and was sidling close to him, her mouth almost level with his own. She was chewing on a twist of caramel.

"We're full up," she said, "if it's a room you're after."

"No, no, it's only that I've come to see a friend" — and Kleinman, chanting this refrain, felt like some traveler in an Oriental tale.

"And who might that be?"

"Her name is Lili."

"I don't know them by how they call themselves, I know them by their looks. And if they pay on time."

"Small. Black hair. And very thin."

"The one he wanted water for, that's the one. Like if I've got the Holy Grail to give away to any tramp that asks. Washed out a vinegar jar and charged him for it too —"

"Him?" Kleinman said.

"Plenty of caterwauling in there, I figure it's been a fight. Not that you're the only one come looking today—the other ran right off. You'd best do the same, I lock up at seven-fifteen."

He climbed the stairs and listened. Lili; and then a man; and then again Lili. Deformed sounds, lifting and dying, lifting and dying, as if their throats were pooling blood. The sounds left him faint-hearted. He did not dare to knock. Instead, he pushed the packet under the sill and went away.

One of those, the landlady said to herself, turning the key in the lock.

51

NOT UNEXPECTEDLY, Bea's principal was a dead end.

—Foreign language tutor? Are you out of your mind, when you of all people know better'n anyone we can't get our guys up to par in their own so-called mother tongue?

—No, Bea said, I was thinking if you still have some connections in that other school where they do French and Latin—where you used to . . .

—Used to, well now I'm here. Better suited as they say. And Bea, from a Commie country, who's gonna stick his neck out these days?

But it was Harold Bienenfeld who came through.

Laura said, "Harold's got this old classmate, not a classmate really, a year ahead, but it's a big accounting firm, does business all over South America and Europe. I'll see if I can get Harold to ask, all right?"

And four days later: "Turns out they could actually use someone, I'm not exactly sure, from Spanish to French to German . . . something like that. The timing's right, they've just lost one of their translators, moved to London—"

So Lili was in luck. Bea took the business card Laura had given her and placed it on her bedroom dresser. Possibly it portended an interview, and how would Lili present herself, how would she be dressed, how would she speak? The card signified hope.

She emptied two of the dresser drawers and crammed the contents into a third. She removed two rows of clothing still on their hangers and transferred them from the bedroom closet to a narrower one in the vestibule. The kitchen cupboards were newly stocked with more than the usual provisions. Where there had been only Bea, now there would be three. Three in a rabbit hutch? The apartment looked oddly small again. She had presentiments of disorder . . . that stocking dangling from a lampshade, from a picture frame — it couldn't have been Lili's stocking. Lili was wrapped too tightly in her sallow skin. Iris's, then; but Iris was closing down her life. Alone with her father in his house, would she ever again throw a stocking over a lamp?

Bea spent the night on the davenport. Her big bed, with its pristinely fresh sheets and big deep pillows, awaited the visitors. Her back hurt a little from the unaccustomed surface — something hard and relentlessly upholstered. The day ahead was uninviting. She was afraid of Julian — perhaps more than she was afraid of Lili. She was afraid of both of them, and of what she was letting herself in for, of what she must say to Julian. And of what she had done! That small covert conflagration. It was covert, it was private; but was it shameful too, was it only to thwart Marvin, or had she more grievously thwarted Julian? Thwarting wasn't the same as vengeance, was it, when it was merely her dignity she was avenging? All her life Marvin had treated her badly. And his son had treated her badly, his barbarian son who was a stranger to her, whom she had looked at no more than twice! Looked at, and barely been looked back at. She had never so much as touched his hand.

She woke into an abnormal early light — a filtered glare, as if her window had been transfigured by some dark galactic radiance. The panes were obscured by starry patterns of crystals. Snow! In the street, humps of whiteness at the curbs, the few cars inching cautiously against a beating slant of white wind. Airports shut down, departures delayed, arrival times unknown. Announcement after announcement; much radio static. The queer light gave off a queer odor — the scent of apprehension.

They were expected before noon. It was after midnight when they came. Their plane had been diverted to another city, Lili could not say which, they had been kept on board for hours, then flown to a different city, where they circled and circled, unable to land. It was all extremely confusing, they were extremely tired, they really didn't want any hot soup, and thank you but please where were they to sleep?

Julian's feet in his scruffy California sandals were soaked to the ankles. Under her coat (it had a sensible hood) Lili wore a blouse suitable for a country house lawn party fifty years before, flounced at the collar, puffed at the shoulder, and ornamented by a double row of ruffles at the wrist. Long sleeves in rough weather, but what a preposterous pair of sleeves! Could Lili herself have chosen such a costume, this daughter of Bucharest who could speak so many of the languages of Europe? The two of them looked impoverished; they *were* impoverished. Lili's pair of worn suitcases, the locks useless, bound with hairy rope. Julian dragging in a stuffed and ponderous duffle bag. Urban nomads, one as outlandish as the other.

Bea led the way to her bedroom. Immediately they shut the door; she heard hushed sibilants; and later, later . . . stifled gasps, broken outcries. Bea had never once shut her bedroom door. What should she have shut it against? Empty air? But these two were, pointedly, man and wife.

The morning was nearly as dark as the night it had left behind. A soundless snowfall had changed, in a few hours, into a haranguing blizzard, pelting the windows with chattering monotony, warning that today too the world outside was going to be closed down — the stores, the offices, the roads, the schools. Viewed from where Bea lay, removed from the amicable mounds of her customary pillows, everything all around had turned unfamiliar, cavelike and dim: a thin crack in the ceiling she had never noticed, the Kollwitz prints freakishly smeary. Her spine felt drilled through; her brain still swarmed with fearsome dream-shreds retreating into oblivion. She had slept hard and wickedly. Her dreams were rife with treacheries.

From a short distance away a rustling and clinking, water running, the kettle's low breathing, the toaster's bruising smell: Lili creeping about in Bea's tiny kitchen. She sat up, unnerved. The table was set, breakfast plates and cutlery; and Julian, huddled over a curl of steam ascending from his teacup, in what had been his father's place, just where Marvin had infamously presided over the expulsion of his son. The storm went on clamoring, hailstones mixed with sleet. Now and then the drumming of wintry thunder. They were walled in together, Bea and her nephew and his wife.

At three o'clock in the afternoon a false dusk was already deepening into the colors of midnight. The lamps were lit. The day had been given over to a desultory decorum—Lili's grateful avowals, Julian's mostly sheepish silence. He yawned; he appeared to brood; he hoarded his thoughts. At times, without provocation, he reddened on either side of his skimpy straw mustache. Was it acknowledgment that the nastiness of Paris was being repaid with Bea's warm New York bed? But it was Lili who admitted to embarrassment.

"You will forgive my husband," she said. Again *my husband*, that supremacy of possession. Or else a restless nervous clinging. "He is so very *fatigué*, the journey it was so difficult, soon he will be better—"

They had almost exhausted the subject of the storm. There was little more to say, and anyhow the icy violence was starting to recede, making way for flying shrouds of rain. A chorus of scraping shovels rose up from the street. The city trucks were out, salting the roads.

"I suppose," Bea intervened, deflecting the apology, "I'll be able to get to work tomorrow. Though maybe not, the way it looks so far. And Lili," she added dutifully, "when this awful weather's over, if you'd like to go for an interview, there may be a job for you. A friend tipped me off, it sounds just right."

The parallel tracks in Lili's forehead tightened.

"But Julian," she began, and let it die.

"I hadn't thought about Julian—I haven't found anything—actually I haven't tried, either—" A callous admission. She *hadn't* thought about Julian, what he could do . . . what he was good for.

"He wishes to study. To learn."

"His father mentioned once that Julian was doing science, some sort of science —"

"His temperament goes elsewhere, I think," Lili said.

They were speaking of him as if he had gone away. Or had turned into a statue, deaf and sightless. All day he had been crouched over a book, remote from the talk. Bea's quiet sociability — willed, forced; Lili's anxious pleasantries. There was no intimacy here.

"Then what does he want to do?" Bea asked.

"Not to do. To be."

But Lili was moving across the room to where Julian sat hunched (Marvin's chair still, no one else had occupied it since), and wound her thin arms around his neck. Docilely, he pulled her fingers down to his lips, and went on reading. The boy and the woman, Bea saw, were densely entangled. They made an old-fashioned domestic picture: all that was required to complete it was a fireside; or a child. The boy (the man, she corrected herself) had a long strong masculine back. One leg splayed outward, the other was twisted around a rung — a boyish posture; but his nape, arched over the page, was aged. Startled, she caught in Julian an evanescent image of her father in his indolent niche at the rear of the shop; her mild, diffident, accommodating father and his perpetual novel; her unworldly father with his rabbinically bookish stoop. She looked at the boy: a bodily gaze, every pore an eye. A longing struck her — a pang. His head had an unexpected beauty, even in the tender curve of the full chin. His flesh held the weight of his feeling; his appetite for meat, she suddenly knew, was a hunger for feeling. She recognized him as someone she had missed; misjudged; passed over. And she had inflicted on him a pitiless blight. Her hand was as gory as Lady Macbeth's. Her hand was a guillotine.

"What have you got there?" she called out — in the gray rainlight that chased vertical rivulets down the streaming panes, he seemed unaccountably far. "You've had your nose in that same book since morning." The friendly aunty tone, meant to ingratiate. In Paris he had hated it.

It was a thick volume, like a school text. The spine was black with yellow lettering—or was it gold? She thought it might be her old college anthology, Beowulf to Wordsworth. He had taken it, she conjectured, from the small stand of shelves in the bedroom, where she kept such things: youth's heirlooms, Leo's abandoned fountain pen, with its rusted nib, still among them; forgotten.

"It's nothing," he said.

It was true: whatever drew him belonged to him and was nothing to her. That sting of compunction, that rise in the ribs—was it regret, was it envy? Envy that there was no one to urge her fingertips into a young man's mouth? Julian's long back, his legs. An old woman coveting a boy. The air was swollen with her nephew and his wife. Their farness and their nearness filled every corner.

In a resolute instant Lili tore away from Julian's grip. She held up her palms to Bea: a mendicant's empty cups. "He carries always many, many books!—heavy! And you see," she appealed, "how he is like a student always, he must study now in a proper way, in a proper school"—here she wavered, it fled her, she could not bring it out; until at last she came on the thing itself—"*théologie.*"

"You can't mean divinity school!"

Impossible for Marvin to suffer such a son. A mistaken shoot grown out of the father's stony seed.

Julian lifted his head. For the first time—for the first time ever—he turned his narrow eyes on Bea. "Not anything like that, you've got me all wrong. I don't believe any of that stuff, why should I? And it's all foreign to Lili. All those denominations, maybe it once meant something to my mother, but I'm nothing, and that's the truth of it."

"But Lili says theology—"

The Tatar lids blinked. "It's only a word. Lili knows what I think. It isn't God I want to think about. It's why there isn't any God."

"There's no school for that." But she meant to oblige him; to cosset. Not to oppose.

"Somewhere there is. Or a teacher. Or maybe," he threw out, "I could found one."

The last was surely ironical, but good grief, the boy's head was skewed, he was in search of no-God! And if there was no God, then he was in search of nothing, and how would he live? Marvin in his wisdom had permitted his son the means—yes, yes, own up to it, Marvin's wisdom, incontrovertible!—and Bea, in all her deviousness, in her wickedness, had immolated it.

And Julian had spoken of his mother.

"Lili is thinking of something more conventional," Bea said.

Lili's small mouth constricted—fitfully, invaded by an erratic beat. In that foolish blouse concealing her bony secretive arms, she looked helpless and clownish.

"No," she said. "Julian must be. I will do."

And again Bea reflected, as she had in the sight of those hanging hooks, coat hooks or butcher's hooks, *She is used to everything. The world is as it is. She is ready to expect anything.* Had Lili imagined that this dreaming boy, restored to his native opportunities, would take on the gravity (*théologie!*) of a serious scholar? Did she harbor the ghost of a lost husband, and hope the new would somehow replicate the old? Still, the world is as it is; it was plain that Lili was prepared to carry this boy—his weight, his hunger—on her frail frame forever. She would work in heartless offices and earn her sparse wages, while Julian sits with his books (whatever they are, black spines with gilt lettering,), meditating on the Great Naught, the no-God that fails to rule the universe. Then Lili was complicit, obdurately complicit; entangled. And perhaps they would have a child? A child fathered by a wraith, by a dreamer of nothingness. Bea could not foresee a child. She grieved for loins without fruit. She grieved for Julian. Something—what? was it only a mood, was it this confinement in the cave of the ebbing storm, what was it?—something in her had shifted; veered. In the deeps of night those sounds behind her bedroom door. She had seen him suckle his wife's fingers, as if he could milk what she was made of. Had he also suckled the black milk of her nightmares?

He shut his book and stood up. His look was not for Lili. It was for Bea.

"Tell me about my mother," he said.

She was in need of steadying; she distrusted her legs. She answered him dully: "I will," and fell back into the chair he had vacated. Marvin's chair: was it a spell? It had bewitched him into speaking so.

"I want to see her. I thought when we go west——"

"What?" Bea said.

"Julian," Lili broke in, "we must wait before you tell this, it is not the way——"

He was quick and terse: "Lili doesn't want that job anyhow."

"But I understood from what she wrote——"

"Change of plans, we've got connecting tickets. We're not staying."

Then Lili, with her pained cautious vigilance: "Please, you are so very kind, this fine hospitality, we are grateful, we make such a difficulty in your home——"

"The thing is," he pushed on, "I don't want to run into my father. I've got to see my mother, even if I have to do it in . . . in that place. But only when he's not around."

Bea was silent: the silence of her fear. It was now; now. It could not be put off. She had schemed, she had played it out—how to begin; over and over she had played it out. But in the scene in her mind it was she who would begin. She was lassoed: he had caught her in a noose.

"My father must've told you how they work it out. Visiting times, when he goes to see her, things like that. So that I don't have to run into him."

"I was there," Bea said finally. "I flew out there when I left Paris."

"You saw my mother?"

"She was painting."

"Painting?"

"A landscape, yes. A night scene, a kind of field. It was . . . lovely. I saw . . . so much talent. My own misunderstanding—or Iris's—I didn't expect it would be the type of place it turned out to be when I got there. I expected—you know, a rest home, it's what your father called it. Marvin's satire—"

"A loony bin. That's where he stashed her, didn't he?"

"She told me she'd chosen to go." In a manic seizure she tacked it on: "*Was* chosen, actually."

"She told you that?"

"It was . . . a kind of retreat. An artists' retreat. Marvin made fun of it, he wouldn't take it seriously. Rows of easels everywhere, all over the lawns. And music! Piano music. Composers, concerts going on. They even had a Blüthner—"

And Julian, fixed, rapt: "What's that?"

"A famous old grand, a sort of European Steinway. Your mother seemed very happy. You have to . . . you have to apply to get into an environment like that, it's an honor to be admitted. It's regarded as a distinction. A prize."

"But Iris . . . you heard her, she said mom was starting to lose it—"

"I don't know about any of that, why Iris would say those things. Resentment, maybe—a falling out. She left, didn't she, without even telling Margaret she was leaving? Your mother and I had a good visit, we hadn't met in years. We talked and talked."

"What about?"

Bea temporized. "Well, she *was* a little angry with your father. You know how sarcastic he can be. She told me she was glad to get away for a while."

A sprinkling of truth in the craze of invention. These mad fabrications, this spigot of fable. It had come on her, an invincible torrent, a devouring, lie, lie, lie, it was corrupt! He believed her, he was ravenous to believe her. She was feeding him joy. The skin of his face glowed around the yellow strands of mustache. He, a poet (*the doves of the Marais*), the scion of a painter, a prizewinner!

Yet all of it risky—a figment too easily contradicted. The son would reliably keep his distance from the father, but if he was heading for California, where Iris would soon be immured, then wouldn't Iris . . . *no!* A senseless contingency. Julian would not be traveling to see his mother, there was no mother to see . . .

It could be evaded no longer.

Tentatively, Bea felt her way. "If the two of you are thinking of going out to L.A.—"

Lili said crisply, "We go first to Texas."

How grotesque the name was in her mouth. It did not accord with nature.

"Texas? Why Texas? Do you know anyone there?"

"Lili's got this friend, not exactly a friend. She heard from him just before we came over, they used to work together. He could be her father, the way he was so pleased when he found out she isn't alone. That she's got me, and a ring on her finger."

"From Poland," Lili said. "A good man."

"And out there's as decent as any other patch of earth," Julian argued. "Better for us than most. This time it won't be only Lili—we'll both be . . . you know . . . outsiders."

"But how will you get on?"

"We'll make out all right. Lili always does. And this Kleinman says the area's full of good chances for someone who can manage Spanish—"

Good chances among the scorpions and desert tracts! And Julian casting himself as a stranger in his own land.

"And then," Julian said, "in a week or two, when we get on our feet, we'll go out to see my mother. I never knew anything about mom's doing art, she never used to, and dad would've sneered anyhow. The way he's been with me—"

Out of the whole cloth, and he believed it! Did Lili? How would she not, and what did it matter, if Margaret was dead?

"Julian," Bea said—she was creeping toward it on her belly, warily, like a frightened dog—"I told your mother you were coming home. I mentioned it in a letter when I got back to New York, she was so looking forward to it—"

This made him bristle. "Well, I haven't come home, have I? As far as we're concerned—Lili and me—Texas is another country, that's the point."

That's the point. Marvin's argot, Marvin's insistence. But under the hard rind, the soft boy.

"They found it in her pocket, it was only a few lines. The pocket of her dress. Somehow . . . somehow . . . an accident on the road, she was hurt, no one knew where she was going—"

Lili gave a cry. It was the same cry Bea had heard in the night.

"On the road?" Julian said. "What road?"

"The one just outside . . . outside the retreat." The lying word disgusted her now. She had fed him gladness only to blight him. Blight upon blight.

"Then she's in the hospital—"

"No," Bea said. "No."

"Julian," Lili murmured, and grasped both his hands, and forced them around her ribs, to lock them there.

He took hold of her with a splintered whinny that was not a whinny—what was it then? A mazy sickened noise not from the pit of the throat but out of some nameless buried misshapen organ—the devil's music—good Lord, the boy was drowning in his father's laughter!

"What a joke, divinity school, are you crazy? I wish, I wish," he scratched out, "there could be a God, and there isn't, there isn't, there's nothing—"

He went trailing after Lili. The shut door became one with the wall. He had left his book on the chair. Now Bea could see what it was: *Purity of Heart Is to Will One Thing.* Soon they would be gone, into that other country of their willed eclipse. She did not regret it. She did not expect to see them ever again. This soft, soft boy . . . infatuation would fade.

The symphony that never was, the God that never is.

52

AT EIGHT O'CLOCK a watery December sun was already turning the gutters into impassable rivers. Bea pulled on her galoshes; she was going to work. The return of the ordinary, the predictable: in an hour or so Caesar would be assassinated, and her young men (they *were* nearly men) would burst into celebratory pandemonium. Shakespeare was teaching them cynicism, and why not?

The bedroom door opened. Lili came out, still in her nightgown.

Bea said, "Is Julian all right?"

"He sleeps now. Today we go."

The nightgown was sleeveless. A hollow in the upper arm. A second mouth, misplaced—lipless, speechless.

"Today? Already?"

"My husband wishes it."

"I thought you'd want to stay on at least a few more days—"

"He wishes it."

"I hurt him, no wonder. I had to," Bea said. "I couldn't not. His mother . . . I had to tell him, he had to know."

"Sometimes," Lili said, "the mad seek death."

"Nobody knows what she had in mind."

The note in her pocket, am I to blame?

"But her mind was not right?"

"Yes and no. It's difficult to say, we were scarcely acquainted. Poor Julian, I've gone and broken his heart—"

"His mother was broken, no?"

The fecal daubs, the barefoot flight.

"I suppose so," Bea said.

"This other woman—she is whole. Whole and clever."

"What are you saying, what other woman?"

"The artist, the woman who paints—"

"Ah," Bea said. How transparent she was to Julian's wife: as if he had married a sibyl.

"He will keep her now, this other woman. The clever mother who paints."

"It isn't true, Lili. You know it isn't true."

"For my husband it is true. How good you are!" she said.

"He won't see through it? *You* have—"

"He is like an angel, like a child, he sees everything and nothing."

Bea said leadenly, "You once called him a man."

In Lili's small dark face the tired grooves made a tigerish delta. "Only a man will weep in his bed," she answered.

And again: "How good you are!"

53

Christmas Eve

Dear Aunt Bea,

    I'm all alone tonight — alone with dad, which is practically
the same thing a lot of the time — and I thought I'd write to
you, since I imagine you're alone too, though you actually
don't do Christmas, or do you? It's just that something odd
happened this afternoon, and you might want to know about
it in advance. Dad was grumpy about putting up the tree this
year, not that I blame him, but our yard man delivered this big
tall Colorado blue spruce just as he's always done as long as I
can remember. Nobody'd told him not to, and here it was, so
I got Mrs. Hruska (she's dad's housekeeper) to help me get
the tree things up from the storeroom in the basement. Two
boxes full of these funny ornaments mom's collected over the
years, little silver donkeys and sheep, and the shiny red and
green balls Julian and I used to want to lick when we were
small, and the orange star for the top. We hung all the deco-
rations except for the lights, because the wires were tangled
in knots, and Mrs. Hruska is afraid of touching anything to
do with electricity, she hates using the vacuum cleaner. Dad
saw the whole thing when it was done — it was looking really
beautiful — and didn't say a word. I can't tell whether this nice
piney smell and having the house all Christmassy gives him

a bit of a lift or makes him even sadder. He's almost stopped
going to the office, but he's on the phone all day, and it's not
as though he's let go of the ropes — it just seems that ever
since the accident he doesn't want to mix with people. By the
time Phillip got back from Milan to bail me out it was way too
late to get to the funeral, but Mrs. Hruska filled me in — mobs
at the church, she said, including these rich hidalgo types up
from Mexico dad does business with. I did go to mom's grave,
though (mom's grave, it's awful having to say that), but dad
wouldn't come with me and I had to stand there by myself and
face what it said on the stone: CHERISHED WIFE, BELOVED
MOTHER. This was so stale and cemetery-ordinary that somehow it didn't feel true to mom, I don't know why. Maybe
because if she could've picked her own epitaph it would've
been something sort of neutral out of the Bible or the Gos-
pels, something semi-religious like that. Just last week dad got
a note in the mail from one of her Boston cousins, someone
I'd never heard of, and took one quick look at the name and
handed it over to me without reading it. It was signed Mal-
colm Alexander Breckinridge III, and went on and on about
how this person remembered mom's parents with so much
respect and admiration, and how he hoped Margaret's children had turned out to be good Christians despite everything,
and it ended with condolences for Julian and me, not a hint
of dad, as if he didn't exist. Dad's been getting lots of other
condolence letters, mainly from connections of the firm and
from the wives of the men on his teams. He barely glances at
them. I can't guess what he's thinking. Even today — Christmas Eve! — he was on the phone for hours, all business talk,
he's spoken of putting in an extra line for me, so that I can get
calls from friends, as if I cared. Ever since I came home — ever
since Phillip — I've mostly lost interest in the way things were
before. And anyhow it doesn't make sense to go back to the

lab when I've missed half the semester — not that they'd let
me — my department chair's nixed it, and my old lab partner,
all on his own, wound up finishing this project we were working on — modifying a protein to get it to crystallize — my idea
to begin with, by the way. We'd had all these protein plates set
up in the cold room, and were waiting — I ought to say hoping
like mad — they'd crystallize and grow enough to get x-rayed.
It can take weeks and weeks, it could be months, for some protein crystals to grow, and sure enough, all that happened while
I was away! Don't think I'm jealous, I'm confident I can get
started again next September, maybe on a different idea, and to
please dad I will. I intend to impress him. It's only that there's
so much dead time until then, alone in this house with how he
is now, all beaten down . . . It might have been the tree that
brought it on, those red and green balls or whatever, but when
he finally got off the phone and gave Mrs. Hruska her Christmas money (she left early, right after we had the star tacked on,
myself up on the ladder and Mrs. Hruska holding it steady),
out of the blue he began to ask a whole lot of questions about
Julian, did I know where he was, and if I ever hear from him. I
said I honestly didn't know anything at all, just whatever it was
that he knew — I didn't dare tell that probably they'd gone to
Lili's uncle — when the doorbell rang, and dad disappeared.
"I'm in no mood, throw them a couple of dollars and get rid
of them," he told me — we both thought it was carolers going
round the neighborhood, the way they always do on Christmas Eve. But it was a man out there, a man in his fifties I think,
looking for dad. He explained that he'd been trying to phone
much of the day and kept getting a busy signal, was our phone
out of order, and since he lived more or less nearby, he figured
he might as well walk over. Well, Aunt Bea, to make a long
story short, he wanted to know whether dad had your address
in New York — and who do you think it was? Your husband!

Or used to be. We got to talking, I even asked him in, he al-most said yes, but in the end he went away. Bea! Your husband! Wanting to be in touch!

I hope your Christmas is a happy one. Happier than ours here, and maybe it will be.

Iris

54

HE HAD WRAPPED it in three layers of tissue paper and shielded it
with a pair of sturdy cardboards and inserted it into a padded mailing
envelope — yet he knew it could not be arrested or suppressed any
more than if he had attempted to encase a flame in a bundle of leaves.
It burned on, it burned through whatever sheltered or concealed it. It
would set her hands on fire! — those hands that had crazed him, the
left stretched far like a cormorant's wing, the right bunched into a ra-
pacious hammer. Her fingerprints would dissolve and her knuckles
turn to blackened dice; she had reaped this punishment, she was an
avenging succubus, she had come on him with a suddenness, an ambush, she had meant to unman him. Her punishment was the blind-
ness of her seeing — the blind clarity of her seeing: she would be
made to look on those round black notes standing on their stems like
black storks shrieking — a cryptogram of blots and filaments deci-
pherable only by sound, and she — she who had mocked him for his
impotence — would not, could not, hear! Her ears were blind to those
black-blooded droplets raining down, tailed, slashed, some confined
to their clef and others freed to race above and beneath it, the chaos
of their terrain secreting syllogisms even as they erupted into a tur-
bulence of crisis . . .

It was accomplished, completed, torn out of the Blüthner, torn out
of his lungs, out of his testes, out of his ambition, his crushed and
desiccated lust. It was vindictive, it was wrathful. And here and there
(he felt this as a philosopher feels Truth) it gave birth to Beauty. The

wrath was inscribed in his flesh, but the sublime had befallen him from a power behind the veil. The sublime was to be her punishment: she was locked away from it in the cage of her unknowing. The clef, the code, the voice of the notes, all mute. She was what he had always understood her to be: a musical imbecile.

And from those blind-deaf imbecile hands, the fist and the splay, had come exultation! He saw past spite to glory. The full orchestra, the concert halls (Chicago, New York), the conductor with his white mane—he ran through the luminaries he preferred—and audiences on their feet, washed over by rapture, a blazing rapture grown out of the spill of his brain-womb, its four movements climaxing in a masterstroke, a chorale of high tiny dwarf-falsettos (such miniature singers could surely be recruited) against the dynamitings of the kettledrums. He expected the work to be known as—the world would call it—*Coopersmith's Symphony in B Minor.*

But this commonplace attribution was hardly satisfactory, and anyhow—from the movie business Leo had long ago learned bitter realism—the likelihood was that it would never be performed: the country pullulates with failed symphonies. Never mind, the thing was done, finished. A victory over her disbelief.

But how to get it to her? Where in New York did she live? After all these years certainly not in that old cramped Bronx atelier?

The brother. The mogul as supplicant. The brother had left him his card—not that he'd ever intended to keep it.

—Take this, it's got all my numbers, and please let me know if you hear of anything that might be a reasonable fit for a kid with a writing flair, my son seems to think he's good at it, movie scripts for all I know. I'll make it worth your while if you can come up with something, anything at all . . .

Leo had sent him packing—a boor trading on his sister's withered connection: a marriage dead, buried, forgotten. Contempt. Disgust. Why should Leo Coopersmith be pursued by a reminder of an ancient whim, a mistaken turn of life? Mistaken and unnecessary—what good had she ever done him? Hounded him with expectations — true enough, they were his own assumptions and beckoning prospects, which made the case all the more irritating. And that this thick-bellied panting boor had the nerve to push his card on a once-upon-a-time brother-in-law, reduced to a stranger! Standing in his front hall (where now and again he thought he could still sniff the stinking aftermath of the silent actor's dog), Leo tossed the card over his shoulder, the way superstitious folk spit behind their backs to ward off a curse. He had got rid of those harassments and entreaties, he had shown the fellow the door.

A month later he discovered *Marvin Nachtigall, Aeronautics Design,* a bit crumpled at the corners, on a kitchen counter — Cora, supposing it something of value, had retrieved it. A fortuitous find: to get to the sister he needed the brother.

But it was a girl who answered his ring. A nervous girl in a long skirt, fidgeting with a barrette in her hair. Hair the color of one of the amber panels of the fanlight above her head.

"Oh," she said, taken aback. "Though I guess it's why we didn't hear any singing —"

"Singing?" he said.

"Carolers. They usually come by around this time."

He looked her over. The nervousness was in the tremor of the nostrils, in the tongue crawling out to moisten the lips. Behind her, in the dim rooms beyond, he glimpsed an unlit tree hung all up and down with trinkets. But no hint of festivity. A darkness in there, a silence.

"Are you collecting for something? Here's five dollars if you are." She was ready to shut him out.

"Marvin Nachtigall," he pronounced. "I think I've got the right house? It's his sister I'm after. Beatrice Nachtigall."

This stopped her.

"But that's my aunt. My father's sister."

"And it's your father I'd like to speak to. About his sister, how to reach her —"

"I can tell you that. Why do you want her?"

"I owe her something." He began again: "I've been trying to phone, so if I could see your father—"

"She isn't called Nachtigall, she has a different name."

The pinch of surprise. "Then she's married?"

"Not anymore, that was ages ago." She stabbed the barrette back into her hair as if the force of it could cow him. What he had taken for nerves was impatience. "What is it you owe her?"

"A present. A musical present." That he should be so unhesitatingly disclosing the momentous thing on a doorstep, in the street, in the open! The recklessness of anonymity. He felt himself to be an impostor.

He said, "I imagine *you're* not musical." How could she be? Her bloodline was against it.

"My mother, maybe a little bit—she once told us that in her teens she had to sing in the choir at church, not that she wanted to. But she's dead, she died." The girl's pale lids flickered. "Almost no one in my family, not really. My aunt Bea's the only one—she has this enormous grand piano that she treats like it's some sort of altar—"

"It used to be mine," he said.

"Yours?" She pondered it.

"I have another one now." He gave out what—perversely—he knew was a dangerous smile. "Another instrument, another life. I've even had other wives."

"Other wives?" Electrified, she was leaving bewilderment behind; she was catching on.

"She was Beatrice Nachtigall when we met," he said.

"She calls herself Nightingale."

"And has the ear of a crow. So if you can let me know where to send—"

"Come in for a minute, I'll write it down for you."

"All right." And then thought better of it. The girl was accommodating enough; it was superfluous to encounter the father. Besides, the tables were turned: who would be the supplicant now, who would be requesting a favor?

241

"And please don't mind my dad," she warned, "if it isn't business he won't want to talk anyhow, he's in a sort of depression. He won't like you, lately he doesn't like anyone."

Petulance. Or was it fury? Boredom, perhaps.

"I'll wait out here," he said.

When she came to the door to hand him a square of notepaper, she asked, "What's this about a crow?"

"Forget the fairy books. In real life," he instructed, "nightingales sing no better than crows."

For this she granted him a grin. A glint of her upper teeth: a comely row of small white keys.

"Do you ever go to the movies?" he said.

"Are you asking me out?"

"I'm afraid not. I'm too old for that."

"In Paris I had a boyfriend who was forty, I wouldn't mind."

"Paris?"

"I get around. Or used to."

"Well, if you happen to see a terrible film called *A Bargain for Betsy*—it's in all the theaters now—I hereby dedicate the score to you."

"Why would you do that?"

"For getting me to your aunt. You'll hear a couple of pretty scherzos."

"What makes you think I should care?"

"I wrote them."

"Really? I'd heard," she whipped out, "you only played the oboe."

He wanted to slap her then. She'd known who he was for ten minutes or more; she'd been playing with him, dangling a string before a cat. Worse, she'd inherited the paternal insult. But she was a pretty thing, a sort of scherzo herself, skipping from mood to mood; she wasn't an innocent. She told him that she was, at least temporarily, out of school. She told him that her mother was in an accident on the freeway and that she'd had to desert Phillip in Paris and that she'd worked in a clinic and that she was exasperated with her father, who was sometimes a bully, even if currently not. And that it was her father who had fancifully christened her in honor of the virgin goddess who lives in the clouds; she let fly this extravagance, though he saw, from the aggressive twisting of her barrette (she was at it again), how she was fabricating it on the spot.

All this on the doorstep under the fanlight.

"In a way," she said — her grin took on a conspiratorial slant — "you're practically my uncle."

This stirred him — it was so like finding the right tempo for some passing trivial tune.

From the bottom of the street the carolers were approaching. "O come, all ye faithful," they sang.

And for a reason he could not tell, it was on Iris Nachtigall's doorstep, and out of some half-remembered tale lodged in the memory of a languidly bookish childhood, that the truth of his grand work fell upon Leo Coopersmith. He would call it — the world would call it — by the name of a questionable bird with a biting beak.

55

IRIS WAS AGAIN feeling absurdly tall, a Gulliver among all these little people wriggling in the ten rows in front of her, and in however many rows there were behind her, and in the long blue chain of plush-covered seats to her left and right; their tiny high peepings, a barrage of needle-pricks, were closing in on her. The man who might have been her uncle had never so much as hinted that *A Bargain for Betsy* was a children's movie, and worse—a cartoon! Betsy turned out to be a plump beaver lady in an abundantly pocketed apron who keeps a jellybean shop in a hollowed-out log alongside a stream and near a dam. The dam is a bulwark against a menacing wood, where a wicked wizard in a leering wolf mask hides his sinister factory in a cobwebby underground vault lined with glass flasks and cruets and urns, each one crammed with brightly colored false jellybeans. But one night, when Betsy is asleep and snoring heartily, he breaks through the beaver-built dam of thick mud and sticks, and invades her shop. His grim purpose is to substitute his own dangerously glittering pellets for Betsy's wholesome beans, flavored like whipped cream but imbued with the vitamin power of carrots and spinach and cabbage. All the neighborhood children are accustomed to flock to Betsy's happy shop—mice and squirrels and raccoons, a comical porcupine or two, and a crew of chatty chickens, as well as Betsy's own brown-furry nieces and nephews excitedly paddling their flat tails. In a charming early scene, accompanied by harp trills, the animal children dance in a ring, with Betsy at its center, as she dips into the depths of her big pockets to toss out a brilliant shower of healthful jellybeans. And here, as the delighted children scramble to scoop them up, the warbling music grows merrier and sprightlier — butterflies lifting in a powdery mass: Leo Coopersmith's scherzo!

But it was not for the sake of this dimpling passage of chordal harmonies that Iris had come, for the second time that day, to sit patiently through all the rest — how the wolf-faced wizard slithers into the darkened shop to replace the salubrious contents of Betsy's jars with his baleful imitations, and how the animal children, innocently ingesting the bad beans, fall into an obedient lockstep stupor and are marched through the ruined dam to toil in the underground factory, and how, coal-eyed and mute, they are made to stir the great steaming vats of faux candies, batch after batch, to lure yet another army of children into serving the wizard's nasty will. And now the rocking bellowing booming of the double bass, a piercing quiver of fifes, the dense slams of a drum — frightening sounds. All around, the human children are gasping and calling out — some are tearfully bawling — when in bursts brave Betsy with a posse of beaver police . . . and so on and so on, until the rescue is achieved and the pretty little scherzo returns.

At the candy stand in the swarming lobby, Iris noticed a large bin of cellophane-packaged red, green, yellow, blue, and purple jellies labeled BETSY'S BARGAIN BEANS. She couldn't remember where in the plot a bargain, or any semblance of a bargain, had occurred: had the film's writers had their central idea cut? Or is it that the newly freed slave children are inveigled into joining in the urgent task of rebuilding the dam? The rescue has its price, one form of servitude traded for another, and what if they had learned to prefer the silent darker life underground? A trick, Iris thought — the slavish toiling on the dam advertised as a jolly communal endeavor. — But the audience, rushing away, didn't care, and in less than five minutes the jellybean bin was sold out.

Iris didn't care either. It was familiar stale Disneyish stuff, the Pied Piper with a stitch or two of the Beanstalk's ogre laced in — the

talking creatures, the whirling colors, the stilted animation, saccharine! Saccharine and poisonous. The busy travail on the screen
was all waste, and nothing to do with . . . *feeling* . . . unless perhaps
those apron pockets unwittingly scattering the wizard's baleful candy
drops . . . *what's carried in a pocket can be deadly.* And suppose it had
been a serious film for adults, *High Noon,* say, with Gary Cooper (Iris
had seen the posters everywhere — it was one of the summer's two
big American movies in Paris, along with *Whispering Winds*), still the
director and the story line and the camera work would have been no
more diverting than this feckless cartoon. The uselessness of such
movie buff's arcana; yet in the past two weeks she had searched out
a classic-film club in Santa Monica and a shabby rerun house in Pas-
adena, and every movie theater that might hurtle her into the swellings and ebbings of Leo Coopersmith's vibrations. It was the vibrations — the shudderings — she was after. In these musics (there were
so many of them) was concealed the private thing she was driven to
unravel: what it was in the husband (the husband!) that had enabled
Bea to cast him away, to let him go. Wizardlike, he had appeared out
of his long, long eclipse expressly to insinuate himself back into
Bea's clean-swept orbit. But Bea was inextricably apart: she could not
be retrieved. She had married a husband and let him go. That pivotal
letting-go, an undisclosed latch giving way: what was it?

The musics would tell. Iris listened and listened: she shut her
eyes, trawling. Lascivious couplings among the swirling flutes — she
fished them out. She was sickened by the world's couplings. Boyfriends, lovers, husbands, idle dallyings (hadn't she come close to
flirting with the man who might have been her uncle?) — while in the
unseen regions of the earth snowy mountains and moon-wrinkled
lakes are waiting, and, in the marble-white city of Rome, Michelangelo's mighty Moses! (Phillip's misbegotten promises, and what had
become of Florence, and Como, and the Alps glimpsed from Milan?)
Instead, all these breeding couplings, the fateful coupling of her father and mother, a pair of unlikes; it had turned her father greedy and
her mother reckless. Her brother and his foreign wife, far away in an-

other country for all she knew, clinging each to each beneath hanging gourds under a boiling Mediterranean sun — and when dark comes, the carrion noises, furious haunted dyings. And Phillip naked, plying his assurances of mountains and lakes, the ugly nighttime nakedness, the naked force of it: the coupling . . . the copulating. The fearsome penetrations. Coitus, a wolfish power to make fecund that tiny secret bean lurking in her belly . . . Her peaceful crystals in the cold room had risen into steepling growths without such fleshly imperatives! She went on listening for the couplings in the many musics, their polluting heat and beat, transitory and changeable. She listened; she saw. Bea's answer lay coiled in those swellings and ebbings, those dartings and retreats, those pulsings and withdrawals, those girdlings and ungirdlings . . . and Bea was released from them, she had let the musics go. The man who had been her husband would never get her back, no matter what he believed he owed her, no matter how he meant to bribe her with his belated bargain tunes.

In the dim-lit movie house, garish coruscations of orange and vermilion and violet flashed down from the illuminated screen to flood the children's intent little faces with rainbow flares. Iris towered over them like some grotesque ruddy ogress. Her thighs were long. Her calves were stone-hard. She wished she could be a child like the children all around her. She wished she could be a small girl, with her smaller brother beside her, secretly licking the red and green Christmas baubles. She wished she could wish away her woman's thighs and the underground factory that was her woman's groin. She would never again plummet into the folly of coupling, she would never have a husband. She would live with her father forever. She wished she could be free. She wished she could be Bea.

56

January 10, 1953
Bea: I've heard from my accountants — it turns out that the check in question hasn't cleared, and I think you owe it to me if you know something — I can't believe he'd spit on a thing of this magnitude, and for sure <u>she</u> wouldn't. Is there any chance he never got it on time, or did it get lost in the mail? For God's sake, you <u>did</u> send it registered air mail special delivery? Anything else would have been goddamned idiotic.

Marvin

•

January 12

Dear Marvin,

Your registered air mail special delivery arrived here early yesterday. I understand that you did this as an object lesson in how to handle long-distance communications. Fine, I take your point, but it has nothing to do with what can only be called a matter of the heart. It's plain your son wants to make his own life as he sees it — can't you grant him that? If he's repudiated your money, that's all there is to it. Which means that <u>she's</u> repudiated it, despite your judgment of her, sight unseen. To tell the truth, Marvin, I've had, on and off, similar suspicions about Julian's marriage. I was thinking just like you — to my surprise, you've had that effect on me. But it could be that those

two are after something else in this world—I don't know how
to describe it or assess it, but when I last saw Julian

Here Bea lifted her pen to concentrate: she was about to place, pre-
cariously, a pebble-sized falsehood atop the mountain of deceptions
that had, stone by stone, been building. Julian in her own apartment,
in Marvin's chair; but she could not admit to this. She wrote instead,

when I last saw Julian—it was the night before I left Paris, at
that dinner I told you about—he was reading Kierkegaard! So
you see where his head is—he has these metaphysical inclina-
tions, how else to say it? It's made him a bit gruff—he doesn't
trouble about ordinary things. And she looks to be nearly the
same—as if being wounded somehow purified her, I can't exactly explain—it's something in the way she talks and thinks,
not that I got to spend much time with either of them. But it
may be that she does him good, and why not let it go at that?
    I hope the New Year brings you some consolation. It must
be a comfort to have your daughter with you again.

As ever,
Bea

•

Jan 17

Bea: I haven't got the goddamnedest idea of what the hell
you're talking about. Kierkeguard, what's that? Sounds like a
deodorant, which is to say that the whole thing smells as far as
I'm concerned. I've stopped payment on the check, so that's
that. I was going to tell Iris what I'd done—I figured she'd
be level enough to see the rightness of it. But since she's come
back I've had second thoughts. A bundle for her brother for
doing nothing, for being nothing—how would she like that,
this kid with a lifetime of steady elbow grease behind her?
She's taking Margaret's death hard, she won't say the word, at

least not when I'm around—she calls it "the accident," as if her mother could be patched up. And by the way, I've got my lawyers right this minute suing the shit out of that so-called Spa and the goddamn bus company, you bet your life they'll be paying through the nose. And that crackpot letter you sent, it keeps on eating at me, what else could have set her off? I won't say it's your fault exactly, maybe I've got over that, but look what happened, so what am I supposed to think?—All right, I'll _tell_ you what I think! It's taken me a while, I had to get my head cleared, and my God, my poor wife, that bloody scrap of shit in her pocket couldn't be the only time you wrote her, there had to be other times before—you told her things, you _knew_ things you never told me and you told them to Margaret behind my back, you told her Julian got married over there! You told her things and I didn't believe her—how could I, nobody believed her, she was sick, it was the way it showed she was sick. The last time I went to see her, didn't I write you this, they'd stopped the imbecile art therapy and had her doing that cockamamie weaving idiocy, _placemats_, can you imagine? Margaret always hated such low stuff, she called it Boston Irish table linen. She tried to hide it from me, but I got a good look at one she'd made—they made her make this shit!—all white, with stars in each corner, blue stars with six points, and in the middle a big yellow cross. No, she tells me, it's not a cross, that just shows how you always think, it's a plus sign and I put it in on purpose to stand for money. Spite, that's what they had her spending hours on, that's their therapy! And while all this was going on you were feeding her things to upset her, about Julian, and that Iris left school, you took advantage of a sick woman! Looking back, if you hadn't been in Paris I could almost get myself to think you'd actually been out here barging in on my wife in some underhanded way, without letting me know—she said so! She said you'd come to her rooms and saw what she'd been painting, it wasn't plausible as far as I knew, you were flying straight back to New York from over there, but she kept insisting on it, how could I believe such a story? Especially when you've never in your life gone off the beaten path, you've been stuck in your godforsaken rut forever. Still, you did make it out to Paris . . . I don't know, I don't know, and I'm telling you now, Bea, if I ever find out for sure exactly how much you've interfered with Margaret, if somehow or other you did manage to sneak out here and play games with my wife's brain, you'll pay for it, don't ask me how. She was sick but she wasn't a liar! I'm almost ready to think it's you who's the liar, and meanwhile I've gathered from Iris that you've made a friend of my daughter, she says she likes to be in touch with you sometimes—just don't you forget I can stop that if I need to. My daughter's my only shaft of light nowadays, that's from a hymn or something Margaret used to sing in church when she was a kid, Lead me out of darkest night, Lord my only shaft of light— You've probably heard that Iris missed the funeral, it had to be for a reason—I cabled her plenty of notice, I guess she thought she couldn't take it. I wouldn't go to the cemetery with her when she finally got home—to see my kid all broken up? Nothing doing. The worst of it is she's got too much time on her hands, she's cut out all her old friends, she won't say why. And on top of everything else she's had to drop back a year or so toward her degree—while she was out of the picture some competitive creep in the crystallography lab finished up that whiz of an experiment she got started. This guy grabbed the credit for it—dog eat dog, same as in the business world, no different. Iris tells me not to take it to heart, she'll make up for it next semester. My daughter's nothing like that boy! She's always had me for a model, for one thing—though I can't go on running the business away from the office—it's how I've been doing it—I expect to pull myself together and get going again. What matters is I've still got a kid with a future, I'm

<u>not</u> worried about her, don't get me wrong — it's no good for a girl like that to be holed up in this empty house — she's got the right idea, she's mostly out the door and off to the movies, sometimes two a day — it beats me that she can stand it. The Hollywood bug, at her age I imagine they've all got it. She says she goes for the music — movie music, who would believe it. If she gets something out of it I can't complain.

I try not to think about the boy. The boy's gone — that's that.

Marvin

57

WHAT WAS IT? Stratum on stratum, swaddled, a mummy's windings, sealed as if for a voyage to eternity — what could it be?

She came to the inmost wrapping and peeled it away. Black blots and spots, some with fragile fishtails, dancing on insect legs along parallel tracks; a marker curved like a scimitar, or rounded like an ampersand's belly; another resembling a hunchback, or else a swollen comma. Treble and bass. *Allegro, legato, sostenuto, sforzando.* Leo speaking in tongues.

On a single unblemished sheet she read:

The Nightingale's Thorn
SYMPHONY IN B MINOR
by
Leo Coopersmith

Thick block of paper. Heavy. Big! What must one call such a stack? A ream? A bale? A quire? (A choir? *"Chorus of little people."*) And among all these thousands of notes, no note, no reason, no why, no key to its coming. Minor — a brooding? a belittlement? How minor she had been in his life. A mote, a fleck of dust. Bea minor, is that what he meant? What was she to do with it? What did he intend her to take from it? He had composed it hastily, oh hastily — it was plain, when she'd surprised him in his gaudy lair, that he had nothing in hand. An empty pot. But how could she know this? It might be the quiet work of years; of decades. A language that kept her out, if it was a language at all. Music the universal language, vibrations that speak—what a lie. Words, the sovereignty of words, their excluding particularity, *this* was language. What was she to make of these scatterings of blotches moving up and down the staff lines like bugs on an escalator? This mutating voiceless Tower of Babel? Foreign matter. She understood nothing. What did he want from her?

She fanned out the loosened sheets, like giant playing cards, on her broad dining table: they were too many not to overlap. Black blisters bursting out of naked stems. Black balloons on thin sticks. Bottomless black wells. Five stripes: a five-lane highway, small black cars speeding. But silent; silent.

What did he want from her, when he was certain she had nothing to give? Symphony in Bea minor: one of his acrid little witticisms, like the *diabolus in musica* that was her crooked toe.

She had sold off the grand and uprooted its shadow. She was rid of him! And here was the grand restored (what might have come out of it anyhow), its stain on her thrown-out carpet returned in these inky tattoos, her devil's exorcism reversed. And yet it was a gift—a kind of gift. Leo's mind! It was the thing she had hoped for, long ago. She went on picking up one sheet after another, gazing, gazing—she was no better than a dog with its muzzle sniffing at an open book.

But there was excitement in it, a glorious wilderness under the breastbone, a metronome charging in her temples—those droplets from the ice-mermaid's tail. Leo burning. Her heart in its cage a foreign body—it had no business stirring up this frenzy, this delirium of knowing and unknowing.

She thought: How hard it is to change one's life.

And again she thought: How terrifyingly simple to change the lives of others.

As flies to wanton boys.

The next morning, against all the odds—her antic young men would soon be sobered into soldiers—she took up *King Lear*. And instantly the buzzing began all around, punctuated by a single high-pitched yell: *Flies, boys! Flies in the wonton soup!*

In the teachers' lounge afterward, she told Laura, "Would you believe it, I've heard from your cousin, and he's actually written a whole symphony—"

"What, for the *movies?*" Laura squealed. "How does that make sense?"

"For the ages," Bea did not say. It would have been a comment too like a thorn; and Laura would only laugh.

Even so, in the long, long war with Leo, wasn't it Bea who'd won?